FUSION

by Kindle Alexander

Fusion

Edited by: Jae Ashley
Mildred Jordan, I Love Books Proofreading
Sandra Shipman,
Cover art by Lori Jackson
Photo by Michelle Lancaster
Cover content is for illustrative purposes only. Any person depicted in the content is a model.
ISBN ebook: 978-1-941450-75-8

Trademark Acknowledgements

Dedication

Kindle, you are forever in our hearts.
Perry, you're missed every day.

Kindle's Krew, thank you.

Author's Note

Fusion has been fully edited by a team of trained editors, but
no manuscript is perfect.
Please email me with any mistakes you find at.
Creative license was taken with this story. Places and situations
reimagined. It's a work of fiction.

Contents

Part 1   1

1. The Booty Bounce, Beau   3

2: The Sweet Daisy Mae, Dash   13

3: The Joy Beau   23

4: The Deed Dash/Beau   35

5: The Arch Nemesis, Beau   46

6: The Windy City, Dash   55

7: The Check, Check Beau   62

8: The Sexy Time Dash/Beau   73

9: The Big Life Beau   85

10: The Taste Dash   97

11: The Anniversary Dash   104

12: The Climb Beau/Dash   111

13: The Surprise Beau/Dash   122

Part 2	130
14: The Fit Beau/Dash	131
15: The Sheets Beau	140
16: The Next Morning Dash	149
17: The New Hire Beau/Dash	160
18: The Court Dash/Beau	168
19: The Pintail Dash/Beau	179
20: The What's Happening? Beau/Dash	189
21: The Chandler Dash/Beau	197
22: The Ocean Dash/Beau	205
23: The Bath	213
24: The Dixie Duke Dash/Beau	220
25: The Practice Dash	229
26: The Walnuts Beau/Dash	235
27: The Fresh Treats Beau	243
28: The Year Beau	252
Note From the Author	258
Books By Kindle Alexander	259

 Part 1

1: The Booty Bounce
Beau

May 2006
Dallas Texas

Enter me into a sexy, all male dance-off, and you'd see me win.

No doubt, I'd bounce my way into a grand prize trophy. Obviously, I needed to hit the dance floor more often, because when I did, the magic happened. My signature move? Hip shaking and butt bouncing. Of course, I didn't do them together. That'd be impossible. Instead, I'd created a synchronized movement to the beat of a funky electronic tune. I didn't even know music like that existed.

Damn, I had to be making Dash proud tonight. I didn't know why I was nervous about coming to his law school's end of semester party. I was the toast of the gathering. The women who attended loved me. Screw Dash's dumb parents. They didn't think I fit into their high-class world. Well, look at me now.

I wish Dash had his fancy cell phone with him instead of leaving it with the checkroom attendant. I needed photographic proof of my greatness tonight. As awesome as I felt, chances leaned to not remembering any of this in the morning. Dash made sure my glass never emptied.

Thanks to Alexis, one of Dash's classmates and my personal twerk coach, I was able to continue drinking while dancing like a professional. It had to do with my shoulders. If I kept them straight and didn't move my upper body, I managed to get more of my cocktail—a total Dash word—into my mouth rather than on the dance floor.

All the ladies cheered me on, adding in an occasional ass slap of appreciation. Dash gave a few of those too, encouraging others to do the same.

The song changed, causing me to be torn with whether I should lean or rock with it. Such a complicated query—another Dash word that stuck inside my head. After at least a solid five seconds of contemplation, I decided to do both. Swaying while shaking my hips. Since I held a glass in my hand, only one arm flew into the air. Apparently, my head wanted in on the action, playfully tilting in the opposite direction of my hips.

An annoying voice inside my head kept trying to harsh my good vibes. Hinting that the spicy dark rum might be responsible for my oddly confident ego. But I knew exactly how to silence all that negativity and took a hearty gulp of the magical elixir Dash had concocted, then made perfect with the help of the bartender.

This drink was basically an RSVP to my hangover in the morning. Since my current life strategy was to live on a second-by-second basis, I'd deal with tomorrow when it came.

I really liked the people Dash went to school with. We were having a blast. I wouldn't call them laid-back, and just like Dash, they had ambition and determination, but not meanness. They also knew how to throw down a good party and went at it hard.

Unlike they had Dash, nobody questioned my age, which was legally below the required twenty-one years old to be inside this club. I liked that too. I never got carded. Dash on the other hand had to show his identification everywhere we went.

My guy and I had given ourselves a forty-eight hour deadline to emotionally get past what Dash's parents had done to us. Actually, we were thirty-six hours into Dash continually apologizing to me. I'd tried my best to make him chill, but that attempt hit an immovable brick wall. His stubbornness knew no bounds, leaving me to count the hours until I never had to hear another *I'm sorry* again.

The club was modern and posh. A ritzy kind of place situated on a floor close to the top of a downtown Dallas high-rise. The three hundred sixty degree view displayed the Dallas skyline from every angle.

In the heart of the shallow swimming pool was a clear, raised, floating dance floor. It had to be close to midnight. Only a couple of hours left before the night came to an end.

"Beau," Dash hollered, weaving like a ninja through the crowded dance floor. He was my hydration hero tonight. He came with two full shots of something that was sure to make my head swim. Without missing much of a beat, he handed me the shot then swiped away my almost empty glass, summoning a waiter as if out of thin air.

"Do you want me to take anything else?" the waiter asked loud enough to be heard over the music. Dash encouraged me to down my shot at the same time he did then passed those glasses to the waiter too. He never broke eye contact with me.

"I love you. I'm sorry for what my parents did," he hollered, angling his body flush against mine. As if destiny had taken hold of the moment, the song changed, slowing everyone down. We moved together as one. I wrapped my free arm casually around his waist. His tight hold held us together. My guy was a silly romantic once he began to drink. And that spoke volumes since Dash knew how to turn on the charm at any given moment.

Just before arriving tonight, Dash and I had made a serious deal. We'd take a shot anytime Dash's heart spilled out of his mouth in either love or apology. This round appeared to be orchestrated and quite possibly the final one that did me in for the night.

"Alexis gave me some hip shakin' lessons." I then backed away from Dash to bust out with my newly acquired skill, bouncing my ass to the slow song. "Come on, boo," I yelled overly loud. "Dance with me."

"Boo? Are you okay? Because you're the one who needs to get us home," Dash said, standing still, watching me. "I'm drunk." He and I twinned in matching swim trunks, hanging low on our hips. No shirts or footwear. "Please don't leave me, Beau. Stay with me. We'll figure it out," Dash said pleadingly, again referencing what his shitty parents had done.

"Stop. Okay? I'm good!" I shouted, not to be heard over the music, but to penetrate Dash's thick skull. I sauntered back to him, slinging my arm around his hip, reaching lower to cup his ass with a playful squeeze. "I'm vibin' with your friends. They're a bunch of drunks, more than we are, but it's fun. You agree?"

Dash's palm swept upward against my chest. "I agree, you're drunk."

"You're drunk," I fired back then boldly leaned down to press my lips against his. The kiss didn't linger. Without missing a beat, I flipped around, bouncing my ass against his semi-firm cock. Over my shoulder, I instructed him on what to do. "I'm twerkin'. Grab my hips and let me dance against you. It's like a standin' lap dance." I dropped my head, leaned forward, and grabbed onto my knees, contracting the muscles in my stomach and lower body. In small, measured movements, I rubbed my butt enticingly against his swelling cock.

After a minute, the grip Dash had on my hips tightened with purpose. He thrust his hard cock against the material covering the crease of my ass. He held me with such force, I could barely move.

When he began to simulate fucking me, I was so there with him. After another minute, it took a bit of force to turn and face him, but this was something I needed to watch. He didn't disappoint. My guy was so damned sexy. His hips continually thrust against my cock. I ran my palms all over his body, feeling and caressing every wonderful inch that made him who he was. My beautiful, gorgeous guy. All mine. So mine.

Dash's strong arm locked around my waist, drawing me flush against his chest. Like a bull in a china shop, he swept us off the dance floor, only taking out about half the dancers as I stumbled where Dash led.

Internally, I knew where we were headed. Dash liked his cuddle time almost as much as he enjoyed a good public display of affection. Loungers lined the outside of the pool, meaning I'd be there shortly with Dash's tongue stuck down my throat for everyone to see.

Had I been a little less intoxicated and far less absorbed in the way his palms caressed all over me, I may have realized that we slipped past a dark curtain.

"I need you moving inside me." His sweet breath, a fruity zephyr, floated over my lips. As his chest bumped against mine, putting space between us, a single packet of lube was tucked into my palm. He closed my fingers over it. "I can't get over what happened. I need you to let me know that we're good."

A solid surge of adrenaline caught me off guard. My heart tripped over itself as uncertainty had me looking around our surroundings. Dark shadows loomed, yet we weren't exactly removed from the party. At any point, one of Dash's friends could wander in and catch us in the act. My drunk brain stopped giving a shit while my wicked cock twitched, all eager to get things started. At the same time, Dash gave a masterful stroke over my swim trunks, running base to tip.

"Is this a good idea?" I murmured, a sober thought trying to edge its way closer.

"Shh," Dash whispered. My chin tilted down at the same moment his lifted to swipe that sinful tongue across my lips. His signature move to demand entrance. Of course, I opened. He drove greedily inside, taking a deep dive into my mouth. The world around us ceased to exist.

All the over-the-top devotion I felt for Dash mixed with the decadent way we kissed. A dominance seeking clash of tongue and teeth. Our special brand of foreplay. Like always, I wanted to please Dash more than myself.

After several long moments, I reluctantly pulled away, surveying the small area. The only items other than us were boxes of glassware. Maybe a storage area. As soon as I locked on my target, a secure place to bend Dash over, I snapped into a more sober state or at least less intoxicated. Dash's wet tongue and soft, supple lips laved my cheek and jaw, aiming to take my mouth again. We had no time for an extended make-out session. We had to focus. Both my palms cupped his cheeks, pushing him away until his gaze met mine. "It'll embarrass you if we get caught."

His sly chuckle implied that I might not know him as well as I thought I did. His answer came with a shimmy, his swim trunks falling to his feet. "Yeah right. You got a lot to learn about me, cowboy." That new nickname caught me by surprise. "My guy's the hottest guy at the party, and he's committed to me. Let the world see."

I doubted the truth of those words, but all was forgotten when his fingers slid into the waistband of my trunks with no underwear to inhibit his touch. My swimwear tumbled down, pooling with his. Dash fisted my shaft, pulling and rubbing until my cock was hard as steel, pre-come already beading at my tip. Alcohol never dulled my physical attraction to Dash.

He'd studied me well, learning details of what I liked, and gave a twist with his tight grip. My eyes rolled into the back of my head, desire echoed in waves through me. My cock grew painfully hard, my hips involuntarily pitched forward. We both had to know my dick sought Dash's warm, wet mouth.

He actually did it. His wicked tongue swiped through the slit in my tip.

"We don't have time," I hissed regretfully, dragging him up to shuffle us several feet backward, between two rows of stacked boxes. My hands roamed freely over his hard body, my mouth suctioned onto his neck. I was so deeply in love, I didn't know where I began and he ended.

With no warning, Dash pivoted a one-eighty. His back was against my chest. All one hundred ninety pounds of him suddenly relaxed against me. The back of his head dropped to my shoulder. The world tilted as I absorbed his weight by taking a small stabilizing step behind me. My eyes closed, my arms wrapped tightly around him. That was when the world truly tumbled off its axis, causing my lids to pop open again. So no closing of the eyes. Shit just got more complicated.

"Bend over the boxes," I encouraged quietly.

"Fuck me, Beau," Dash murmured, swiveling his head toward me. "Hard and fast. Hurry." That was my plan, but I understood its implication. I did generally like to take my time, building his pleasure before I ever sank inside his ass. Even with his directive, I had to nudge him between the shoulder blades to drop his chest forward.

As I tore the corner of the lube packet, Dash shot up that perfect ass, spread his legs, and stood on his tiptoes. He wrapped his fingers around his cock, stroking. Overwhelming desire flooded me at that sight. There was never a time I didn't want him, but I loved this position.

Without a second thought, I slicked my cock then pushed my hand through the inviting crease. Three fingers easily breached his hole.

Dash reared back, driving my digits deeper inside. His handsome face twisted my direction, his plump lips opened into an O, an almost silent moan escaped. His eyelids screwed closed. What a beautiful guy in the throes of passion.

My hand on one hip moved to his shoulder, gripping him there to keep him in place. He wanted to be dominated, I was up for the task. I bent my knees, positioned my cock at his entrance, and thrust balls deep straight into my love's ass.

Jeez, what a fucking feeling. Dash's channel surrounded me, both tight yet pliant. The pumping music and loud chatter faded away. Dash's audible groan was all I needed to hear, a loving stroke to my soul.

"Shh," I managed to say. With no buildup, I drove my hips in and out of my guy.

"So good," Dash whispered or maybe I said that. The thundering in my ears drowned out all reason. This was good. A perfect end to our date night. Why hadn't I thought of this three shots ago?

A wild frenzy built inside me, rough and eager. My hips pistoned. My thighs burned from the pace I kept. I punched up into him, drawing Dash off his feet with my pummeling tempo.

"You good?" I asked, unsure if I said the words loud enough to be heard. Nothing intelligible left his mouth. His body went limp, causing me to grab his hips, keeping him in place as the blinding pleasure of my release tingled in my balls.

My body hummed as I continued to pump my hips. I went deep and hard, snapping my pelvis, slapping against Dash with every thrust. He was going to feel the impact of this fucking for days. I was in complete rapture, my fingertips digging into Dash's skin, holding him roughly in place.

Fire engulfed me from the inside out. Goosebumps erupted like tiny fireworks across my skin, even if we had time, I couldn't hold back a second longer. My orgasm blasted from me, ribbons of come filling his ass. The off-the-charts intensity sent my body into spasm mode, lurching me around on a wild ride as I tried to regain control. I stumbled forward, tumbling down on top of Dash's back, helpless to do more than absorb the intense pleasure careening through my system.

In unison, we slipped off the boxes. Dash's entire limp body landed on top of mine. Normally, I could absorb Dash's body weight, but the fingers I used on the ground below me for balance weren't on my side.

"Dash, what're you doin'? Help me out," I said. He didn't respond. Then I noticed his chest slowly rising and falling. He was asleep, or passed out, or both. Gently, I slapped his cheek to wake him. "Do you hear me?"

A loud snore rumbled from my guy, his head turning a minuscule amount. Or maybe his slight movement came from my quivering muscles.

"Well, hell." My ass hit the cool concrete. At the same time, my release began trickling out of him. What the fuck was I supposed to do with that?

I read the contents of the boxes around us. There was no reference to anything more than glass stamped on the outside. No cloth anything. Another slip in the plan of our secret hideaway. Fuck, Dash slumped over, slowly sliding off me as his snores grew louder.

Carefully, I laid him out beside me with his swim trunks still hanging off one foot. I manhandled the shorts up his legs, then yanked harder to get them over his ass to his hips. Mine were still a few feet away. Had I realized how intoxicated he was before starting all this?

Maybe.

I'd enjoyed myself thoroughly.

I tugged my trunks on then took the moment to straighten the few displaced boxes. With a giant heave-ho and one fluid move, I repositioned Dash from the floor to land over my shoulder. He hung there like a rag doll. One karate chop later, and I shoved the material of his swimwear deep inside his crease. Nobody needed to see my little swimmers slipping down his legs.

Off we went. I bravely pushed through the curtain and, just like Dash predicted, our disappearance had gone completely unnoticed.

"You're not as light as you were the last time I did this."

Dash gave no response, but his body did begin to slide down my arm, making me have to hoist him more securely over my shoulder. A sudden cheer erupted from the dance floor. I had no idea what they were celebrating, but lifted a fist pump high in the air. My own tiredness was getting the best of me too.

"Do you need help?" A host came racing over as I reached the elevator doors.

"Probably need a cab," I said, edging past her onto the elevator. "And we checked our stuff." She followed me into the elevator car. On the descent, the world tilted, requiring another stabilizing step from me. My stomach did a full somersault on the way down.

"I'll meet you at the front doors. There should be a cab there." She went one way, and I the other. As predicted, the doorman motioned a cab that pulled to the front of the building. The host returned as I did my best to lower Dash into the seat without doing too much damage.

"Dash, right? Here you go." She handed over one large clear bag full of everything we brought with us. Cool. "Did we tip you?"

"Yes, sir. Before you started. You two were generous." Cool again, and I gave a thumbs-up, pushing Dash's legs up to slide into the seat. We probably weren't going to be the big-tippers for too much longer.

2: The Sweet Daisy Mae Dash

"Mornin'," Beau chirped, slamming his cell phone on the kitchen counter. Well, not so much a forceful drop as a placement. But with my head pounding like a rock concert, it echoed like shattering glass falling down on me.

"Good morning," I replied, but only because it was Beau. Anyone else might have received a cold shoulder. "We need to tackle the hangover cure again. You're right, it feels very much like swine flu."

"Told you," Beau said. "You drinkin' that?"

I glanced down at the Keurig, busy filling my cup with coffee. The answer seemed obvious, but I replied anyway. "Yeah?"

"Want me to get a couple of raw eggs to put inside?"

My dry heave was violent and instant. I pressed a hand to my stomach and took big breaths through my nose. Luckily, I got it under control. Beau wasn't near as funny as he thought he was.

"I came home and hydrated. I feel okay, I guess." Beau opened the refrigerator door as if to follow through with his threat. He better not... I watched as his hand reached for the side of the door. I didn't need to see the bottle to know it was blue Powerade, Beau's constant sidekick for his outdoor activities and these types of occasions. One bottle slid across the counter toward me, and he took another.

"I had one a few minutes ago and took the ibuprofen you left out. How did we get home last night?" I asked, pouring loads of honey into my hot coffee.

"That was all on me. I didn't think about camera phones catching us leaving. Those are weird to me..." he said, then began chugging the drink.

His comment left me with more questions than answers. "The new phone I got you has a camera. If only you'd use it," I said dryly. Speaking of dry, so was my throat.

I didn't know what was so funny, but he'd just taken a sip, and his body pitched forward. I couldn't tell if the droplets flying everywhere were from his mouth or the bottle he quickly jerked away. Without missing a beat, I tossed the hand towel on the cabinet to the floor. Amelia's stern expressions, and years of training, reminded me that even a small spill could lead to chaos throughout the house.

"Why did you waste your money? My phone's fine."

"Your phone's based on minutes and it's six years old. They've stopped updating your operating system. I'd love to text you during the day..." I said, echoing the reasoning I gave at least three times a week since I bought the silly phone.

My oh-so-frustrating guy shut me down like it was his favorite pastime. "We're not havin' this conversation again. If we yap all day, what do we talk about at dinner? We'd already know everything the other did for the day." His index finger and thumb went to the crease above his nose, telling me what a challenge I was to him. I'd show him a challenge... Just when I was ready to blast an argument, his hand did a slither movement from the top of his face to the bottom until it popped out at me, insinuating he was tired of the many times we had this conversation. That I was the problematic one, not him. As I opened my mouth to unleash the demons of my hangover, he raised said hand to silence me. Only the intensity of my love sealed my lips.

"As I was sayin'..." Beau shot me a look that could curdle milk, daring me to interrupt him. I rolled my eyes and clutched the coffee cup like a lifeline to better days. "Your buddies snapped a picture of me carryin' you out. Got a call this mornin' and used your phone to receive it." The hydration drink was back at his lips as he sucked it down until the bottle was empty.

A million questions popped into my head as I tried to piece the puzzle together. "You're going to have to tell me more. I don't remember what happened. You carried me out of the club? How?"

"Tossed you over my shoulder like a sack of potatoes. For the record, potatoes are easier to carry than you are," Beau said, discarding the plastic bottle on the counter and crossing his arms over his chest.

I nodded, already questioning the consequences of my actions. How was I ever going to be taken seriously again? I moved to stand in front of Beau where he leaned against the edge of the granite island countertop.

"Well, that was after you made me fuck you like I hated you..."

My heart skipped a stuttering beat. *No.* Please no. "You did that at the party?" Oh holy hell, I already knew the answer. Heat built over my body at lightning speed. Warmth crept into my cheeks. My breath shifted to shallow puffs. If anyone saw me in such a compromising position, my reputation would be ruined. I was sure to have a permanent code of conduct disciplinary action on my school record. Pain spiked through my headache to what I assumed was an unhealthy level.

"Yup." Beau reached for the second bottle of Powerade. "I didn't realize you were that drunk when we started. You passed out probably in the middle. I guess that's about the time I started holding you up. It's sketchy. I had too much to drink."

"Explains my sore ass," I murmured, willing myself to remember any of it. "Did anyone see us?"

"Not that I'm aware. You found an alcove. Curtains closed us in." The pause felt designed to let that claim settle over me before he continued. "Alexis has claimed a spot as my new best friend. She called this mornin' to let me know they caught evidence of me sneakin' us out. She wanted me to tell you. And she taught me to twerk. I was solid. She kept slappin' my ass. But that's not all."

Oh holy hell, not more. My brows furrowed. I had to brace my nerves. They couldn't take much more. A key to my success was a constant representation of being a gentleman and a professional. Dammit. I blamed my family for last night's transgressions too.

"Scott and Lauren and their baby are makin' a pit stop in Dallas on their way home from a family reunion. They're swingin' by so we can meet the baby. They want to crash here for the night and leave tomorrow mornin'."

"When?" I asked.

"Soon," he said, reaching for my untouched Powerade bottle, flicking the lid open. "They'll be here in about two to three hours. I couldn't find a way to tell them no."

"Right. Don't tell them no." I took a deep, steadying breath to dispel the lingering nausea. It didn't help. "I'll need to order in food. I'm not up to cooking. Do we need any baby supplies?"

"Nope." Something in his tone had my gaze lifting to his cocked brow.

What now?

"They're comin' with the portable baby bed we sent when she was born."

Dammit, I was outed. Beau had insisted I not spend over thirty or forty dollars on presents when the baby arrived. What could you even buy with such a low limit?

"I don't think portable baby beds cost forty dollars max with delivery."

"I got a deal."

"You're lyin'," Beau countered. Damn straight. I rolled my eyes, then my head, and finally my body followed, turning to move between Beau's spread legs, and placed my coffee cup on the counter behind him. I didn't want him to be mad at me, mainly due to his cheap ass nature. He needed to leave future gift giving to me.

"Ding, ding, ding, some detective you are. Hold me."

"Naughty boys don't get lovin'" Beau replied, his lip curving up on the edge.

Ignoring that ridiculous edict, I wrapped my arms around his waist. It didn't take much more than a few seconds for him to pull me closer.

"So we had sex at the party?" I asked, my cheek landing on his chest, staring out the back windows at the swimming pool. "Did I enjoy it?"

"'Course."

"The way my ass feels, I'd say you hit it out of the park."

Beau caressed a hand down my back. I was in desperate need of a shower and our guest drink options required an inventory check. The thought of booze ruined the small amount of willpower I'd managed to rally.

I shrugged off Beau with a yawn and started for the bedroom. My guy grabbed me by the wrist. "I'm goin' to the store to get Scott some beer."

"Give me twenty minutes, and I'll go with you." That suggestion seemed ambitious, but we'd see how it went.

Beau just shook his head and let me go. "It'll take you longer. The shower alone takes you twenty minutes."

"Make scrambled eggs. I'll be fast." I left him there to argue with himself. Meanwhile, the clock was ticking, and my hair wasn't going to style itself.

I never imagined I could adore Beau more than I did, but boy, I got it wrong. The way he cradled Daisy Mae, Scott's baby daughter, melted my heart in the most gratifying way. We needed to have children of our own someday.

"Sir, your credit card has been declined." I had to rewind those words in my mind as I shifted my attention from the peaceful scene to focus on the phone call.

"That's not possible," I finally answered. "Can you try again?"

"I did, three times," she said. "You're a good customer."

Sure, I appreciated the sentiment, but how did being a good customer have anything to do with my credit card? "Thank you?" I answered.

My shoulders tightened, and my belly knotted. It had to be a power play from my father. Were all my credit cards suspended now? "Can I pay cash to the delivery driver?"

"Absolutely. The total's seventy-five twenty."

"Great," I said. Seventy-five dollars seemed a high price to feed four people.

"Give us about thirty minutes. Thank you, Dash."

"You too." I ended the call and brought myself back to the present. I'd delve further into this tomorrow.

With barely a toe through the door onto the patio, Beau's gaze locked on mine. He swayed back and forth, cradling the baby like a pro. My heart did a somersault. "At first he was all like, nope, not touching her, and now I'm not sure he'll ever let her go."

"I feel like bein' a godparent is like being a grandparent. I can love on her then give her back." Beau's genuine grin and heartfelt words hit me right in the feels. What a loving man. A good mix of loyalty, strength, and tenderness. No matter what curveballs my parents tossed our way, we would manage it together.

"Her face scrunches up at any noise or change in the breeze. I can tell she's a fighter with a warrior's heart." He ran the tips of his fingers in small circles over her heart. "But I think she's done somethin' in her diaper." He walked slowly toward Scott, suddenly ready to hand her off.

"I've got this one," Lauren said as if anyone else was trying to take on the duty. Beau gently handed Daisy Mae to her mama who cradled her just as tenderly as Beau. "I'm gonna feed her. Maybe we can both take a quick power nap. I'm tired."

Scott rose, giving Lauren then the baby a quick kiss. Even more endearingly, he went ahead of his family to open the door. "We'll be quiet out here. If Daisy Mae doesn't go to sleep, text me and I'll come get her."

They were sweet. Scott barely shut the door before he jerked his head toward Beau, superiority in his expression. "Just closed a ten-thousand-dollar contract. My cut is ten percent. I'm definitely gonna win." Scott's tone held confidence and determination. I'd only heard stories about this rivalry between Scott and Beau. I'd never seen it head-on. My brow crinkled, having no idea what he was talking about.

"Ha," Beau shot back, not in a happy way. Condescension laced every word he said. "I put my application into buyin' a FedEx ground route. When I get it, you'll be left in the dust."

Beau buying a route was news to me.

"Ha," Scott mimicked. "You can't afford a route. Good luck with that. And we agreed you weren't usin' his money." With the way Scott pointed a finger at me, I felt suddenly and unwittingly included.

"I know nothing about any of this," I said, my tone suggesting Scott and Beau were insane. The guy I lived with was trying to buy a ground route, and I didn't know? We spent every available free minute together. The sweet emotions rolling through me from earlier turned into confusion and maybe a little hurt thrown in. I kept very little from Beau.

Before I could react, Beau started scanning the roof. I followed his gaze, wondering what he saw. Within seconds, he started toward the corner where one side of the house connected to the other. With one foot on the edge of a patio chair, he grabbed the ledge and was off, hoisting his body onto the roof. His balance was insanely good. With that same fluidity of movement, he fearlessly ran across the roof.

He repeated the same maneuver onto the second floor. A sudden memory of a younger Beau climbing in and out of his grandparents' window helped me deal with the overwhelming burst of anxiety at Beau's recklessness.

Another leap had him landing on the peak of the dormer window. He was as far up on the house as he could go. He mimicked Scott's confident attitude as he glanced down at us. Well mainly at Scott as Beau splayed his arms and hands out. "I win."

Besides the beads of sweat forming in my pits, all I could think about was how ridiculous they were, and how selfish Beau was being. What happened to our relationship if he miscalculated a step? Was I destined to pine for him for the rest of my life?

"Beau, get your ass down here," I said firmly.

"Oh yeah, watch this." Scott's challenging tone had me looking away from the crazy guy on the roof to the other one shaking his fist, loosening his wrist and arm. A stone began to skip across the water in the pool. It managed to stay on top of the water for three quarters of the way before sinking to the bottom. The gauntlet was thrown. "I took the stone-skippin' crown at the Dog River Festival three years runnin'. I didn't want to rub it in at the time, but I win."

Oh no, that was Beau's old title. I felt to my bones the depth of how badly Scott got under Beau's skin. He didn't hesitate to respond and ran the few feet across the peak. Remarkably, he didn't lose his balance before leaping into the water. A perfect cannon-ball off the roof into the deep end of the swimming pool.

My heart dropped to my feet. The seconds it took for him to emerge from the water were the longest of my life. When he popped up in a grand splash, his fist darted above his head. Scott mimicked the same fist pumping raise. Loud whoops and hollers came from both guys.

I reared back, grasping behind me for the arm of a patio chair, landing blindly on the seat. This was too much. "Scott, you can't come back. You're a bad influence."

Lauren's head poked out the back door. "Seriously? That's quiet?" she called.

"Sorry, babe." It was as if Scott instantly flipped a switch, transforming into the attentive husband again. "Did I wake her?"

Honestly, Lauren might have more attitude than either of them. "Well, of course you did. Come help me." With no hesitation, he obliged, following her inside. She held an extraordinary grip on Scott.

My guy had that same kind of captivating control over me. My gaze fixed on Beau ascending the swimming pool's steps with a smile larger than life. For me, the vision of my muscled-up guy coming toward me with water cascading down his body was an alluring treat. He made me forget why I was upset.

When he started toward me, I recognized his playful, predatory intent. He had a thing for enveloping me in one of his bear hugs that would wrinkle my clothing.

I leaped up, ready to dart away. Luckily, the doorbell chimed, giving me an excuse to leave. "Dinner," I said. "I'll be back."

In almost a jog, I dipped back into the house. I couldn't believe he'd jumped from the roof. We had to dial back his crazy adventurous spirit to a safer setting, if there was one. I shook my head, smiling.

3: The Joy
Beau

Monday

I released a jaw-cracking yawn and focused on the country music playing from my truck's radio. The workday hadn't been particularly rough, FedEx was in chill season, but the events of the past few days were piling up. A quiet night at home then a good night's sleep should do the trick, making me feel right as rain tomorrow.

With one elbow resting on the edge of my rolled-down window and the other on the steering wheel, I maneuvered onto Dash's street with what I considered an expert one-handed turn.

I saw the events unfolding instantly, but it seemed so wrong that it didn't make sense. A beater tow truck was in the process of leaving the driveway with Dash's sleek ride on top of the steel bed. I braked in the middle of the road until the tow truck was out of the driveway.

Dread coiled the muscles in my shoulders. Stop assuming. Maybe Dash had some sort of vehicle malfunction. I hadn't heard from him since this morning. Now, that seemed suspicious. I saw Dash standing on the porch, one hand fisted on his hip, the other grasping his cell phone, the crease between his brows deepened. He saw me and didn't smile. Whoever he spoke with held all his attention.

The garage door was wide open. I parked in the driveway and got out of the truck. The closer I got to Dash the more I felt waves of anxiety wafting off him. I was slow on the approach just in case he was on a private call. Before I made it halfway to the porch, Amelia's car, Dash's nanny now housekeeper, came to a screeching halt at the curb in front of the house.

Oh, that couldn't be good. Something nefarious was a foot.

"Is Dash all right?" Amelia asked from her open window, concern in her voice and tears in her eyes.

"Can you help her?" Dash asked me. To him, Amelia was like a mother. She'd been by his side since the night his parents brought him home as a newborn. Their bond was unbreakable. Whatever happened to her was bound to be a catalyst that drove Dash to the brink.

"I just got home. What's happenin'?" I asked her, crossing the yard to help her out of the car. I glanced over at Dash. Who now had a finger stuck in his free ear. He turned away, retreating into the house.

"I've been terminated without any explanation. I had a letter dropped off at the place where I'm staying. Is Dash all right? This wasn't his decision, right?" she asked, her deep concern evident in her tone. Ah, power plays of the rich and famous. That was what was afoot this afternoon. This one was low, even for Dash's family. Amelia was a dedicated employee to the Richmonds.

"Let's go inside and wait for Dash. I don't know what's happenin'. We haven't talked much today, but his car was just hauled off." I wrapped an arm around her shoulders and began walking her toward the front door.

"His phone isn't working," she clarified. "That's why I'm here. I've worked for the Richmonds for twenty-five years," she explained with tears running down her cheeks. The gravity of the situation became clearer.

"His cell phone was turned off?" I asked.

"Yes, he's using that fancy phone you refuse to use. He bought the service himself. That's why it's operational," she explained. "He told me what his parents did. I made him a good lunch to help him feel better." She gave a hiccuped tsk and shook her head in distaste.

I pushed open the front door, finding that none of the lights were on.

Oh no.

Dash's office door swung open, revealing the deep concern etched on his face. His efforts to conceal it from us failed mightily. His grin that usually helped him get his way, lacked its normal radiance. "I was hoping to have all this resolved before you got home," he said, his voice tense, but he did come toward me, placing both palms on my chest, lifting for a quick peck. "What's going on, Amelia?"

"Your father fired me. His secretary called and gave no explanation except they won't fight unemployment. I don't understand," she said, tears amping up again. "He's being too mean. You're his son. You've been good to him."

Any attempt to hide his worry fell from his face as he gave a heavy exhale. Amelia and Dash never hid the depth of what they meant to each other. Amelia being closer to him than anyone else in his family. His sorrow was palpable, taking her into his arms, hugging her tightly. "Give me time. I promise to figure this out. Until then, I'll pay your salary. Leave your sister's house and move in here. I've wanted you to for a long time."

"I can't be a burden to you. It's my job to take care of you, not the other way around," she said and opened her purse, pulling out a tissue that she'd technically needed several moments ago.

"If you stay here, your money goes farther. Stay upstairs, you'll have a private entrance."

In all the years I'd known both of them, I knew very little about Amelia or her life. Only that she was devoted to Dash, and Dash to her. Not that I was asked, but of course, she should live here.

"What's goin' on with the electricity?" I asked, interrupting the sadness between these two.

Dash sighed. "I've transferred all the utilities into my name. The bills come with me as the payor. The electric company said they'd turn it back on tonight. I'm not sure when," Dash answered. He rubbed his temples with the thumb and forefinger of one hand.

"The utilities weren't in your name?" I asked. That was different information than what I'd heard the numerous times before when I wanted to pay them.

"I believed them to be," Dash answered, waving a hand dismissively. He refocused his attention on Amelia. "What will your family think if you decide to stay here for the foreseeable future? I can talk to them personally."

"Dasham." The use of his real name caught both our undivided attention. "I don't want to be a burden to you. You're like a son to me." Her focus turned to me, distaste on her face. "I've never liked the way his mother and father treated him. Dash didn't agree with me, but I knew they were no good."

Her confession left Dash scrubbing his hands down his face in dismay, and perhaps agreement. "I need to catch Beau up. Give your notice that you're moving out. Beau and I will help you move your things, whenever you're ready." His next words seemed designed to relieve the tension. At least they worked to alleviate the tears. "Beau has a truck and strong muscles, it'll go fast. Are you safe to drive home tonight?"

She nodded, drawing him into a hug as he spoke to me.

"I need to secure some sort of transportation and get a new cell number." Lines of worry creased the corners of his eyes and mouth. "We've also lost the landline and internet service. I haven't had time to reconnect those. Utility companies take a long time to deal with on something pretty straight forward."

"He took your car?" I asked.

The hug released. Amelia lowered her head, wiping away her tears. No way that single tissue could stand up against the waterfall coming from her eyes again. Without saying a word, she started for the small bathroom off the entry.

"Yes. The electricity was off when the tow truck driver arrived. He had to battle the garage door open," Dash answered, and swiveled his neck, trying to release the strain there. He gave another deep centering breath and slow, steady exhale. The hits kept coming. My poor guy.

"You have the truck. Maybe drop me off at work in the mornin', or is there a bus route I can take? I've ridden the bus before." While Dash typically controlled his facial expressions, he couldn't help but let them slip when he perceived I said something absurd, like right then.

"You're not taking a bus," Dash said sternly. "Of course, you're not. Everything will be fine. Right now, things are complicated, but once it's managed, we'll be independent and done with them."

"I'll let you two be alone," Amelia said. The tears had subsided, leaving behind a pair of puffy eyes as the only proof they were ever there. "I'll be here first thing in the morning, like always." She offered me one of her rare side hugs then embraced Dash with something more substantial. "You're a better person than all of them combined. Your choices are the right ones. We'll get through this together." It was the kind of comfort only a mother could provide. She brought her face close to his. "If I need to take a second job to help pay the bills around here, I happily will."

Oh man, that was dedication, and something Dash would never allow to happen. "I'm sorry this has affected you," Dash said on a sigh.

I left them in the foyer to finish their private conversation and went to the bedroom, my brow furrowed in concern. My most immediate goals included a shower because it was like a furnace outside today. Then I needed time to process why I shouldn't take off tonight. The only reason this was happening to Dash was because of me. His parents didn't like me around. It felt irresponsible and selfish to stay, but I promised Dash I would. So how did this end?

The tension knots in my neck became rock hard. The mere workday exhaustion from minutes ago felt like boulders on my shoulders. I had four months' salary saved. I'd be okay until I found another place to settle. Perhaps now Dash would see the merit in our separation.

"Your ball cap's on backward. I haven't seen it like that since we were in Sea Springs," Dash said fondly from the bedroom doorway.

How could he focus on something so ordinary while his life was crumbling down around him? Perhaps Dash was genuinely struggling with mental illness, just as his parents and all the counselors they had sent him to suggested.

"You're correct in whatever you're thinking, but it was a fond memory I hung onto. You wore a cap like that when I first met you at the party in the field. It frames your face really well."

"Since I chopped off my hair, the ball cap is the only way to keep it off my face..." Wait. I let Dash distract me. I waved my hands in the air to show my frustration. "Stop. What you're dealin' with is ridiculous. How much more can your father do to you before you open your eyes?"

Dash's shoulders slumped in defeat. "I'll acknowledge I wasn't as prepared as I believed when I severed ties with my family, but I'm sorting it out. I apologize for the inconvenience this causes you. You work hard..."

"You're worried about the inconvenience to me?" I asked incredulously. "When's it gonna feel right to say goodbye to me? You don't have a *car*."

"Hush. We made the decision to stick together. Fuck the world for keeping us apart. Let me change, then come and help me open the back doors. They have a manual locking system that I'm certain you can reach easier than I can. We have plenty of cold cuts, cheeses, and chips. I think Amelia made a pasta salad this morning..."

The more Dash spoke, the better his mood became. He began the process of removing his snug shirt. Something I really enjoyed watching. A private strip tease only for me. Each shimmy and shake captured all my destructive thoughts and tossed them away.

"We'll rough it until the electricity turns back on," Dash continued. "Be cowboys from the wild west. Hang out by the pool, the lights out there are solar operated." I followed him into the dark closet. A pair of swim trunks hit my chest before Dash wriggled out of his expensive khakis. The shadows added extra flair to his undressing.

I was such a pig, ogling Dash on such a difficult day. Even with no utilities, this house was still comfortable with lots of natural light. At least to me. And maybe to the guy now standing nude in front of me.

Several hours later

Dash was back. My quintessential doting guy. We shared a meal, swam, relaxed, and had an overall good time. He cracked his usual silly jokes and acted as if every word I said mattered, which it didn't. I listened as he broke down his day.

As the evening turned to night, the electricity was still out. We laid contently in bed together. We left the glass wall panels that lined the back of the house open to allow the cooler night air to filter through the bedroom.

I held Dash with my eyes closed, and as if by magic, the electricity flipped on. Music played quietly in the background, as it always did, followed by a succession of beeps from every direction. The security monitor on the wall initiated its operating system, signaling its status as it went.

"I have money," I murmured into Dash's hair, not ready to let the closeness go. "We also have Mom's check for the truck. They'd be a good downpayment on a nice ride for you."

Dash trailed his fingertips across my chest, lulling me into a trance with every swipe. "Maybe it's time to have a joint checking and savings account. We've defined ourselves as a committed couple to the world."

"I'm fine with that. I want to be a partner, not a dependent," I said. They were words I'd uttered many times since we'd gotten back together.

"Why didn't I know about your application to own a FedEx route?"

I had kept it quiet, not allowing myself to dwell too much. No doubt the fear of failure held my tongue. My application had a very solid chance of being denied, and what if I couldn't handle the load of being a small business owner? I was young, almost twenty-one. Money and loans were concerns I didn't know about. My mom had agreed to back the loan and be a co-owner if my age and lack of business experience were a problem.

If I answered honestly, I risked Dash throwing a full-fledged tantrum over how I hadn't asked him to be my money tree.

A sudden ding on the monitor indicated the garage door was being opened. We both tilted our heads in that direction as if we might see what was happening. In seconds, Dash was out of bed, dried swim trunks pulled back on and running his fingers through his hair.

"Hang on, I'll go with you," I said.

"Stay in bed. Besides you and Amelia, only Chandler knows the security code to come inside. Let me go see what's happened." Those words were said as he left the room.

Of course I didn't listen, dressing quickly. For the first time, I was glad for Dash's eccentric glass walls throughout the house. As I went to join them, I watched Joy, Dash's niece come into the living room. With Dash the last and unexpected baby of ten children, it created lots of nieces, nephews, and cousins slightly older than him. Chandler, Dash's longtime friend, followed behind her. Joy was dressed in a one-piece Jiffy Lube coverall, her hair neatly tucked underneath a matching ball cap.

The scene seemed weird. Dread coiled in my gut based on their grim expressions.

"What's happening?" Dash asked. Joy removed the cap, her long, straight blonde hair unwinding in a cascade down her back. It had been years since I saw her last. She had matured. Her face now featured defined angles. Yet, she continued to radiate a striking beauty, a characteristic that ran in their family.

Her blue-eyed gaze landed on me, worry clearly etched on her face. A mirror to Dash's expression. Yet, when she saw me, her face softened.

All else faded into the background when she came to me, wrapping her arms around me. "Despite all that's happening, I was happy and relieved to hear you've returned to Dash," she said.

"Thank you," I said, my arm easily encircling her, savoring the sincerity of her words.

"No one understood what Dash was waiting on, but I did. I saw you two together. I got it." With the attitude that was all Joy, she flipped around to Dash. "He comes back, and you don't tell me?"

Dash's lips quirked up. I appreciated his ability to remain level-headed despite everything being thrown at him. "I was keeping us in a bubble. I didn't want to share him."

"Maybe stayin' hidden a little longer, or like forever, would have been wiser," I added, my grin growing broad. I felt lighter in that moment, which was a wonderful feeling since I'd been carrying the blame for every shitty thing that went down with Dash and his family.

"I knew he was back," Chandler said, pointing a finger at me. "But he doesn't like me at all. Notice how quickly his smile faded."

"It's not that he doesn't like you," Dash said, responding to Chandler. However, even Dash couldn't maintain the overused lie when he turned to my stern face. Joy laughed a musical sound at the change of my expression. "When Beau first arrived, there was confusion."

"Yeah, that was the day I got my walking papers," Chandler quipped. "Anytime we crossed paths, I was surprised I didn't vaporize where I stood." No matter how hard I tried, I couldn't hold in my grin. The way he spoke the truth made me feel like I'd won. I didn't say it aloud, but my core knew the win counted.

"So what's going on?" Dash asked.

Chandler dropped his hands in his fancy pants pocket. Joy moved to stand in front of Dash. The room's vibe turned serious again. "If Granddad or my parents find out I was here, I'll be excommunicated like you." She air-quoted the word excommunicated. "Granddad actually used that word about you. He's so arrogant. That's the reason I came over. He's crazier than normal. He's unleashing all his power on you. You're going to be evicted from your house..."

"This is my home," Dash stated firmly. "It was a graduation gift that I personally went down and signed the paperwork for. The title is in my name."

Joy shook her head. "I don't understand it all, but something about shell companies that you've been removed from?"

I certainly had no knowledge about business, but Dash's expression transformed into that of a fierce opponent. He planned to fight where maybe he hadn't before.

"There's more. I eavesdropped on Dad and Grandad's lunch chat. He's having you watched. That's where we were told about your situation and under no circumstance are we to communicate or see you. If we do, we're out of the family too," she added. "He's planning to bring you home on your knees, begging to be reinstated. He's not going to let you back in, but he wants to see you grovel."

"The rumor circulating through Dedman suggests that you have been removed from further classes," Chandler said. The pain those words obviously caused him to say may have mollified my dislike of him by a tad.

"What?" Dash erupted. His anger was tangible, sending a surge through the room. "I'm a student with an impeccable record. How can they justify removing me?"

"Dr. Harris advocated for you. He's someone good to have at your back. He didn't let it go, but your father threatened to pull his funding for the entire school, saying you'll be the last Richmond to enter SMU. Of course Dr. Harris didn't stand a chance after that."

Typically composed, Dash had reached his tipping point. A hot flush spread from his neck to his face. The cords and muscles in his shoulders visibly strained. "My utilities were disconnected, my car's been taken, and they terminated Amelia's position. She was the person who raised me."

"Why did he terminate Amelia?" Joy asked, just as concerned. "Why didn't he reassign her?"

"To hurt me," Dash said in a steely tone. "What're my options?" he asked Chandler.

"I don't know but use Dr. Harris's advice. He's reaching out to you in the next couple of days," Chandler said. "Be honest with him. If the gossip's to be believed, and the source is his assistant, Dr. Harris said some pretty nasty things about your family."

"We have to go," Joy said, winding her hair back up and shoving it under the cap. "I'll get a phone I can text you on. For whatever it's worth, I'm glad you're here," she said to me with a faint, sweet grin, before she turned to Dash. "I know you were over the moon when he arrived. I'm sorry for what's happened. Granddad's completely in the wrong."

Dash nodded. The anger remained in every line of his body. He needed space to vent to Joy and Chandler.

"I'll give you some privacy to talk. He won't do it in front of me," I said.

I raised my hand in goodbye and held Chandler's gaze. If I read his expression properly, he blamed me and wondered why I was still there after everything that went down. He wasn't wrong.

My retreat to the bedroom was swift, closing the door behind me. I had to find a way to sleep. My morning started in seven hours. If not, when Dash returned, he'd take time to talk to me, let me know it was going to be all right, when it so clearly wasn't.

4: The Deed
Dash/Beau

Dash

Two days later

My father was a master manipulator. It appeared he'd chosen attorneys of the same ilk. I reclined in my office chair, rocking in measured movements, confronted with an incredibly convoluted mess. I inhaled deeply then gave a slow, controlled exhale, going through the steps I'd learned in counseling to keep my anxiety at a distance. Then I repeated the action. This time, the inhalation lingered on the inside until I slowly let it go as a sigh. Confusion was rare for me, but my father had certainly managed to create it.

What more was he hiding? Why was he determined to cut me off at the knees? My kneecaps ached at the possibility. How had I become the very client I wanted to help in the future?

I shook my head. My father had been busy. It hadn't taken long to find the fraudulent information on the shell company that now supposedly owned my house. If I deciphered all the vague legal jargon correctly, the front company that owned this property was now being dissolved. The assets, meaning my home and the land it was on, were being transferred into Richmond Holdings.

Somehow, my name was listed as the founder of the shell company but was now being removed from the business altogether. I needed time to quietly reflect, to consider my next move. I probably needed to find an attorney who specialized in real estate to counsel me. Someone who wasn't afraid of my father.

My chair popped forward as I reached for the keyboard. The concern of keeping my house was a minor annoyance compared to the upheaval with my law school. Based on an email I received yesterday from the assistant dean of admissions, I was no longer enrolled at Dedman School of Law. This tragic turn of events was followed by a complete refusal to speak to me by any leadership. I sneered at my computer screen, seeing red as I planned another probable lawsuit in my future.

I might not have my father's wealth backing me, or his conniving, mean-spirited, cutthroat attitude, but I was steadfast and stubborn as fuck. Smarter than my father too. His day was coming. I'd sit and wait for the opportunity to pounce when the moment was right.

As I logged into my email account, conviction steeled my spine. Out of the dozen or so emails of interest I'd sent to various law schools across the country, I hadn't heard a peep back. A move from the DFW area seemed imperative. A prospect needed to firm up quickly before Beau's application for a FedEx route began to process.

Another far worse realization settled like a heavy blanket on top of me. What if no law school was interested in me? What happened to my future? With a glance at the large decorative clock on the wall, I had about thirty minutes before Beau was due home. A strong, jaw cracking yawn overtook me, revealing my exhaustion. Relentless hours spent on finding the answers were to blame.

My eyes drifted closed as I sorted through the devastation of the last week. The worry didn't last long as assorted images of Beau flitted across my mind. My love had only grown stronger even amidst all the chaos. I cherished him in a way I didn't fully understand but drove me to be a better man. Right now in our lives, the unsettled emotion Beau held in his gaze bothered me a lot more than having to figure out how to stop my father's destructive actions.

I saw the strain he was under. He believed he was the cause of my current problems. Of course, it didn't help that I had spent every waking moment for the last two or three days fixated on countering my father's moves before he destroyed me. The dark edges of sleep lulled the running commentary in my head to nothing more than a background hum. I let it take me under.

Beau

"Dash," I murmured, resting a firm hand on his shoulder, gently shaking him awake. "You can't keep goin' like this. It's time to go to bed."

His head tilted toward me, eyes closed, smiling in the direction of my voice. Then his eyelashes fluttered open. One of my hands rested on his shoulder, the other on the desk. What Dash tried to hide, I could still see written all over the concerned set of his handsome face. He was worried over the lengths his father was taking.

"I like your ball cap on backward. It fits your face. Reminds me of the night we met," Dash said with fatigue still in his voice. He found my hand and threaded our fingers together. "You look tired."

"I am. It's been an exhaustin' week. Did you find anything new?" I asked, taking a seat on the edge of the desk, forced there because Dash didn't let go of my hand.

"Yes and no," he said vaguely, slowly rising to his feet. "Dr. Harris contacted me today and wants to stop by our house tomorrow evening. I want you to be here to listen to what he has to say. Does that sound all right?" he asked, swiveling our hand-hold until he began to pull me from the office. "You've been shouldering a lot—"

My sudden burst of laughter startled him, halting his ridiculous words and his steps. He pivoted around on the heels of his loafers, his quizzical gaze locked on mine. "What?"

"Nothin'," I answered, no amount of talking could change his thoughts, I'd tried. I continued moving us to the bedroom. "You've been goin' at it from mornin' to night. You're going to bed. I brought home pork and beans and hot dogs." I winked at him to show my confidence, paired with an unwavering belief in my skill at creating a delicious homemade dinner for the two of us. "I'm on supper duty. I mastered my skill at makin' a mean beanie-weenie while in my dorm room. I also make a pretty decent Kraft Mac & Cheese."

Dash's brows lifted in faux excitement as he circled an arm around me. We walked side-by-side toward the bedroom. "Mmm, that sounds delicious. I was thinking of ordering in from the dumpling house, but your idea's good too. I guess. I've never eaten a beanie-weenie."

Once we reached the bedroom, Dash released me, but I didn't let go of him, drawing him into the circle of my arms. He automatically wrapped his arms around me.

"You need to take better care of yourself," I said.

With a thump, his forehead hit my chest, a heavy breath exhaled slowly. "I'm honestly getting worried. I've sent messages to different law schools, none are responding. But that's not the worst of it. If I lose this house..." He lifted his gaze to meet mine, his head falling between his shoulder blades. "I designed this home for us, envisioning years together here. Nothing's going as planned. I apologize for everything."

"Don't say that," I told him firmly. "You know what to do to stop all this."

"Please don't leave me," Dash pleaded, cutting to the chase, his voice filled with emotion.

"It'd be the right thing to do, but I can't unless you tell me to. And we see where that's at." I bent to kiss his lips and reached for the hem of his polo shirt, freeing it from his waistband. "Every day that I come home and you're consumed with worry, that's only there because you wanted a relationship with me... Dash, it's hard."

"I love you, and you're right, I have to loosen up about all this. Tomorrow night we'll form a good plan. I'll do better," he said.

He always took all the blame from me and landed it on his shoulders. "Stop. You're perfect. We'll eat dinner in bed, maybe watch one of the documentaries you like, and go to sleep early." I tugged on his shirt, his arms flailed as I pulled it over his head. I tossed it to the nearby armchair.

He also gave me a cheeky, inviting grin.

"I think you're trying to seduce me?" Dash unbuttoned the top button of my uniform shirt then removed my ball cap. "You're so tanned."

I ended up shooing his hands away. "Tonight's all about making you feel good. Let me handle it. Why wear all these clothes when you're home all day?" I aimed to release his belt buckle, eager to move him into more comfortable attire.

I knew he knew I was teasing. Dash dressed to impress all of the time. Apparently, I moved too slow, because his hands swooped in to finish my task. In a flash, Dash popped his feet from his loafers. His slacks were caught in one hand to be tossed over the chair. "I've gotta give you a reason to come home, right?"

Ridiculous. In a move I'd performed plenty before, I placed both hands on his biceps and backed Dash to the bed. About a foot away, I pushed, and he let out a yelp, landing down with a bounce on the mattress. "What the hell, Brooks? You trying to seduce me or break my neck?"

His plump cock was a second or two behind the rest of him, landing on his lower belly with a bounce. I grinned, liking that a lot. "So dramatic."

Sex hadn't been on the menu tonight, but as I stared at his hard, toned body, I couldn't stop from pulling off more of my clothing.

"I like to watch you undress," Dash said, appreciatively.

"Yeah, me too." I dropped my dirty clothes onto the floor where I stood, pooling around my work boots. They'd find their way into the laundry room soon enough.

"You like to watch you undress too?" Dash gave a thoughtful nod, teasing me. "That's another thing we have in common."

Dash gripped his shaft, pulling up and down. I couldn't look away. My lip tucked between my teeth and my mouth watered as I zeroed in on the small bead of pre-come already on his tip. It had only been a few days since I'd felt my guy's intimate touch, but man, I missed it.

I reached down to untie my laces and remove my boots. What should have been an easy task was made monumentally more difficult with the way my gaze continued to shift between Dash and my laces. "I thought I'd bring you to bed, maybe suck you, then cook dinner. I wanted you to be asleep by now."

"Yeah, right," Dash chastised. "I'm determined it'll always be like this between us. Finish undressing and join me."

Following orders, I unbuckled my belt, then let the shorts fall to my feet. "Now, turn around."

Surprisingly, Dash listened and gave in to my request. Sure, I'd seen this view of his backside every day, but tonight felt different somehow. It was as if I'd finally committed to sticking around. He wanted me with him, and I wanted to be here too.

A pump bottle of lubricant was a permanent fixture on the nightstand within reach of my position. I crawled onto the mattress, pressing my lips to the edge of where his ass and thighs met before settling down beside him.

"I'd give everything for you too," I purred against his ear. I massaged and caressed across his back. "How do you want me tonight?"

"You know," he said, laying his cheek on the bedspread, looking at me. "Own me. The rougher the better."

I lifted my hand to his shoulder, digging my thumb into the tight muscles there. I rose, single-handedly pumping a generous portion of the lube into my palm, while straddling his ass. Rubbing my palms together, I spread the slick over my hands before digging my fingers into Dash's hard traps. "You've gotta relax more. You'll think better if you do."

"I'm struggling to get past how I misjudged my father so completely. Both my parents knew how much you mean to me. My intentions were clear. Yet they were fine with destroying you and ruining me. They stripped me of my standing in a university that finally began to judge me for me. I know that shell company wasn't in place when I signed for this house. Someone on the inside of the courts had to change ownership. They had to. "

"Shh," I said quietly, working my hands in the same manner football trainers had done to untie me after a game. "You're a clever guy. You'll know what to do when the time comes. Rest. If you fall asleep, I won't wake you."

Dash closed his eyes and leaned into my touch. "Don't stop. We haven't been together in days. I need this."

What I had to do was keep my wits about me if I planned to get through the next few minutes of sensual torture. With every roll of my hips, my cock rubbed against the crack of Dash's ass cheeks. I should let him rest, and I was determined to let that happen, but he always wanted me ready and rough. Yeah, I was up to the task.

Dash

Thousands of twinkling lights threw a party inside my head as Beau worked his magic with those talented hands.

"I love you," he murmured softly in my ear. His raspy voice sent a shiver down my spine. When he leaned in, I could feel the evidence of his desire pressing against my spine. His strong hand traced the length of my shoulder, neck, and hairline.

I shivered under the intimacy. A smile akin to the over-the-top love I had for our lives spread across my face. Tingles sprinted over me with the romance of it all, certain to have my guy inside me before too much longer.

The sexy sensation of his body pressed along the length of mine, going skin-on-skin, sent another shiver as he drew me from behind into one of his giant bear hugs. Those sinful, pleasure-filled lips nipped at my neck.

"You're a good guy. You need to remember that. Do you hear me?"

It wasn't the question it seemed. Instead of waiting for a response, I rode the waves of emotion Beau so easily conjured inside me. My thoughts drifted to a peaceful, committed life with my love. Something far easier than anything in our past. Nothing mattered more than the dream of our lives together. A bright blue sky and churning waves were the backdrop of the images ruffling through my mind.

"The place that drives me is building a vendetta against my father," I murmured in contrast to the serene imagery inside my head. My toes dug into the sandy beach, the ocean's give and take sent water cascading over my feet then back again. "I've never been focused on anything so mean. I want Jackson Richmond to pay for what he's done." I spoke those words in a soft tone, failing to convey the determination and strength of will I'd used to get my way. Maybe I wasn't as calm as I thought.

"You're so smart and focused. You challenge everything." He gently touched my shoulder with a simple kiss. His hands continued roaming, caressing, and massaging freely. As I relaxed, my cock responded, growing harder with the way he pleased me. "I think the best way to get to your dad is for us to thrive in a great life together."

He slid his hand beneath my chest, covering my heart. I could sense his heartbeat aligning with mine. He made an incredible point. My happiness mattered and would drive my father crazy.

I lifted my head, puckering, waiting for his lips. Beau sweetly obliged.

"Let's move back to our roots. Close to water. Chase your fishing charter dreams. I need a plan to hold on to," I murmured.

"I do too," Beau agreed. When I tried to shift to face Beau, he denied me, and repositioned to fully cover my back. Beau read my silence correctly and latched onto my neck, sucking there, determined to leave his mark. My guy liked to tag me.

I arched my back up, pushing to my knees. The move dislodged Beau. He effortlessly repositioned, slipping a hand beneath my hips to grip the shaft of my cock. He glided smoothly back and forth, easily undoing me.

"Mmm," I moaned, signaling my readiness. Three lubricated fingers entered my hole. *Fuck*. The sudden intrusion felt good. One of his skilled fingers curled, intimately knowing the direction of my gland. Instant blinding pleasure caused my hips to buck and my body to arch. Beau's grip on my cock tightened to keep me from coming early.

"You're so fuckin' hot, baby." The hissed and husky delivery of the words sent a thrill through me.

Beau's lips latched onto the skin on the side of my back, sucking tenderly as his fingers continued to move inside me, readying me from the inside out.

"You tease too much," I muttered under my breath, but I didn't mean a word of it. Every building second through my release incited pure pleasure. Beau spread my cheeks wide, giving a single swipe of his tongue, bottom to top. I fucking loved that move.

His broad, mushroomed tip poked at my entrance. And here we went. My head reared backward as Beau expertly sheathed his cock fully inside my channel. Exactly the way I wanted, in one sure thrust. He played me like a fiddle.

Stars peppered my vision. Goddamn, how did this mean so fucking much every single time? I got on all fours, lifting my chest off the mattress, clenching the duvet with my fists. I relished the way my body stretched and encased Beau's moving cock.

I spread my thighs farther apart and dropped my head to lock eyes on Beau's swinging balls. I needed a camcorder placed right under Beau's sac to watch his body move in and out of me. Then the real pleasure came. Beau gripped my shoulder tightly, doing his best to keep me in place while he pummeled my ass.

My knees weakened at the cadence Beau created. My pants huffed, a bead of sweat trickled down my cheek, and my ass slapped against Beau's groin. He did a motherfucking deep dive with every single thrust. Something new happened... Beau circled his arms around my body, hoisting me up until my back hit the hard muscles of his chest. Holy hell, I sank down onto his cock to sit fully on top of him. A burst of bright light tore through me, causing my mind to blip. My only recourse was to will the neurons back inside my head in order to retain every second about the pleasure of this moment.

I gripped my cock to help steady myself, squeezing tightly as Beau shifted to better absorb the weight of my body.

"Ohmigod," I hissed.

Beau's heavy breath huffed against my ear as my being betrayed me. I went limp, caught between both of Beau's strong arms. The decadent way he destroyed my ass continued, bouncing me up and down at his will.

My head swayed back and forth as he worked me over.

"Only you." Beau's sweet husky vow melted me.

As soon as I could form words again, I'd tell him the same thing.

Beau

The sensual hums and moans whispered from Dash spurred me on. A new twist in our bedroom play was that Dash consistently wanted me to go at him hard and fast. The rise and fall of my body exerted energy that I'd apparently been saving during our brief stint of abstinence.

I writhed, moving instinctually in the way Dash wanted, but, hell, I did have my limits. Sweat trickled from my hairline, also coating my chest. The silky feel of his skin rubbing against mine resonated in a place that belonged entirely to him.

Dash's slack arm circled my neck, holding him up.

The way my arms caged him in, he wasn't going anywhere until we were through.

The crescendo of dazzling pleasure and total dominance kept me rocking up into Dash's ass, then taking him down with me, ass to heels. The pace was wild and frenzied, my stomach muscles working with my thighs to make this perfect for the purring man in my arms.

The moment was beautifully devastating. The binds between us tightened a notch. Where did I begin and he end? We were one. Always to be one.

Dash

"I'm close... Be ready," Beau said, his husky command hoarse and gravelly. He gently knocked my head off his shoulder to carefully place me down on the mattress. I'd lost all focus. My body exquisitely vibrated and hummed. My guy owned me, body and soul. When I woke up in the morning, I'd be centered and balanced, ready to find the answers I sought to establish our future.

Beau never stopped grinding against me, but he used his strong grip to lift my hips, shoving a pillow underneath me. This was his signature move to get me where he wanted me. He plundered my ass, both his hands gripping my shoulders as I huffed and puffed, grunting loudly with each driving thrust. He drove harder and deeper. He was so damned good at hitting my prostate every single time.

"Touch yourself...Dash."

The bed frame rattled, taking a solid beating as my body bounced up and down under his demanding thrusts. The musky scent of our sex reached my soul. The sounds of flesh slapping against flesh echoed throughout the room.

I whimpered, begging him to finish, so I could too. I shuddered involuntarily before I tensed from head to toe. My ass contracted tightly around him. Darkness engulfed the bright fireworks show behind my lids. It was all it took. His wild thrusts never slowed, but his rhythm faltered.

Rapture crashed over me in mind-numbing waves of ecstasy. I rode wave after wave. Beau's shout and spilling seed somehow made it better.

In the deepest of trances, darkness claimed me into an inviting sleep.

5: The Arch Nemesis
Beau

Dallas, Texas

I lounged against the sofa, one arm casually draped over the back. With Dash's cell phone in hand, I gave up the pretense of listening to the conversation in front of me. Two important findings to note: Who knew cell phones had *Tetris*? And legal jargon was mind numbing and impossible to follow. Dr. Harris's visit created some issues for me. The most important one was how many stifled yawns I could hide in one night.

My thumbs danced deftly over the phone's keypad, my gaze glued to the small screen. *Tetris* had never been my thing, but as well as I played, maybe I was some sort of prodigy. I pondered if gaming might be the career path for my future. Maybe I needed the new Xbox.

"Babe," Dash said, his palm resting on my thigh. That touch was the only thing that could tear me away from the game. In a split second, I glanced at his hand, then up to his face, before shifting my concentration back to the phone.

Maybe as long as a minute passed when the silence in the room drew my stare back to Dash. If I read his expression correctly, he was astonished or maybe incredulous.

"What?" I said, defensively raising the hand resting along the back of the sofa, not nearly ready to part with the phone.

"You weren't listening to Dr. Harris?" Dash snapped. My eyes narrowed a small degree as I judged the sincerity of the question.

Since Dr. Harris had arrived, a whole new side of Dash emerged. He was polished, poised, and an extreme gentleman. From his polite manners to serving coffee and dainty snacks, he had serious social game. Me, on the other hand? I was a clumsy, unsophisticated ox. I decided honesty was the best answer.

"You lost me after you told Dr. Harris to have a seat."

Dr. Harris and Dash spoke a language I'd never heard before, so I sat there quietly. That should be considered a win in my favor.

Dash continued to stare at me as if I'd suddenly grown two heads. Heads... He'd love me having two heads... I was hilarious.

"What?" I said, defensively. "I didn't fall asleep, that has to count."

I took Dr. Harris's low chuckle as a vote in my favor. "I've given Dash some hope."

"More like a lifeline," Dash replied, his tone clipped with his irritation at me. "He's contacted Wesley Carter who's apparently my father's arch nemesis. Overall, Carter has a completely different take on life than my father. Dr. Harris wants me to contact him. Dr. Harris thinks he might help me find a law school that'll accept me."

"That's a positive, right?" I interpreted Dash's newest look to mean *you're a dumbass*. So I glanced at Dr. Harris for a nod of approval. He gave it, and I beamed at my mister, unwinding my arm until I clamped my palm over the back of his hand, still on my thigh.

"I respect Carter. He and Dash share similar ideologies. We can make the call now."

Great. My hand tightened around Dash's. Good news had been hard to find over the last week.

"And the house, did you figure out a way for him to keep it?" I asked. Based on the sheer volume of paperwork scattered over the coffee table and everywhere else, they had to have gone over every possibility.

"Dr. Harris believes we have a path forward. I'll, of course, handle the work which will save us significant money. It'll drive my father insane which is an added benefit." Dash's lip quirked up on one side, which let me know he enjoyed that thought.

Dr. Harris dialed a number on his cell phone and set it to speaker mode before laying it on the center of the coffee table. Shrill ringing filled the room but was silenced almost immediately by someone answering on the other end.

"Carter." The tone was similar to the one Dash had used moments ago to reprimand me for my inattention.

"Carter, this a good time?" Dr. Harris asked.

"Sure," Wesley said, his tone changing in seconds. "I didn't recognize this number. Is Dasham with you?"

Dr. Harris lifted a hand, gesturing for Dash to respond. "I'm here."

"Great. I'll be brief as I'm interrupting my date to take this call." The commotion in the background grew quieter as he spoke. "Dasham, there's an opportunity for you in Chicago. Summer classes begin soon. You'll need to make a quick decision, but they're pleased to have you considering them. You've built quite a reputation among your peers."

My quick glance at Dash revealed instant relief easing the tension on his face, a small smile even appeared. I moved my hand to Dash's back, caressing there. Proud that others knew how hard Dash had worked in his studies.

"I'm relieved for the chance, but Chicago's a long commute from Dallas, and my resources are becoming more limited with each passing day."

"I've heard about that as well. Don't worry. I've got you covered. I own a building in Hyde Park that can house you. It's my personal suite that I haven't used in years. Stay as long as you need—forever, if possible. A home needs someone looking out for it. It's not an inconvenience at all."

Dash's smile broadened, his eyelids closing as he took a centering breath. Silence fell over the room.

"Based on what I'm seeing, Carter," Dr. Harris said. "You've overwhelmed him."

"Very good."

"Mr. Carter, I have a partner now. Is there any issue with him joining me?" Dash asked. He reached for my hand. The phone I'd been using to pass the time while Dash and Dr. Harris discussed all the issues tumbled from my hand, allowing Dash and me to link our fingers together.

"Sure. No problem," Carter replied. "Drop the mister. That's a term your father requires, not me."

"Yes, sir," Dash said.

"Lose the sir," Carter said with a chuckle. "I'm not near old enough to be called a sir. I need to end this call. Dr. Harris believes in you, and I trust him. I also don't like your father. He'll not appreciate my interfering in his appalling decision, so it works out for both of us." I could've sworn I heard a touch of glee in Carter's voice with that last statement.

Dash gave a single nod and tilted his chin in my direction. "I need to discuss this with my partner. He has a job here in Dallas that he loves."

Carter chuckled this time. "I fully understand the importance of having your partner on board. If it helps, I'm certain I can work out a position for him in his chosen field. Dr. Harris has my contact information. Take your time but call me in the morning with your decision. We can get you to Chicago to begin the process."

"Yes, sir," Dash said, his gaze locked on mine.

"Aaa..." Carter's admonishment made me laugh. Dash was trained so well that he only murmured a quiet contrite apology.

"I'm sorry. I'll touch base first thing in the morning. We appreciate this offer. My situation was turning more dire than I anticipated. Thank you for the lifeline."

"Truly, it's a win/win for both of us," Carter said, and the call ended abruptly.

My beautiful guy broke his composed demeanor, placing his hands over his face. I watched his chest give a slight shudder and reached for a napkin, tucking it inside the bottom of his palms.

"This has been a difficult time for him," I offered to Dr. Harris, pushing over in the seat to wrap my arm around Dash.

"I assumed so. I've been in the circle of Richmond children attending SMU for most of my tenure. I had figured I'd have to pass him due to the financial help his father gives the college." Dr. Harris tsked his disapproval of that action. With a nod toward the man wrapped securely in my arm, he added, "His siblings have nothing on Dash."

Dash dropped his hands, but kept his face downturned, dabbing the napkin at his eyes.

"I'm sorry. I wasn't sure I'd be able to continue law school." He released a shaky breath and stood. "Excuse me." He didn't wait for an answer. Instead, he headed toward the small bathroom off the foyer. His eyes were red, his composure struggling.

"I'm going to leave," Dr. Harris said, rising and starting toward the front door. "Tell Dash I'll email him Carter's details tonight. Once his father makes his official move, we'll work together to secure this property. Unfortunately, he'll have to make these decisions quickly. Classes begin in Chicago a week before Dedman."

At the front door, I extended my right hand to shake his. Dr. Harris obliged. He seemed like a very down to earth guy. In a lowered voice, he said, "I'm uncertain if he'll go without you, and he'll need a good support system in Chicago. It's a different world there. Make your decisions quickly. If given the opportunity, Dash has a tremendous future, but he needs to be decisive either way."

I appreciated how direct Dr. Harris gave his advice and nodded my understanding. Of course, I'd go if Dash needed to move. I'd never abandon him. Those decisions were made. Perhaps I could transfer with FedEx. If not, I'd find some place to work. I was employable even if only for a pack mule position.

"I understand, and I'm committed. Thank you for comin'."

"Good night," Dr. Harris, he left without looking back when I opened the door. When he made it to his car parked on the street, I shut the door and twisted the lock. Dash emerged from the bathroom within seconds. He had been crying, pretty significantly, based on the flushed cheeks and glassy eyes. My heart twisted. Dash had been so loyal to the ones he loved and was barely given that back in return. I lifted my thumb over my shoulder to the front door.

"He said he'll send the information to you tonight through email."

My guy came to me, arms spread. The simple embrace we gave one another all the time had more meaning now. I wasn't sure I'd ever seen Dash tearful before.

"Everything that happened tonight is good, right?" I asked, squeezing him tightly.

"I'm nervous. It seems too good to be true on such a shitty week," he said, releasing me with one arm, the other guiding us toward the living room. "When I lost you, I was determined to see you again. With my parents, they've made choices that I can't forgive, and they continue to ensure I never will. I didn't share with you all the rejections and non-answers I was getting from my transfer requests."

Dash let me go to clean the paperwork off the coffee table. I started with the coffee cups and saucers, adding them to the serving tray he'd brought out. "I'll eat the snacks."

His grin softened his expression. "Keeping you fed will cost us quite a bit of money."

"Untrue. The beanie-weenies you missed last night only cost a couple bucks," I countered, deciding those weren't near as good as I remembered them being. Dash fed me too well these days.

"I regret missing such a delicious meal," Dash said, stacking the pages together.

"I've never seen you sleep so deeply before." I took the tray to the sink. "I knew it was rough for you."

I filled the sink with soapy water. These dainty cups had to be china. Dash placed the three-tiered snack serving tray beside me.

"I decided last night that I'm not into secrets," I said, turning enough to give him a wink. Dash needed no extra pressure right now, but he also had to learn to keep things real.

"I slept so hard because you're a god in the bedroom," Dash said and turned to lean against the counter, arms crossing over his chest, facing me.

I executed a dramatic eye roll and began washing the dishes.

"If it works out, how do you feel about moving to Chicago?"

"If that's where you are, then I'll figure it out," I said. "I don't want to be without you, but if you need me to stay in the house, I will."

"I guess you're right." Dash reached for a hand towel, encouraging me to give him each rinsed dish. In the lull of conversation, I could almost hear the cogwheels turning in his head.

I gave him time and space. He went toward the china cabinet, and I grabbed the tiered snack tray and headed for the bedroom, my stomach growling. Among the leftovers were assorted tiny sandwiches, a fruity array, and mixed cheeses and assorted crackers. A plump, mild blueberry landed in my mouth, but it only accentuated my hunger.

After placing the tray on the mattress, I headed to the closet to change out of the nice clothes Dash had laid out for me earlier. He entered the closet, clearly still lost in thought. Usually, I'd accost Dash as he undressed, but I gave him a break tonight, no matter how sexy unfastening those cufflinks looked.

I felt strange about having cufflinks turning me on, and made a beeline for the tray. My stomach upped its game, rumbling like a snare drum in a homecoming parade. Each tier tray came off the base, so I carefully put everything on the duvet and took a seat with them.

Dash was so preoccupied that he even sported a pair of pajama pants, going against his own rule of being naked while inside this room. He went for his laptop and brought it to bed with him.

"Do you know anything about Wesley Carter?"

The bite of cheese lodged in my throat as I laughed then coughed my answer. "Of course, not."

"What do you think his angle is?" Dash asked, sitting across from me with the computer in his lap as he typed on the keyboard.

"I feel like he was pretty straightforward about it," I answered, rolling off the bed to get a glass of water from the mini bar.

"And what do you believe he said?"

Here we went, the many questions began. Of course, Dash had the answers in his head, but he wanted a different perspective. I always played along. "Okay, I believe what he said about stickin' it to your father. You two have that in common. I do too."

Dash nodded his acceptance of that premise. "That was my interpretation too."

"I don't understand money on that level," I said. "But helpin' you live and go to law school seems like pennies for guys like that. How do you feel about it all?"

Dash's gaze turned speculative, thinking through the answer as he spoke. "Better than I anticipated. I'm not sure it'll upset my father. He seems to be finished with me."

"Your old man wants you destroyed, so if this gets under his skin, then you have a win."

"What does it say about me that the prospect excites me?" Dash asked, a gleam in his eye. I loved that sparkle. It meant he was happy.

"If there was any way I could have gotten my father back, no question, I'd already have signed on the dotted line." Those were facts.

I chose a couple of sandwiches to try. With the first bite, my taste buds questioned my choices. I sniffed the sandwich, unsure what to make of it. I glanced over at Dash. "What's this?"

Dash's gaze locked on the sandwich in my hand. "Leek, prosciutto, topped with a sour cream spread. It's my favorite."

Well then, I'd save the rest for him. I definitely didn't have the refined taste buds to swallow another bite.

"Come over here, sit by me. I'll share my food," I said, patting the bed closer to my side..

But I'd lost him again. Dash's eyes moved quickly, scanning the screen, reading in that quick way he always did. I dropped to my back, staring at the ceiling. It sure seemed like I was moving to Chicago. The country boy inside me rejected such a big city. Depending on where we lived, maybe we'd be close enough to get to the lake easily. If so, it'd be better than living in Dallas. Pushing all thoughts aside but the food in front of me, I decided to take it day by day.

6: The Windy City Dash

Chicago, Illinois

It was one thing to be consumed by a desire for retribution against my father, but quite another to act so blatantly on that impulse. After spending most of the night studying the history of the Richmond/Carter public feud, it became apparent that there was a deep-seated loathing between the two men. Like Dr. Harris suggested, my ideology aligned more closely with that of Carter. If I accepted Wesley Carter's offer, I'd be jumping the line of no return. But was there a point to return to anyway?

I had vowed to cease all communication with my parents until Beau received an apology and a plan in place to earn our trust. Of course, that was never going to happen. Joy had made my family's position clear. What they hadn't counted on, I was just as stubborn as my father. I had youth and education on my side to combat his aging experience. Wow, that was a damned bold statement, but true, nonetheless.

So why did I persist in wrestling with this decision?

I paced the living room. The sunrise edged through the glass walls, making the time and expense I'd invested in my backyard worth every dime. What an extraordinary view. The brief reprieve from my thoughts allowed the truth to emerge. I'd always been a positive, assertive, somewhat obsessive person. What happened if the goodness inside me turned into a consuming vengeance? At that point, what happened to the man I wanted to be?

I knew that answer. Fuck a meaningful life. I'd spend my time searching for a way to destroy my father. Where others failed to bring him to his knees, I'd find the way and act swiftly.

However, I couldn't let this opportunity slip by. No other law school wanted me. I abruptly stopped walking as a light bulb moment struck. There was no other choice. Over the last six years, I'd painstakingly planned every part of Beau and my life together. It hurt me to think I had to give up on those dreams.

I was confident in my ability to outperform my father's lawyers in court. It wasn't just my intelligence, but more the lack of effort from the men on his team. They relied on my father's reputation and ability to bribe the officials. I'd bury them, no question. Especially with Dr. Harris at my back.

The one crucial person I hadn't given enough thought to was my guy. Could being with me compensate for his relocation across the country, and the sacrifice of losing his dream job? The effect on Beau couldn't be ignored. Finishing my degree meant we'd be far closer to achieving the charter boat service Beau had always dreamed of establishing.

My cell phone rang, interrupting my ruminations. I strode into my office, glancing at the wall clock, not yet seven in the morning. Hmm. I swiped the small screen, putting the call on the speaker option. "Dash Richmond."

"Dash," Carter said, and dove right in. "I needed to initiate this call before starting my workday. A plane's being readied for you at the Dallas Executive Airport. Joanie, one of our employees, will rendezvous with you in Chicago to get you where you need to be. She's scheduled meetings with the school, then you'll check out the living conditions, and take a tour around the immediate area. You're scheduled to return to Dallas tomorrow morning," he said, his no-nonsense voice grew softer to a whisper as he spoke to someone else near him. "Did I get that right?"

"Yes. Only add that Joanie will take him to the airport in the morning too. He'll stay in your place tonight," a female voice said.

"Did you catch that?" Carter asked.

"I did." I thought this was a discussion on my commitment to the idea, but instead the wheels were in motion.

"You still there?" Carter asked.

"I am."

"What's got you silent?"

"The offer's exciting," I started, my mind racing to process everything while considering all angles. "Your help aligns with my goals to thrive in spite of my father and family. It'll make him crazy."

"Whenever it happens, I want to be there when you confront him, so it's settled. I'm traveling today. Don't take the first offer given from the school and carefully consider everything. Chicago is a very different place than Dallas. We'll continue this conversation this evening," Carter said.

I nodded a few seconds before speaking. "Thank you. Let me talk to Beau and then I'll head to the airport. We're a package deal."

"That's right, I remember. Dr. Harris explained the fucked up things your old man did to you two. I don't abide by the class structure. Tell me again what his needs are." I heard the call switch from speakerphone to a direct conversation. Good. I didn't want anyone to think badly of Beau. "My personal assistant is with me. I'll transfer the phone to her. Let her know what he needs?"

"Hi, Dash, I'm Lisa. Tell me what he needs."

"Beau likes his job." My smile grew as I ensured he'd be as happy as possible with the move. "It'd be nice if he could transfer with FedEx or get a job with UPS."

"What does he do?" she asked.

"He's a delivery driver. He's currently employed with FedEx, and he may be able to transfer. Perhaps I'm getting ahead of myself," I explained, lifting my gaze as the front door opened and Amelia came through.

"It's no problem to secure employment. I'll have answers for you two this evening," Lisa said.

"Thank you," I said.

"No, thank you. Carter's been grinning ear to ear this morning in the office. It's a real treat," she said in a tone that showed happiness or maybe that was just her natural way.

"I even brought donuts today," Carter said, taking the phone back. "I need to leave. I'll call you tonight. Enjoy yourself." The call ended. All my excessive contemplations were futile. I was heading to Chicago. I had to call Beau, schedule a cab, and pack a bag.

"What's going on?" Amelia asked as I came out of my office with the phone in hand. At the same time, it dinged with a notification. The message had to be from Beau. I opened it as I nodded toward my bedroom.

"Come with me and I'll explain. I feel like things are finally going our way again." As I went, I opened the message.

"*Stop fretting and make the call*," Beau texted.

My wonderful guy knew me well. As I set my thumbs to typing on the small keyboard, I felt like moving to Chicago was the best idea. Fingers crossed it turned out that way.

"The place is stunning," I said to Beau. "Look at these appliances and the way the whole kitchen's seamlessly put together. It's beautiful and functional," I explained, happy with the way my day had gone. Hope filled my being, something I desperately needed. "I'll go to the bedroom."

I walked the length of the contemporary dining room then up the sweeping stairs, curved along a wall, directly facing Lake Michigan. At the top, one way went in the direction of a large guest bedroom, the other way was the main bedroom. The entire house flowed well together in both the architecture and interior design. The colors and decor were much like my home in Texas. Beige, cowboy brown, black, and whites. The pop of color came from different layers of blue all across the spectrum.

"Close your eyes." I paused at the doorway to make sure Beau's eyes were closed, then pushed the door open with my foot. "Open." I slowly scanned the room with the laptop camera.

"Are those windows?" Yes, they were large windows with an unobstructed view of Lake Michigan.

"Nothing gets past my guy. The bed's soft yet firm. The closet's huge..."

"Is that a bar?" It took me a second to find what he saw. Maybe an armoire in the corner of the room. I hadn't paid attention. I went there and opened the handle, and yes, it was a complete bar with a sink and ice machine. Shelves moved in and out, filled with everything from Grey Goose to a professional grade espresso machine. We only had to leave the room to eat. That explained the armchair facing toward the windows.

"Why do rich people have bars in their bedroom?" Well, the answer seemed easy enough, so I gave him time to think it through.

"Stop distracting me. The closet's something else." I walked through the door and soft light lit the small room. There wasn't much in the way of personal things inside. A suit, athletic pants, a dress shirt, and a nice long coat. I stood still and let him take it all in. "It has many tie drawers and a shoe cabinet. Look at this." I went to another built-in cabinet and pulled out a thin row of drawers with one T-shirt folded there. "It keeps your T-shirts organized."

"That's cool."

Beside the closet was the bathroom. Again, decorated in the same colors throughout the home. It was gorgeous with a large sunken bathtub, and a sauna on the back wall. On the other side, there was a nice-size shower with jets pointing in different directions from the ceiling. The shower walls were glass from top to bottom. I imagined we'd spend a lot of time there.

"That almost looks like a muscle recovery bathroom. There's gotta be an ice machine in there. Is he fit?"

"In the pictures I found, he was always in a suit. But I agree, it's the perfect place for relaxing." I went back through the closet to the windows. "You can't see it, but we're close to the top floor, the view of the lake is spectacular, and from the other side of the living room, we can see the front of the building and the parking garage. The pool's on the seventh floor, so we shouldn't have too much noise. We're one of two residents on this floor. Each suite is accessed separately. It's gorgeous here. Everything we need is within walking distance. My school's pretty close. A UPS facility is nearby, and the FedEx facility's a decent drive, but not too far."

"Cool." The doorbell rang on Beau's end.

Seconds later, Carter's name appeared on my cell phone screen. I didn't immediately answer. "Who's at the door? Check before you open it."

"To Amelia's frustration, I ordered a pizza. It's them." Beau's sudden grin spoke of how angry Amelia truly was. "She wanted to spend the night, so I didn't get lonely."

"Babe, Carter's calling," I said and lifted a hand to wave goodbye. "I'll call you back."

"Give me a few minutes," Beau said. My desktop computer in Dallas instantly clicked off without even a goodbye.

"I love you too. I miss you," I teased the blank screen and answered Carter's call. I plopped my ass in the first available chair I found.

"I hear you've accepted the UC Law offer," Carter said. "You got a full scholarship out of them." He sounded proud, and I definitely was.

"What kind of law student would I be if I couldn't handle a simple negotiation of who was paying for my education?" I quipped. "They've accepted my fast track needs, making an exception that allows for summer school classes to help me finish by December. I enrolled in the program and spent about an hour in the bursar's office. Beau's good with it, so I locked myself in."

Carter barked out a loud, boisterous laugh. The chatter on his end silenced for a couple of long seconds. He didn't seem to notice. "Good job."

"I've been to Chicago many times over my life, but I haven't ever seen it like this before," I said. "What an eclectic part of town. I'm truly in debt to you."

"No, you aren't. But I wouldn't mind getting under your father's skin now. Post pictures on whatever social sites you're on. My team will pick 'em up and run with it in a positive light."

I nodded, my grin turning as devious as his. Since I'd gotten a guarantee from the school, my father couldn't ruin this for me. I too was ready to show dear ole Dad that I was still standing, maybe even better than before.

"Deal. I have a friend who can also drop the news," I said, thinking about Chandler's parents. If I spoke to Chandler, it wouldn't take more than a couple of hours before my mom found out, she'd handle spreading it throughout the family.

"All right, you've got your marching orders. I've got to go, but I wanted to add, I have a vehicle there in the garage. Use it," Carter offered.

This deal just got sweeter and sweeter. "Thank you," I said.

"Stop saying that." Carter disconnected without waiting for a reply. I ended the call. The quiet allowed me a moment to consider everything. What I didn't know was how long this good fortune might last. It didn't matter. My target was set, and I could achieve it. I only needed the opportunity.

7: The Check, Check
Beau

Dallas, Texas

The to-do list that Dash and I created for ourselves was longer than I realized. A full page each, single spaced. We'd put pen to paper after he returned home. The list just kept growing as we talked about the future and moving across country. Currently, I watched from my perch at the kitchen table as he paced the living room, landline phone to his ear. The open floorplan of our Dallas home let me see and hear it all. He spoke to Dr. Harris. A lengthy conversation, much like the one a few days ago that lost my attention completely.

I palmed his cell phone, spending way too much of my free time playing games. The same thing happened this time that did the last. I tuned everything out as my thumbs worked the keypad until Dash's shadow broke my tunnel vision.

"Video games while I'm talking to Dr. Harris. I'm beginning to see the pattern," Dash said, grinning like the Cheshire cat. The call with Dr. Harris must have gone his way. He took my list and rapidly scanned the page. "Let's call your mom together. That'll remove something off both our lists. Then call Scott to see if he can ride with you."

"I don't need Scott. I'll drive by myself," I said. There were several points of contention between him and I regarding this move, and we ran smack into one of them right now. He was so damned hard-headed. "Drivin's what I do for a livin'."

"I don't like the idea of you driving alone. Anything could happen. I'd be more comfortable if he were there with you."

How was I only now seeing the old man who resided inside Dash? Everything we did was through the perspective of a risk manager.

"Sit down," I said, nodding to the seat beside me. "Let's call my mom. I haven't told her anything. So, we'll catch her up, but only hit the high points. Otherwise, she'll worry."

"We don't have to tell her," Dash offered. "She doesn't need more stress. It's turning out good for us."

Yeah, right. My mom never let anything go. "She's like a bloodhound. She'll sniff out the truth. Just follow my lead," I said. "Don't offer anything extra."

"Got it," Dash said.

I placed the phone in the middle of the table and found my mom's contact information. After another follow-my-lead stare, I pushed call while Dash grinned. Based on his smile, maybe my look didn't convey what I wanted. Dash often gave that same expression during our sexy time.

"You like that phone, don't you?" he asked. Adding a dramatic flair, I rolled my eyes. Of course, I liked the phone—who wouldn't. I lifted a finger, silencing him.

"Hey, babe. I didn't expect your call," she said as if we ever had a plan to talk, and as if we didn't say something to each other every day.

"Mom, it's me and Dash, listen, we need to catch you up on what's goin' on now with us. He's here with me." Like a good boy, he stayed silent, listening until I gave him permission to speak.

"Hey, Dash. How're you this evening?" she asked. My chin nodded, encouraging him to answer.

"Hi, Linda. Beau hasn't given me permission to say anything more." The way his eyebrows waggled had me upping my conversational game and my irritation.

"What?" she asked. Dash had garnered her full attention. The bloodhound began sniffing. "Dash, why can't you speak?"

The way my palm shot out, halting any response he had to give, caught us both off guard.

"I'm gonna bullet point what's happened over the last week, then I'll tell you the solutions we've found. You can ask questions after that," I explained.

"Dash, does he do this to you all the time? Is my boy a control freak now?" Her tone held humor, and Dash grinned again. He and I both knew who the true control freak was, which was why I was handling the call. Otherwise, we'd be here until tomorrow, lists left undone. I shook my head. My mom and Dash liked each other so much.

"Here we go, Mom. Pay attention," I said and had to look down to my hands to keep from losing focus. "We finally told Dash's parents about us. Apparently, Dash's dad worked with my father to break us up. Probably the reason for all the money he had."

The interruption was immediate. "Beau, no. Are you certain?"

"He's very certain," Dash said. "My parents explained their actions in front of both of us."

"Hang on. Stay focused," I said, taking back control of this conversation. "The result of that discussion is that Dash has been cut off from his family. His father's done a complete job of removin' him from their lives, takin' his car, canceling the utilities, turnin' off his cell phone, just on and on."

"Because he's with you? They'd do all this to Dash because you returned?" she asked incredulously.

"Yeah," Dash answered. "It was shocking to me. They watched the way I mourned for my guy..." Dash's hand came across the table to cover mine.

"Mom, there's more. His father had Dash removed from his law school. The employment contract he'd secured for after graduation was terminated too."

"You've got to be kidding. What kind of parent..."

"Save it, Mom. Long story short, through Dash's professor, he found a person willin' to help him, but we have to move to Chicago for him to attend classes." I ticked off the list inside my head, feeling like I was covering the basics. "Dash starts class on Monday. He's flyin' to Chicago in the morning."

"Are you selling your house, Dash?" she asked.

"No. I've arranged for Amelia to stay here until I know better what our future holds. My father fired her to get back at me," Dash said, squeezing my hand tighter. His stated devotion from moments ago was forgotten. This grip held frustration.

The way she gave a deep intake of breath, made me do the same. It was a lot. For a woman who'd lost everything fighting for me, this had to be hard to hear.

"But it's turned into a positive. Dash is goin' to the top law school in the country on a full ride. A guy that can't stand his father is offerin' help," I explained.

"So you're moving?" she asked. "What about your job? I know you like what you do."

"There's a UPS hub close by, a FedEx station a little further out. We think I have an in," I said, glancing up at Dash for confirmation. He nodded. My main goal was to be supportive, not questioning how this was going to impact me. The hell Dash had been through meant a breakdown was coming. I'd give to him what he gave to me: a quiet, stable space in the storm.

"When's this happening?" she asked.

"In a couple of weeks. I'll pack up the truck with what we want to take with us and head up there. Amelia's going to move into this Dallas home to keep an eye on the place. The Chicago home we're stayin' at is fully furnished. It's not like I'm takin' a movin' van worth of stuff with me. And then we'll stay until Dash finds a place to land."

"I'll probably fly home then ride up there with him," Dash offered, exactly like he wasn't supposed to do. Adding to the plan or the explanation was a previously stated hard *no*. How did he not remember since it was only moments ago?

"I'll ride with you," my mom suggested. "I want to see where you're living. Make sure it's safe, in a safe neighborhood." The crazy-eyed expression and tilting head I gave to Dash better have conveyed my utter irritation with him. I mouthed, *stick to the facts.*

"Mom, I want you to come up there, but I think Scott's gonna help us. Maybe you can come the next week. I'll have time to show you around while Dash is in class. It's different than SMU. He's gonna be really busy."

"Not too busy to explore Chicago with you, Linda," Dash corrected, charmingly. "Beau's going to try and keep me away from you, so you'll like him more than me."

"I have two sons now. I love you both equally, but I have questions. All this money your father had, did it come from Dash's father?" she asked. Pretty much my most immediate thought too after learning the truth.

"Probably, but we don't know," I answered. Honestly, I knew her too well. She'd think this through and want to give the money back. Dash and I had talked about that possibility last night. The money needed to stay with her. She had also suffered mightily under our fathers' cruelty.

"Linda, we don't know, but I'll say my father owes it to you and much more. He took everything from you. We want you to keep the money," Dash said, and I gave him props for the warm reassurance in his tone.

Silence ensued for several long moments. "This is why your father turned to alcohol. He couldn't bear what he had done," she said.

"That's our guess too, and ultimately, he might not like what he'd done, but he still did it," I said. "I'm not givin' him any breaks. He did this along with Mr. Richmond."

"I know, son. And I agree."

"We have a lot to do before Dash leaves," I said, drawing the phone closer to me. "We should probably go. I gotta call Scott."

"Son, if he can't ride with you, I will. You don't need to make the trip by yourself," she said, mimicking Dash who nodded exaggeratingly. They were ridiculous. Like either one of them could protect me or themselves if things went south. "Then I'll plan to be there for your birthday. Twenty-one is a big one. We'll go have a drink."

Dash chuckled under his breath. I'd never been the one carded. My resting bitch face scared people. Dash, on the other hand, had to show his ID everywhere we went.

"Sounds good, Linda. I can't wait to see you," Dash said.

I cocked a brow at him while understanding she was the only parent figure we had left, and Dash was buttering her up, because that was what he did.

"Mom, I gotta go. We have a million things to do before he leaves. I'll call you next week," I said.

"Dash, you call me too, honey," she said. "I'm sorry for the trouble your parents have caused you. I'll never understand being gifted such joy with your children then doing everything possible to tear them down."

Dash ducked his head, probably not wanting me to see his vulnerability.

"I'm sorry for the pain it caused Beau," he finally said. His words less forceful than moments ago as a well of emotion clogged his throat. Dash let go of an unsteady sigh, and continued, "But I've been given a gift with you and Beau standing with me." Well, that might be laying it on too thick. I laughed but his hand reached for mine again, gently squeezing. "You know I feel that way."

"I agree," my mom said. "We're family. I'll always be there for both of you."

"Thanks, Mom. Dash has turned into a crybaby. I see a tear forming," I teased, giving Dash a minute to compose himself. "Bye, Mom."

"Be careful, Dash. Text me when your flight lands," she said in another turn in our relationship. Our family unit just grew stronger.

The following Monday evening.
Dallas, Texas

Who knew how much I enjoyed the quiet? And honestly, props to me over how far I'd come emotionally in the last five months. No matter how hard my dad tried, he hadn't destroyed the inner fabric of my being. The negativity was gone. I was growing and developing into the person I always hoped to be. A good guy with values and honesty. Dash was the conductor, orchestrating the power of healing inside me. I truly hoped I was helping him in the same ways too.

Dash. His name echoed over all the restored spaces inside me. Since he'd made me believe that this was my home too, my soul found contentment by simply breathing in the Dash-infused scents surrounding me. From the front door, the closest entry from my parking spot in the driveway, to the kitchen stove where I stood right now, I was in a familiar, secure, loved territory.

I peeked underneath a foil-wrapped plate, still warm, so Amelia hadn't been gone all that long. Tonight's dinner, a plate of her homemade from scratch tacos and tamales. My absolute favorite. My taste buds watered at the sight. She was slowly bringing me into her native flavorings, which were spicy, earthy blends, something I'd never been exposed to before. I loved it so much, and Amelia was the queen of landing an excellent meal every single time.

After checking the refrigerator to see if she had left more, I pulled out a second plate, putting it close to the first. No reason for it to grow cold. I'd eat both of them soon enough. I went through my normal routine, stopping by the laundry room and undressing, then on to the bedroom to wash the day's grime from my body. I stopped short when I saw a new box on my side of the bed. Based on size and shape, something I'd gotten very good at judging due to my employment, it was a cell phone.

I shook my head and grinned. My guy had to go big, hitting it hard right now, because there was no way he'd make it as a lower income individual. The box called to me like a siren, guiding me in that direction. A Sony Ericsson box. My ass hit the bedspread as I lifted the box, shimmying off the lid. Inside was a ridiculously nice gadget-filled cell with a full keyboard and camera lens along the back. There was no way this was a free-with-contract device.

The phone had some weight to it with a row of lenses along the back, a plastic flap covering them. What would I ever do with so much phone? Back inside the box, different compartments held earbuds, a charger, and an instruction pamphlet. A handwritten note fluttered from the folds. It held an easy-to-follow guide on how to start the device and what the different key combinations meant.

With a press of the power button, I started the phone and waited for it to begin. The charge was one hundred percent. Dash had thought of everything. Of course, he had, when didn't he?

I tossed the phone aside and took a quick shower, letting my hair go wild, before grabbing my athletic shorts. The entire time, my thoughts remained on how much it cost. How long of a contract did he have to sign? Did it have the same video game options Dash's phone had? I hoped it did. I'd enjoy that feature. Except the cell needed to go back. My old phone was good enough. It had a long life still to go.

As I pulled up my shorts, the musical ringtone startled the shit out of me. I'm ashamed to say it took a second to figure it out. My mind first went to a new fire alarm tone because Dash loved music. I feared for the tacos before my own life. Then, I was drawn to the bed on the second ring. I leaped there and answered on the third peal.

"Why did you get me this phone?" I asked in lieu of a standard greeting.

Dash's immediate chuckle said everything I needed to hear. "I don't know why, because you're generally ungrateful for my efforts, and maybe that your old phone barely works. We're going to need better communication while being apart like this."

In theory, I agreed, but wasn't willing to let my side of this argument go. "Then call me on the landline," I suggested.

"No, it's not my preferred way to communicate with you. I'd only have a few hours when you're off at night." The way he said those words made them sound reasonable and thoughtful, which they weren't at all.

"Dash, this is too fancy and we're on a budget." I did my best to remind him gently.

"We're in a better financial place now, and I miss you. I can't believe how hard it was to leave you again. I think it's easier if I just take a cab to the airport next time. I'm a big crybaby. Now say it back," he explained. He had turned on the waterworks this morning when I dropped him off, but outside of that, I sensed the positivity, relief, and happiness in his tone. The first day of school had to have started off great.

"You're a big crybaby," I repeated, staring at the ceiling tiles that always drew my attention. They were pretty and mind occupying while following their paths.

"Ha. You're not very good with the jokes. You need to leave that to me. Now say it back," he teased. I could hear the smile in his tone.

"I love you. Is that it? Do I add I miss you?" I said.

"No, you did real good. I've learned more about my father's practices. What happened in Sea Springs is my father's normal business habit. Every time he builds, the trajectory of his business dealings end with the community's destruction. It's only gotten worse over time." It was hard to believe that Jack Richmond's company could be meaner than what he did to my grandparents' lives and livelihood.

I didn't voice my thoughts aloud. It'd bring Dash's happy mood too low. Best to let him sift through the ugliness on his own. "Hmm, that's too bad."

"Joy says my dad heard about UC Law and Carter's help. His face turned bright red. I guess all this worked out for Carter." Again, another loop into a conversation we didn't need to have now, or ever again for that matter. "Let's change the subject. I've decided to come home Friday night to finish my to do list and talk to Amelia's family about her moving into the house. And I'm coming home because I miss you," he added, sounding like an afterthought. I could almost hear the cogwheels turning inside his head. "Did you find out about a transfer with work?"

"No, I only put in the request on Friday," I said. "It'll take a minute."

"Can you go to my desktop computer in my office?" he asked. "We can Skype. I wanna see you. This is truly a beautiful home. The city has so much to do. I think I may want to live here forever, but the sparkle in my life is sitting at home in Dallas. I need you here with me."

"Can I eat before we Skype?" I asked, stunned that those words left my lips. I liked my time with him too. "It's just that Amelia made her tacos and tamales. They're still warm, smell great, and look even better."

"Oh, man, I'll miss those things. We'll have to request she make them when we come home to visit. It appears the only real flavoring they use here is butter," Dash said with a chuckle. "Give me twenty minutes. I'm starving too, and I need to see what restaurants are around me. We can have dinner together. When we're away from each other, I want us to keep our routines. Eat together, unwind from the day together, sleep with the phones on together. It'll be what makes our separation bearable."

"That sounds good. I need to put some clothes on and dry my hair..." I said, but he interrupted me.

"Don't. I like you all natural and rugged," Dash said. I guessed we were the same then. I liked him a little mussed-up, which he refused to be most of the time.

"Only if you do the same," I said, knowing full well that was never going to happen. Dash gave a sudden bark of loud laughter as my answer.

"Twenty minutes. I'll call you, or call me, I guess." The humor was still in his voice. "I don't want you to be lonely while I'm gone."

"It feels like you're here except I'll go to bed earlier. Might actually get a full eight hours of sleep," I said. Four-thirty in the morning came early when staying up late on the computer at his desk..

"Good. Can't have you forgetting me while I'm gone," Dash said, quietly, with meaning.

"You're unforgettable," I said to his tiny amount of insecurity. "Nineteen minutes now. Get moving."

"On it," he said and abruptly disconnected the call. I loved that silly man, and I was getting homemade tacos. I'd have the first plate gone by the time he called me back. Then the second plate would become my first, and we'd eat that together. Screw portion control.

My happiness was full-fledged back. My guy was being well taken care of, which mattered. I lifted off the bed and took the phone with me. We were going to be okay.

8: The Sexy Time
Dash/Beau

Dash

Eleven days later
Chicago, Illinois

"No, I'm not doin' that," Beau said firmly, giving his final say in the matter.

A long yawn followed his unyielding negation of a simple suggestion. Turned out, it was a good thing I understood the language of talking through a yawn because most of his explanation was given that way.

"It's already weird that we're sleepin' together online like this. And besides, you're spendin' too much money. Why did I need a laptop after that expensive phone you purchased?"

"I disagree." I paused as I watched my guy dramatically flip to his back and interrupt an ensuing argument forming on my lips.

"Of course, you do," he said sarcastically, giving the same drama-filled hand movements that were now becoming part of the way he spoke. Then a final hand slashed through the air to drive his decision home. So much attitude that if I didn't know better, I'd consider him Italian. Which was my favorite country to visit.

"Will you let me finish a sentence? I let you say your peace. Now, it's my turn," I explained as patiently as possible. And dammit if my guy didn't cut me off again. Beau was so challenging at times.

"You only get a say when you're not tryin' to change my mind. All you do is continually try to do things that make me uncomfortable. Have you ever considered you're a pervert?" He tossed the question out like that was new information. I did enjoy a little of the kinky stuff—his words, not mine.

"It's been days and days since I held you last. I haven't kissed you or made love to you..." I countered, changing tactics.

"I'll be there in thirty hours max. If you'd allow me to go to sleep, I'd be far safer on the drive tomorrow." He sounded reasonable, even right, but I wasn't in the same mindset. My turn-around trip the previous weekend hadn't even allowed for an overnight. My schedule had been cut short due to a group project that I needed to be present to complete. I missed my guy. We'd been living our life through Skype. Everything we did, eating dinner, packing the things I wanted to bring, falling asleep at night, all done on video. What was truly influencing my current quest was that I wanted to have video sex at least once in my lifetime. Beau's refusal consistently came by way of safety concerns. He didn't do technology and didn't trust the process. He wanted our privates to stay private, not potentially out for the world to see.

The thought behind his rejection was sweet. He didn't want anyone else to see me that way. I, though, didn't have those hangups. I liked watching my guy come. Many times, I encouraged him to jack off, only helping his release in order to catch him in the throes of passion. Beau Brooks did it for me in every way. I missed him.

Instead of trying to battle this out, I put my money where my mouth was, or better said, I put my laptop on my thighs. My hard, ready cock on display. I clutched around my shaft, giving one sure tug. Based on my limited view, I only caught Beau's head coming closer to the screen.

"You're always so responsive. I like that a lot," he said, his tone turning husky and rough, his bottom lip sliding between his teeth. I needed to remember that Beau responded better to action than words. My guy liked our sex as much as I did, maybe more now that he'd found the joys of bottoming.

"Then join me, Beau. Touch yourself for me. Don't hold back. I'm not." The groan that left my lips was from the way he stared at me like a prime piece of meat. His gaze turned needy and appreciative. The fight vanished. He lowered, pushing several pillows underneath his head to see me better.

"Hey, where did you go?" he asked, my laptop sliding off my thighs as I shifted my upper body to see better.

Elation and frustration flowed through me at finally getting my way. Elation because of a naked Beau and video sex. Frustration because I could've been doing this every night before bed if Beau had allowed it sooner.

"I'm here." And, boy, was I completely there.

Beau stroked his swollen, ruddy cock.

"You're sexy as hell. I knew you'd be. I wish I was there to taste your tip. You're like an ambrosia..."

Beau chuckled at me, stopping my attempt to dirty talk us through the deed. "I appreciate your effort, but my come tastes like ambrosia?"

All right, he caused me to laugh too. "Delicious a better word?"

"Still probably a stretch," Beau said, his voice growing husky while he gave into the friction of his fist. I wished I was there to jerk him off. "I love watching you, Beau. Your cock's the pinnacle of my dreams."

"Pinnacle?" Beau murmured. Always ready to give me shit about something.

I didn't have an opportunity to respond as my guy began a measured pumping of his hips, riding the pleasure wave he created. He dropped his head back, amping up the rhythm of his skilled hand. He'd recently gotten into tugging at his balls, that proved true again tonight.

My gaze riveted on Beau, I didn't want to miss a single visual of my big guy working his release. Even when his full body splayed across our bed, and the laptop fell cockeyed—funny choice of words—I didn't ask him to correct the position. The new vantage point made Beau's cock and sac the feature of my screen. I swiped my thumb over the beads building in my slit, spreading the pre-come over my tip.

"You like rubbing one off for me, don't you?" I whispered huskily. My tone sounded more like a purr as my body heated, lost to the show of my gorgeous guy getting off.

"Always do." The view changed again. The laptop was left on the bed, showing me a direct shot of his ass. Jesus, I had nothing on Beau's ability to entice as his wet fingers came into view. My gaze locked on the screen. I lifted on an elbow to see better. Beau spread his ass cheeks open and pushed his fingers inside his hole.

"You're beautiful. That's my hand driving in your ass."

"Oh," he began, saying the whisper on repeat.

"Find the gland, Beau. Like I'd do if I was there." He did what I asked, taking his fingers deeper. His undulating hips didn't disappoint. I knew they wouldn't, I'd seen that same reaction during our sex, over and over again. "Fuck, that's hot."

"I'm not fightin' it. I'm strokin' my cock too," Beau hissed, turning his head toward the screen. The pump of his hips swayed with his fingers driving into his ass. His narrowed eyes had me back to forcing my cock through my fist. Dammit, if the look on Beau's face wasn't enough to force my orgasm free.

I joined Beau's moment, imagining his calloused palm working me to my end. The image of Beau gripping me, stroking my pulsating cock to completion became the only thing I saw. My nerve endings tingled and their electric tentacles raced over my body, which hummed in response. I gripped my cock tighter, bucking up and down as my release surged from my balls.

"I'm gonna come..." The universe knew that I tried to watch him, but when I started this, I'd had no idea how completely this would get me off. I fisted the bed sheets, my feet drawing up under my bent legs. I was on fire as I reached for my sac, my balls drawn into my body. The intensity of pleasure proved to be too much.

How did he still fill me with such blinding need?

I didn't want to miss Beau's release expression—it was hot as fuck—but my orgasm erupted of its own will, splattering come against my belly and chest. I rode the orgasm out with my jaw clamped, my muscles seizing, my breath stuck between exhale and inhale. Somehow, I caught the moment Beau plopped to his back, his cock straining as his orgasm emptied in the same way mine did.

"Aghh...*yes!*" Beau exclaimed. I watched in awe as Beau screwed his eyes shut tightly, his head thrown back, his chest arching off the mattress. What I didn't see, but knew without question was there, were his full lips parted slightly as he mumbled incoherently. The same gestures he made every single time we were together intimately. My body shook at the intensity of my emotions, proud to have captured such a beautiful man's love. Beau was exceptionally put together.

"Fuck," Beau panted. The expected yawn followed.

"Use the wipes," I instructed. Usually, cleaning us after sex was my job. "You'll sleep better if you're clean."

Beau barely moved, only lifting a hand to the wipe-warmer on top of the nightstand. He gave one swipe up his chest. Another followed the same path as the first before wadding the towelettes together. I felt certain that his toss didn't make it to the wastebasket tucked close to the mattress.

"Did you set your alarm to pick Scott up at the airport?" I asked. Beau turned on his side, facing the laptop, drawing the soft, plush throw over his body.

"I wish you were here. I like to cuddle you after we do it," he said. "Don't tell Scott my secret."

I grinned while watching him draw a pillow into his arms, knowing that it would be me anchored there, usually not in a comfortable way.

"I liked tonight. Thank you. Keep the laptop on, I wanna watch you sleep."

"You gotta stop spendin'. We're on a budget." A heavy breath followed as Beau fell asleep. I left the mattress for the bathroom and was back within a minute. I enjoyed watching Beau at rest. He always looked so peaceful and relaxed. I missed him desperately.

He had seven and a half hours before he had to rise and go to the airport to pick Scott up. For the first time in a long time, I didn't grab a book or use my laptop to study. I lay there, alone, watching Beau, so thankful for the life we were forging together.

"I love you," I said quietly. I received a perfectly timed snore in return. "I can't wait for you to get here. We're starting over again. Funny how we keep doing that. Maybe this time will stick." My hand fisted in reaction to the need to reach out and touch my guy. I tucked the pillow under my cheek and continued to stare for several hours. What a love we shared.

Beau

Dallas, Texas

A rare cool front pushed through Dallas, making today, late in May, feel almost like early springtime. The sun shone, a gentle breeze blew over us every now and again, and the birds were chirping their little tunes. All positive signs for the official relocation day.

"Fuck, Brooks," Scott said in his most annoying whiny tone. "Why couldn't you move from Dallas when it wasn't so fuckin' hot?" Clearly, he had no idea how truly heated the DFW area got this time of year. He also followed right on my tail from the house to the bed of my pickup truck, a couple packed boxes in his hands.

"What did he say?" Dash asked from the earbud currently stuck inside my ear.

"He said it's hot here," I said. This back and forth, repeating what the other said was getting old fast. Since Dash had insisted on being on the phone every leg of the trip, I felt like twenty hours from now was going to be my breaking point.

"Right?" Dash answered. "But it's chilly here. I'm still wearing a jacket and long pants. Make sure you have your jackets or coats handy. It's not expected to warm up for another few weeks."

"We got 'em in the cab." I hoisted myself into the truck bed, scooting the boxes in was like playing a game of Tetris.

"What'd he say?" Scott asked, pushing each of his loads toward me. I rose to my full height, stretching out my shoulder and arm to help release the tightness there.

"He said it's cold there," I repeated, keeping the rotation of my arm circling. This muscle ache could be due to the stress both men were putting on me as opposed to an actual strained muscle.

"Mr. Beau, is this rod in the backseat for Dash's clothes?" Amelia asked. She'd taken responsibility for Dash's clothing herself. She understood firsthand how carefully he treated them, so she wrapped each piece by itself, mindful of any potential long drags. Since it'd be a while before he was able to commission a new bespoke anything, he had been silly careful with what he had available.

"What did she ask?" Dash questioned. My shoulders drooped in the beat down I was experiencing. What happened to my chirping birds and gentle breeze?

"She asked about the rod in the backseat, and yes, Amelia's the only one hangin' your clothes there," I said, starting for the tailgate to jump to the driveway. "Why do you need to be on the phone through this phase of the move? It'd be so much faster..."

"Because I desperately wish I was there. I should've taken the day off and flown home," he said, giving the perfect sorrowful inflection to his tone.

My response to the many different ways Dash had attempted to come home for this move played like a loop out of my mouth. "Since neither of us has a job, I think it's best for you to stay put. I'll handle this leg, but it'd be so much smoother if I could hang up the phone. These earbuds are startin' to hurt my ears."

"You'll get used to it," Dash said dryly. "The earbuds take time for the ear to adapt." Like I thought, the sad tone was all a manipulation tactic. The new voice in place spoke of something more akin to "buck up, buttercup."

"If Amelia gets lonely, me and Lauren and Daisy Mae can come stay with her," Scott said good-naturedly.

"Do they need a place to stay?" Dash asked, apparently having heard Scott just fine. "Amelia won't mind."

I didn't bother responding. That was the other side of the communication problem we were experiencing. Scott and I messed around with each other all the time. What Dash was missing was all of Scott's facial cues. I'd have to explain those too.

"We started with about fifteen boxes to load then we'll tie it all down. Amelia's at least halfway through. Her short legs move pretty quickly. We'll probably have to help there—" Dash cut him off.

"Please use care," Dash reinforced. "How did you pack my shoes?" Oh man, like we hadn't discussed these things at length, several times over.

"She put the shoes wrapped in tissue paper inside the shoeboxes. They'll be on the floorboard stacked on top of each other to reach the ceilin'." I felt the wind on my face while, rooted in my spot, I chose my words carefully. If I didn't say exactly the right thing, I'd be in for a ten-minute instructional one-sided chat.

"Hush. I don't have that many shoes," he corrected, but he did, and we both knew it.

"I decided to pack your cologne collection. We had room for it," I said and started inside to gather two more boxes off the stack.

"Good. I tried to be an adult about leaving those at home, but I'm all for mixing it up. Everything smells good on you." As he rambled on, my eyes did a dramatic somersault into the back of my head. Luckily, I stopped just shy of labeling his words as the horseshit they were. I had to admit, way back when we first met, Dash was a primper in training. Now, he was determined to be a runway model every time he left the house. I found those fragrances had become his mood ring, and I was learning to crack those codes too.

"He gonna be on the phone until we get there?" Scott asked, shimming past to avoid my slow pace.

"Yes," Dash called out in my ear. "I've got to go to class in about twenty-minutes, then I'll be on the phone with you the whole way here. Tell him."

I stared at Scott, nodding him back inside the house. "We'd most likely be on the road if I could concentrate and pick up the pace. Call us when you leave class."

"The laptop comes with an internet stick..." Dash reiterated.

"Babe, you've gotta rein in the spendin'. Our cash is gonna run out too fast if you don't," I urged, plopping my load of boxes on the bed then hoisting myself up to carefully stack them alongside the others.

"I've been brainstorming some pet names for us. I like Bobo for you, what do you think?"

I couldn't hold back my sudden howl of laughter, drawing both Amelia and Scott's attention.

"I'll never be called Bobo. Got it? You've called me handsome, babe, and cowboy, I believe. Pick from those." This time, I went to the edge and jumped over the side. Before I heard Dash's answer, the earbud dislodged and fell from my ear. "Hang on." I worked the hard ear bud back into my now sensitive ear. "Before you repeat what you said, I feel like I like the word *baby*. Baby. It feels right on my tongue. What do you think?"

"I think it's perfect. I like it a lot," Dash said quietly. "I'm going to keep thinking about it. I want a special name. Something that rolls off my lips too. I'll hang up so you can finish, but there's no more breaks until you sleep on the ride. Then I still want to be on the phone."

I stopped dead in my tracks in the middle of the yard and closed my eyes at all the effort it took to have Dash with us in this way. But no matter my irritation, I did like his willingness to spend his free time with me. Falling asleep with his face next to me meant the world to me. "We'll see."

"I guess we will."

"Cocky, aren't you?"

"Confident in my ability to persuade my guy."

I laughed a crazy sounding chuckle, knowing no truer words had ever been spoken, and started for the house. "Be safe," I murmured.

"That's you. I've seen how the FedEx truck bounces around the road when you drive," Dash teased. He probably wasn't wrong, but he also hadn't seen me drive.

"Ha, ha. I'm a better driver than you," I teased.

"All right, hot stuff." Dash stopped speaking, then changed the subject. "What about that name?"

"Nope," I said, grinning. Hot stuff. Oh, lord. "Keep thinkin'."

"I've got you six to two. I'm almost finished," Scott said, edging past me where I had stopped in the middle of the walkway.

"Go to school. Make good grades. Call me when you get home," I said.

"Tell him goodbye," Amelia said, also passing me with an attempt to stay on the sidewalk. She held several coat hangers in her hands.

"You hear that?" I asked and started back inside the house.

"I did. I'll call her on my way home," Dash said. "I love you. I can't wait for you to arrive. It truly feels like a new start."

"Dude," Scott confronted me in the foyer. "I didn't know I was coming here to do all the work. I appreciate the money y'all sent, but being the bitch isn't my way."

"What money?" I immediately asked Dash, not Scott who had an instant chuckle and muttered *I win*.

"I always wondered if you knew. You're pretty damned cheap to be so generous," Scott said, lifting two more moving boxes, only four left to carry out.

"I'm going," Dash said. He mimicked the sounds of faux static in the dead air space.

"Stop. I wanna hear everything you've done. We don't have the money..." I started in earnest this time.

"You did it. You're making me leave the call," Dash said, his humor clear in that tone. "I love you."

"Was it more than a hundred dollars?" I asked, determined to get to the bottom of this.

Dash's laughter turned downright hysterical. He loved my guess, meaning it was so much more than that. "Be careful. I'll call you when I'm done. Be halfway here by then."

This did feel like a healthy reawakening happening to us, a shedding of the past, in the best possible way. "I'll do my best."

The call ended with a smile that lasted about five seconds. Scott's grisly self came through the door.

"Oh no, I got the last two boxes while you talked on the phone. Come stack 'em. Amelia's makin' us food for the road. We gotta finish loadin' his clothes. But we can't tell Dash we did." The grumble in his voice was wholly unnecessary. So was the way his boots stomped across the ground.

"Did he pay you to be here?" I asked, following behind him.

"'Course not. He put money in an investment account for Daisy Mae. It's that college fund deal. If it all works out, she's gonna be taken care of for college. It happened right after she was born. He hopes she'll call you both uncles," Scott said, lifting the last two. "Are you mad?"

We worked in silence as I considered the question.

"I'll give it back," he offered.

My "no" was immediate. "I want her to have it. I just wish the money had come from me. Does that make sense? I planned to do something like that when our situation evened out."

"Yeah, so maybe it's time to tell you Lauren's pregnant again."

I gave myself whiplash, jerking my head in his direction. Another baby? It didn't seem like he was pulling my leg.

"Yeah, I know. And I'm gonna cross boundaries with you, but I like more meat on her bones. She's the most beautiful woman in the world to me. I'm always chasing after her. Sometimes the condom's there, most of the time it's not. I can't help it."

Nobody understood that better than me. "I don't know what to say. How far along is she?"

"We haven't told anyone. She's in her first trimester, we think. It could have happened anytime. You're the first to hear." Scott placed his boxes on the tailgate, next to mine. "I'm freaked out."

"Don't be," I said, jumping into the truck bed. "You wanted kids, and it'll be easier to have them back-to-back. You'll still be young when they grow up." Honestly, I was pretty proud of the logic because I was terrified for him.

"Maybe," he said, this time watching me work. "Dash acts older than he is," Scott said.

"You think?" I asked, teasingly. "We live like we're thirty years old and it's awesome. He's constantly lookin' out for me, and I don't make it easy." I lifted and stretched. The truck bed was packed solidly. No room to be had. It worked out perfectly. I jumped down and Scott lifted the tailgate to lock it in place. "How you feel about Lauren's pretty much what happens here."

"I love you, guy," Scott said, clamping a hand on my shoulder as he went past me for the house. "And you know I'm so cool with everything, but I'm not ready to hear about your sex life. It seems painful. My ass clenches when I think about it. Not that I'm thinkin' about it."

I followed behind him, trying my best to hide my smile. "When the ass clenches, that's the sweet spot."

"Nope, not listenin'. I'm gettin' the food. You go anywhere else," Scott said, diverting toward the kitchen.

Yup, this was, in fact, a great day.

9: The Big Life
Beau

Chicago, Illinois

"Fuck, the traffic's bad," Scott said with aggravation, driving the last leg of the trip. I stayed focused on the street signs and the MapQuest directions that I'd printed before we left the house. Dash was still in my ear, asking all sorts of questions I ignored. He was standing out front of the parking garage, waiting to guide us in.

There were too many cars on the street and none of them cared about basic consideration. Somebody had to let us over. Scott needed to change lanes, but this truck was pretty massive compared to the smaller vehicles weaving through traffic. We also needed another minute to signal a turn just ahead.

"Left at the light. Dash's out front waitin' for us," I said, pointing toward the streetlamp just ahead. "Force your way over. They're not gonna let you in."

"I don't want to wreck your truck," Scott said, hesitating.

"We're bigger than all the cars on the road. Get over," I said, turning to look out the back window. "You got a chance comin' up." Seconds later, I shouted, "Now. Put the truck in that lane." Of course, there was a crescendo of annoyed honks coming from behind us. I didn't care. I was tired of being inside this cab, but I easily admitted the large lake just to our right soothed some of my irritation.

"Do we park in the garage to unload?" Scott asked.

"Yes. Pick me up and I'll guide us to the service elevator," Dash said. "I can't wait to see you."

"We'll pick him up, and he'll guide us into the garage to where the service elevators are," I explained again, maybe for the fourth time. At the light, I could feel the tension in the truck. The only noise in the cab came from the blinker, ticking over and over again.

"Tell him I miss you," Dash instructed, clearly not picking up what was happening inside this truck.

"I'm not saying that to him," I said, watching Scott bust a move, turning left before oncoming traffic began to roll forward. The cars in those lanes started with their long honks and clearly given hand gestures showing what they thought of us. Dealing with this kind of traffic was going to be a lot to handle every day.

"I see you," Dash said. I spotted him too. He was handsome in crisp blue jeans, white runners, and a blue jacket zipped to the collar. When we left Dallas, it was shorts and T-shirt weather. The temperature had dropped by thirty degrees on the way up.

"You see him, right?" I asked Scott. My gaze focused on Dash, raising his hand to make sure we saw him.

"'Course, I do. Do I pull up in front of him?" he asked.

"Yes," Dash answered, walking a few steps into the street.

"Yeah," I said, repeating Dash's word. We barely had the gearshift in park, with Dash rounding the hood of the truck in my direction, before the phone call ended, and my door was yanked open. The cool air blew inside the cab as I was enveloped into his arms. His lips and face buried into the crook of my neck. I felt his love to my core.

"I missed you." I circled my arm around his back while releasing the seatbelt holding me in with my other hand.

"How could you miss me? We've spent most of our free time on the phone together." The words were intended to come off as playfully sarcastic, but with the way my arm stayed locked around his back, he had to know my truth. His palms came to my cheeks as I turned, putting a foot out the door. He didn't let me out but stayed in my face as he drank me in.

"We don't do this again. I like you being with me. Promise," he said.

I leaned forward to kiss his lips and forced myself out of the cab. A loud honk came from behind that instantly grated on my last nerve. The agitation was quick and thorough. I believed Dallas had some bad road rage, but they seemed downright hospitable compared to these drivers.

"Come on, guys. We gotta move," Scott said, lifting a hand high to flip the driver off through the back window.

"Get in the middle of the front seat," I said, ushering Dash inside. I climbed in beside him. Based on the next honk, then the foul language shouted at us, I wasn't moving fast enough for the driver's liking. That last nerve snapped, halting my progress to sit beside Dash.

My guy grabbed my wrist before I could move a solid step in the other car's direction. I'd teach that motherfucker how to be patient when necessary. Scott's door opened, he began to leave the driver's seat, ready to have my back.

"No, no. No fighting today," Dash said loudly.

"We aren't fightin'. We're explainin'," Scott said, but he stopped, waiting to see what I was going to do. The trip had been long and the drive into Chicago had been awful. Seconds passed. Dammit if Dash wasn't right. We didn't need all this tension in front of our new home.

"Lee, get in the truck," I said, forcing myself to follow my own instruction, regardless of the way the guy tossed his hands in the air, brushing us off as a non-threat.

"Take the left into the parking garage and circle to the ninth floor. There're freight elevators that go directly to our floor. It'll be faster to use them," Dash said. His joy erased my frustration. "Did you bring your jackets?"

"Yeah, but it was hard to believe we'd need them," I said, threading our fingers together.

"I think we're going to need an update in our wardrobe. We'll have snow in the winter," Dash said. He bent his head to my shoulder, lying there. "I missed you."

"I missed you too," I murmured. Luckily, Scott didn't utter a word, probably still mad at all the horn-blowing and fuck-you hand gestures. That was okay. He'd take off back home early tomorrow morning.

"Park there." Dash pointed to the empty space with Carter's name on it.

"What kind of car is that?" Scott asked about the one parked next to the truck.

"It's a Saleen S7. It's Carter's. He wants us to drive it. It's a 2005 and hasn't been driven in a year," Dash explained nonchalantly.

Scott's weird expression locked on mine. "What's a Saleen?"

I shrugged. "Fancy usually follows Dash."

"Y'all are strange men. Get out. I have a cart waiting beside the elevator. It'll help limit the trips," Dash said and hip-bumped me to get moving. The cool air from below was colder up here, causing me to reach for my jacket.

"How much does that thing cost?" Scott asked, nodding to the Saleen. Dash didn't answer until he was pushing the cart toward the bed of the truck. I had no idea of the expense, but I knew it had to be high.

"More than most people make in a lifetime, I'm sure," Dash said, lowering the tailgate.

Rope crisscrossed the top of the bed, securing the boxes in place. I made quick work of untying the knots while Scott assisted my guy in filling the cart eight boxes high. He and I grabbed more to carry, following where Dash led. My experience at FedEx had me familiar with the inner workings of high-rise buildings. This freight elevator was no different than any others. The hallway was good enough too. It was the entrance to the apartment that took my breath away and kept it that way as we put the boxes in the foyer and began exploring the place.

"Is this an apartment?" Scott asked, his head moving different directions, seemingly stunned by what he saw.

"I believe it's a penthouse apartment," Dash answered from behind, allowing us the raw advantage of taking in the picturesque furnishings and design. I'd seen parts of the home through Skype, but nothing prepared me for the luxury of the home. The highlight for me was the expansive windows in the living room. I assumed that was what they called this formal sitting room overlooking Lake Michigan. I was captivated, staring out at the churning lake. Large bodies of water always make me feel a little bit better about life.

Dash caressed a hand up my back until he gripped the nape of my neck. "I wanted to surprise you. There's a boat dock to the right. We can rent something to fish on or buy a boat when we can. There are loads of free fishing docks around."

"Fuck, Brooks. This place is nicer than your home in Dallas," Scott said from the catwalk above us. "You got those waterspouts, ass cleaners in every bathroom."

I pointed my finger toward the lake. "Check it out."

"There's some sort of transit heading in every direction. Even with the stops, it can be faster than driving," Dash said, trailing his fingers down my arm to link our hands. "The kitchen's in the other direction from where you entered. There's a guest suite beyond the kitchen and two bedrooms upstairs," he said, pulling me in the direction of Scott.

"The showers have jets all over the place," Scott added. "And a detachable wand. I landed on the bed and it's soft as shit. Lauren needs to see this place, or maybe not. She'll want us to live this way." Each syllable Scott spoke held more and more awe.

Dash acted as my tour guide, but I'd spent a lot of time on video in the main bedroom. Scott hadn't gotten it wrong. The rooms were just as remarkable as the rest of the house.

"The downstairs loops around into a dining room, a gym, an office, and another sitting room. It took me a few days to find them. It was a whole closed-door issue that I didn't feel comfortable breaching," Dash explained. His happiness was evident with the giant grin on his face. He tucked his hands into his jeans, patiently watching us discover the cool amenities that neither of us had ever seen before.

"What a badass place to live, Brooks," Scott said on our ride down to finish unloading the truck. "And his old man's gonna have a fit when he finds out?"

"I guess he already did," I said when Dash didn't immediately answer. "It went over like Dash and Carter expected."

"Good, he's a motherfucker," Scott tossed over his shoulder. The unloading didn't take nearly as long as the loading had. Not having to relay to Dash everything everyone said helped too.

"I made tentative arrangements to eat deep dish pizza at Lou Malnati's. It's been recommended. At least that's where I've been pointed. I printed an online guide to experience Chicago in a day. I thought Scott might like to explore the area before he leaves," Dash explained, pulling the last remaining clothing onto the cart then taking us back to the elevator.

"Whatever you want to do. I'm sure Lauren's gonna drag my ass back here soon enough," Scott said, pushing the floor button as the elevator doors closed behind us. "If you guys wanna unpack, that's cool too."

"I could eat," I said, winking at my guy.

"When can't you eat?" Dash retorted.

"Wait," I said with enough urgency that drew both Scott's and Dash's attention. "Lauren's pregnant."

"What?" Dash said, having the same shocked response as me.

At the same time, Scott said, "Brooks, it's a fucking secret. You failed." Scott punched me in the arm when I scooted past him. It wasn't necessarily a hard hit but added to the happiness of my moment.

"I win," I said to Scott's sputtering.

"How was that a win? Loose lips don't constitute a win of anything," Scott said, following me out.

"I win."

Days later

"Where are you now?" Dash asked again for at least the hundredth time. I honestly had no idea. Besides everything looking the same over the whole entire city, and this being one of the first times that I'd ever had to maneuver mass transit, the bus I was now on was packed to the gills. It was hard to judge distance and harder to learn the stops with Dash talking in my ear.

Whatever. I was done trying to figure it out, so I stepped out onto the street when the doors opened again. The cooler air hit immediately, a welcome relief from the sauna I'd been standing in. The phone was stuck to my ear, the people around me on a perpetual power walk, and I stood in the middle of the chaos, trying to catch my bearings.

"I'm not sure. I gotta move closer to the street signs," I said and started that direction.

"Stop right there. Now turn around." Although I couldn't see him, I heard the scraping of a chair against a hard floor. I did turn but uncertain of what I was meant to find. Another challenge of being in Chicago. Every building appeared identical from the street view. "Babe!"

It took a moment more to scan the first-floor restaurants to see Dash's head poking out of a doorway. Like a magnet, I was drawn to him. So much had changed in my life in such a short amount of time. Birmingham to Dallas had taken a minute to get used to, but Dallas to Chicago was an entirely different level of change. The two major cities were ridiculously different from each other. Even navigating through the crowds to reach Dash felt like a monumental task.

"It's crazy out here," I called steps away from my guy. The way he looked at me calmed my slightly ruffled feathers. With all his charm focused on me, he effortlessly drew a smile as he leaned against my chest and lifted. He had no reservations about public displays of affection. He was like a magic balm, turning my souring mood into joy. He kissed me short and sweet.

Like so many other restaurants and bars we had tried, Chicago's long history hung on the dark interior walls and poorly lit space. Another common feature, the doorknob had a large bell attached, rattling as if the door's bang wasn't enough of an indicator that someone had arrived.

"Our booth's over here," Dash said, threading our fingers together and guiding us to the seat. I'd recently confessed to him how much I liked U-shaped booths. I could easily slide in next to Dash. Since then, all our dinner spots had that kind of set up. This one was no different. "He's here," Dash called to the bartender who raised a single brow as he looked at me.

"Draft?" he asked.

I nodded and took my seat, scooting around to meet Dash in the middle. We'd spent three full days in Chicago, and two of my personality traits firmly established themselves. First, I could pinch a penny. While this habit annoyed Dash, I felt a sense of pride at my thriftiness. Second, this move had brought Dash and me closer than ever. With no familiar faces, every aspect of our lives was a new experience. We loved exploring the city's layout together.

"Tell me about the job interview. Were the blue jeans a bold choice?" Dash asked, scooting closer to me, his cocktail moving with him. "I've been here awhile. I've had a few." The glass lifted as if I might not understand he meant drinks and not interviews. His beautifully masculine face, staring only at me, held no signs of the worry that had plagued him for weeks. Only love and contentment.

From this point forward, he'd focus on my happiness. He was determined to make our lives as comfortable and joyful as possible. Oh man, I loved him.

I backed away long enough to shrug off the suit coat he'd made me wear. "Most of them were wearin' their uniforms. I did get a couple of under the breath *fancies* when I was bein' toured around..."

"Tour, meaning you got a job?" Dash asked excitedly.

"Don't know yet. I have to go through the process. They processed my transfer request and my application to buy a route. At least, it's not off the table. The distribution center is about twenty minutes away from here. Maybe in LaGrange? I'd start in Downers Grove, I think. They said the roads change names through every city, did you know that? It's kind of weird."

"I didn't know," Dash said, still lovingly staring at me. "And yes, it's weird. But it straightens out some of my confusion. I'll talk about somewhere I want to go and say the street name, but they always correct me. It's not easy to navigate around here."

"Draft for you," the bartender said with a strong Italian accent, handing the beer over. "Another vodka soda for you. Do I still keep them coming?" A new cocktail glass was placed in front of Dash, who responded with a thumbs-up while finishing the remainder of his previous drink. "You ready to order food? Or are you here for the game?"

"Both." Dash kept his eyes pointed toward me. "Dallas vs Phoenix. The Mavericks are expected to sweep. We might have some people from school join us," he said. This was a date to mark since Dash never spoke of sports. "We'll have a little bit of home. The sign outside says this place has the best pizza in Chicago. What do you want?" he asked me, finally turning his attention to the bartender, ready to order.

"Somethin' with a variety of meats. I like it all," I said, lifting the beer for a pretty decent size swallow.

"I got cha," he said and left us having no idea what we'd ordered. Another Chicago way.

"Who's comin'?" I asked.

"Just a few people I've met," Dash explained. "I invited them casually. I doubt they'll come."

"Well, you're mistaken then." A female voice drew both our attention as I draped my arm over the ledge behind Dash. Without hesitation, she dropped down in the booth, scooting toward me, a guy trailing her. "Pierce is on his way." She regarded me with direct curiosity in that particular way lawyers had at looking at something. "I'm Mandy." She extended her hand for a formal handshake. I hadn't expected that but obliged. "This is my husband, Denver." I understood his acknowledgement way better when I received a nod.

"This is my guy, Beau," Dash stated proudly.

"Thank God you're here," Mandy said with flair while looking at me. "We thought he was insane with the way he talked about you all of the time."

"We've all heard the story of how you met," Denver added, lifting a hand to gain the bartender's attention. "We got trapped one night at your condo, hearing about all the years he waited on you." Denver turned a playful stare at Mandy. "I'd've moved on, for sure." She knocked him in the chest with the back of her hand.

Well, this was news to me. Since Dash had me on call most evenings and into the night, he never mentioned having friends over or that he wasn't right there with me all night. I tilted my chin toward Dash, but didn't get much of a reply. My guy was on his way to a solid drunk. "They came over a couple of times. Always late. Study sessions."

"That turned into quite the party," Mandy added. "Dash knows how to have a good time. We played guess the name of the song and indulged ourselves into oblivion." Something caught her attention as she spoke and never missed a conversational beat as she added, "Hey, Jay, we're here. The group's together again." Their confidence levels were insane. Jay ordered a drink at the bar then took the seat next to Dash.

"Hey, buddy. I'm Jay. I'm glad you're here." Jay's hand also came across the table, forcing my arm from around Dash to shake his. "Beau, right? We've all heard about you. Maybe our team lead can focus now."

"Ha ha," Dash responded, sitting up a little straighter. "I'm already carrying you all."

"Grey Goose and tonic, extra lime?" a new waitress asked at the head of the table.

"That's mine," Mandy said. She waggled her fingers to get her drink.

The waitress passed that over and set Denver's drink in front of him. "Goose Island for you. The volume on the game is going up."

As if she had mind control, the TV's volume increased, and the game began. Less than minutes later, our pizza was delivered to the table. After a *thank you*, I pretty much didn't say another word for the evening. I attempted to keep up with their discussions; they were incredibly intellectual, and so far out of my intelligence league. The needling poking around my head wanted me to worry, and I would. Though, maybe not. Dash needed this regardless of how well I fit into his crowd.

I was damned good at silence, which I planned to be, all of the time.

10: The Taste Dash

July 3rd, 2006
Grant Park, Chicago

My belly was rarely ever full, but today it was after a fun afternoon at the Taste of Chicago. We sampled many different cuisines from the area, and listened to several local live bands perform. I was certain this was the best day I'd had since arriving in Illinois. So much so, I said the words aloud, taking tastes of the gelato from both my mini cup and Beau's.

"You gotta taste this." I wanted Beau to try them all too. Today, my official birthday celebration day, meant that saying no wasn't an option for Beau. I lifted my tiny spoon to his lips, waiting for him to take the bite. When he did, I said, "Best day since we moved here."

"You say that every day," Beau said, eyeing my gelato. "That's good. Better than mine. Let me get one."

I didn't get a say or even an acknowledgement, Beau simply walked away, returning to the booth we had just visited. We'd been lucky all day. Besides the beautiful, warm weather with not a cloud in the sky, we never experienced more than a handful of people in any restaurant vendor's line. Watching him leave wasn't the hardship I pretended it to be. I couldn't help but admire his ass in the cargo shorts he wore.

He effortlessly pulled off the casual yet cool vibe, better than anyone I'd ever seen before. He wore sandals, and a T-shirt, with a backward ball cap, hiding much of his growing out hair, and a pair of aviator sunglasses to block the bright sun. The stud earrings added to his mystique. All the clothes I'd secretly added into his side of the closet before the situation with my family had gone down.

Honestly, screw the legal field, I should have been a stylist with how completely I nailed Beau's clothing to his personality. I gave myself a nod while taking credit for Beau's beauty.

What about beauty for his nickname? Nah, he'd cancel that in less than a second.

"Is the gelato food like an ice cream or is it ice, like ice?" Linda asked, coming to my side, curiously glancing in my cup. I was reminded of the melting treat in my hand after being lost in how defined Beau's thighs and calves were.

"Mom, you want one?" Beau called out.

She shook her head, "I'm stuffed."

After spending the last thirty days with Beau and his mom, I saw where his personality came from. Linda was a little more open to suggestions than Beau, and her son was significantly taller than his mom, but they were cut from the same cloth. A very pretty fabric based on the changes Linda had gone through since I last saw her. She was thin, the aging on her face was gone—completely erased—and she wore a bohemian style dress that fit her frame remarkably well. She smiled easily, charming the people, mainly men, around her. Beau had a fit every time it happened.

Beau came back to us, handing a cup to his mom. "Son, I'm full."

"Just take a bite," he said. His spoon was already scooping a bite from his small bowl. "I'll eat whatever you don't."

Right. The real reason he purchased the extra cup was so he could finish it off.

"My tickets are all used," Beau said.

"I have five tickets left," I said, reaching into my pocket, handing over what was left.

"We're going to the John Hancock Building next, right?" she asked, finally taking the bite, no doubt only because her son wanted her to. The love and commitment each shared for the other was inspiring. I'd work every day to ensure they both continued to love me so completely. Her eyes grew surprised as she glanced down at the cup. "This is delicious. Gelato. I've never had it before. I didn't understand what it was. There has to be milk or cream in here."

"It's the way they process the milk fat, right?" Beau asked me. I'd given him a long lesson on the difference between ice cream and gelato, taking my time to explain how it was made. The air content and calorie differences took about three long minutes for me to describe. I knew he hadn't listened.

"Yeah," I answered. Neither picked up my sarcastic intent with the single word used. "It's time to head to the Signature Lounge and find our seats. I heard it gets crowded fast." We had a twenty-five-minute walk. For today only, Beau somehow secured a reservation for the Fourth of July firework show that included the Signature Lounge, a bar in the building. Our allotted time of arrival was in about thirty minutes.

We'd have a few hours to drink and enjoy the party before going up to our reserved spot at the observatory to watch the fireworks from the best vantage point in the city. Today marked the beginning of my birthday celebration, even though I still had tomorrow to look forward to. The same day that I claimed as mine and Beau's anniversary.

I started in that direction, but then glanced back, noticing Linda and Beau moved at a snail's pace. Their meandering this time was caused by a second run through of the vendors, collecting paper menus from the various restaurants. I followed a strict schedule, one I had created inside my head, and they continually threw a wrench in it over and again, making me have to remind myself that I loved them both dearly.

So I paused for each of them to remember me, especially since the entire day was about me and my birthday. Apparently, easygoing and reasonable weren't part of my emotional makeup this day.

"Y'all can meet me there," I offered when they drew closer.

"Because you have a change of clothing in your backpack," Beau teased aloud, drawing the attention of everyone within hearing distance. Damn, I'd claimed the bundle in my backpack as a picnic blanket, just in case. I'd hoped to stave off the teasing until I changed at the bar. Of course, Beau knew the truth. We spent every available second together. No one knew me as well as my guy.

"It took you long enough," I replied, deciding I'd give him shit about being slow on the uptake.

"I've known. I was waiting for the right time to reveal the truth, you liar," Beau said, grinning as he walked straight to me and pressed a kiss on my lips. Since I loved that he was now instigating the PDAs, I gave in. I guessed it wasn't too challenging to discover my backpack filled with clothes and toiletries.

"I'll share them with you if you're nice," I offered. As I turned around again, he grabbed my wrist. My body was brought back to Beau's. "Stop being a baby and walk with us. Enjoy the day."

Well, I sure had done that. Beau slid an arm under my backpack, circling a hand to my hip. We were walking side-by-side. Linda grinned at me.

"He's sweaty," I said, ready to forfeit our plans in order to crawl underneath his T-shirt and stay locked around him.

"Let's go," Beau prompted. "We still have lots of birthday time left." I was completely appeased. My guy was more relaxed here which made me remember I needed to slow my roll and smell the flowers too.

"Come on, guys." In unison, we glanced over toward Linda's voice who had big city living down. She'd hailed a cab, ducking into the backseat. "He's going to drop me off at the condo and you at the John Hancock Building."

I'd planned to walk, but this was much better. Beau took off for the ride, I followed. I'd have more time to primp this way.

The observation deck in the John Hancock Building's ninety-fourth floor was an incredible way to watch the city celebrate my birthday. It was also much chillier than I'd expected since it was in a climate-controlled building. Beau was prepared though. He'd packed a jacket. I, on the other hand, had worried too much about my appearance and not enough about practicality.

"Take my jacket," Beau said again.

"I'm not going to. You'll be cold," I said, glancing up and behind me. This time, Beau opened the coat and pulled me back against his chest, wrapping it around my body as far as it would go. His arms followed, and I warmed slightly.

The fireworks show began with a loud booming pop drawing our attention. Suddenly the dark sky crackled under the opener's bright beauty. We stood just that way, Beau's arms encircling me, my hands gripping his forearms to keep him close. I lost myself to the feel of being here with my guy.

I loved everything about the fireworks. At some point, Beau clasped something around my wrist and pulled back from our hold. The lights on the observation deck were mostly off for the show, but I glanced back as best I could, lifting a questioning brow at his actions. Beau only nodded me forward to watch the display. Then he placed his jacket sloppily on my shoulders and held it there to allow me time to shove each of my arms through the sleeves. His warmth and smell still permeated the jacket ensuring the moment was romantic and cozy. The palms of his big hands ran up and down my arms, helping to warm me up.

The thoughts of the Fourth of July we'd spent together six years ago came flooding through my mind. That had been the first time we had made love with not only each other but with anyone. The only man I ever wanted to make love with for the rest of my life. As if he heard my memories, he tightened his arms around me just as the finale began its booming chorus. We stood there even after the smoke cleared and the other patrons began to leave. Our position didn't change, still staring out at the dark, alluring night.

"I love you. Thank you for today," I said quietly.

"I love you too," he said all breathy and warm against my ear.

"Can I see what you put on my wrist?" This time I fully turned, lifting my hand.

"It's your birthday present," he said. "I know it's tomorrow, but I believe you deserve your own day to celebrate."

"Gentlemen, the observation deck's closed," a security guard called out behind us. I reluctantly let the surprise on my arm wait. We needed a moment of alone time. In all probability, I was going to love this present and needed a make-out session of appreciation.

"Come on," I murmured. "I want to see what you got me."

I didn't resist reaching out to him, taking his hand as we walked toward the brightly lit elevator with its doors wide open. Beau offered a quiet apology to the security guard, and we ascended two floors, my anticipation growing with each moment. This perfect day was far more than I thought we'd share. Beau genuinely surprised me with a material gift.

With much difficulty, hell, everyone knew I wasn't a patient guy, I managed to wait until we were seated in the lounge again to shrug off his jacket and finally take a look at the bracelet hanging off my wrist. That wasn't exactly true, it fit to size comfortably. I recognized the antique silver chain styled in open block links, which I had occasionally selected for myself, but needed to trace my finger along the material that threaded through the chain.

"Is it wood?" I asked, instantly rejecting the thought.

"Yeah. I knew you'd figure it out," Beau said proudly. "Now what kind?"

I stared at the unusual piece, trying to identify the source. Nothing came to mind as I retraced the grain.

"Black walnut from Sea Springs," Beau answered excitedly, unable to hold back the response any longer. He was proud of his gift, which made it better in every way. "I bought the bracelet from a group trying to make money to help the Houston flood victims. I saw it and thought of where we started."

The gorgeous piece of jewelry became the most treasured I'd ever received. "The trees are ones that were uprooted, none were harmed to make this." Beau covered my hand with his, drawing my gaze up to his. "Do you like it, or was it dumb?"

"I love it. Try to get it off me."

Beau's eyes turned doe-eyed sweet, and I leaned across the small table for a kiss.

"Take me home. Let's finish the celebration in bed tonight. It's my turn to top."

He was already scooting out of the chair before I finished the sentence.

"So, no new drinks?" a waitress asked.

"No," I said. Forward thinking was my new jam. I purposely hadn't opened a tab, so we'd have a faster escape route when we needed to leave. "We're done with the table."

"Got it. Be careful out there," she said.

Careful was the last thing I intended for the rest of this night.

11: The Anniversary Dash

July 4

Something in the way Beau's expression softened while sleeping was incredibly endearing to me. The sweep of his hair fell across his forehead. His strong jawline and wide lips fascinated something inside me. His masculine, rugged beauty drew me like bees to honey.

My head rested on one hand while the other gently moved the swipe of hair off his forehead. Slowly, his eyes fluttered open. Tired confusion furrowed his brow as his gaze sought me out, not that finding me was hard as I lay snuggled against his side.

"Is it time to wake up?" A yawn followed.

"It's our sixth anniversary." I raised a festively bowed jewelry box that I'd been eager to give to him for well over a month. However, at this moment, I began to doubt my decision, uncertain this was a good idea.

"What time is it?" Beau asked, another yawn followed.

"I think somewhere around six fifteen," I said.

"In the morning?" Beau asked, blinking wildly, a hint more awake than seconds before.

"Yes." A smile spread across my face, aware of how much my guy cherished his sleep. I, on the other hand, worried about missing something important during my few hours of rest at night.

"We've only been asleep for four hours. The alarm's set for nine o'clock. Let's do this again, then," he said, turning to bring our bodies flush. His strong arm wrapped around me, tucking me firmly against his chest. A familiar move Beau did all the time, and one that gave me cramps from the different angles my body was forced to lie.

"I don't want to miss a single minute of today." I gently placed a hand on his chest, pushing backward to make space between us. "You can caffeine your way through the next twenty-four hours."

Beau remained soundless, but also didn't give a long intake of breath, reminiscent of sleep. I patiently waited to see if he'd drift off or choose to wake. It took a full minute for him to make up his mind.

"Vacations are meant to be relaxing," Beau muttered against my hair.

By vacation, he meant the day before the fourth to the day after, but as busy as we'd been, spending all day and all night together was harder to do.

"It's only the second time we've spent the entire day together. And I'm becoming an older man who needs to properly celebrate an anniversary."

Beau chuckled, his body vibrating against mine. "Shouldn't an anniversary start a year after we've been together full time?"

"What? No. Never." I jerked my head back only to see Beau grinning broadly. His tender gaze met mine. "Our anniversary was set years ago. I like the idea of sharing my birthday with my love."

"I like messing with you." To prove the point, he lifted a hand to ruffle my hair. Since it was bedhead anyway, I didn't give him grief. "It's better to be awake. I like our lives too much to miss a second of the day."

"Me too. And there's been some updates and schedule changes for today."

Beau immediately pushed back against the headboard to sit up. I followed, positioning myself to face him better.

"Like how?" he said. The furrowed brow now spoke of possible irritation. It wasn't a completely mad look, but it was loading. My hand rested on Beau's cheek, keeping his attention on me.

"Carter's coming in today," I started, this being the simplest of the two changes.

"Why?"

"He wanted to meet us. I told him about the anniversary, and he said he'd be scarce. He's going to take the downstairs bedroom and leave early tomorrow morning."

Beau's brows lifted about a millimeter and a half. We'd see how fast they dropped after the next schedule change.

"Then after lunch we've been invited to a beach volleyball tournament."

His brows slammed down like they did when Scott challenged Beau to any sort of competition that ended in a win.

"Babe, no. This can't be an I-win moment. It'll be more relaxed. Just fun. They're law students, not super athletes driven to win."

He was silent for several long seconds. "I don't believe that. You're more competitive than me, making my wins sweeter. I'm calling it. We're on separate teams."

"No," I said and shook my head to drive home my answer. "Only casual play. I have a short time to gain lots of ground with these people. They can push me to headhunters or firms that I should have been courting for years."

"We're still pier fishing?" Beau questioned.

"Yes and hitting up the street food vendors," I added.

"For sure," he said, giving me a subtle hint of encouragement with the way his lip quirked in the corner.

"And we're still wearing the clothes I picked out?" I said, trying to get his agreement on this well-battled idea I'd had about a month ago.

"Matching shirts? I feel like that's not my personality," he hedged *again*.

"I believe it is your personality, and you're just not understanding it yet," I countered, fully aware that since conception of the idea that he'd scoff at wearing matching anything. "I got an anniversary present for you too," I said, extending my arm to reach the oversized ring box hidden in the folds of the bedspread. I was excited for the next few minutes. I'd planned this for more years than I could say. Now a favorite memory of the way I passed my time, waiting for my guy to return. "Here."

Beau's brow lifted critically. "What's in there?"

"Take it and see," I encouraged.

"It looks like a ring," he said, still skeptical. Of what? Who knew.

"It's not a ring," I said and lifted one of his heavy hands and placed the box on his palm. "Open it."

I couldn't tell if this new facial expression was one of relief or *why not*. Beau clasped the box and manipulated it until the opening faced him. He gave me a disbelieving quizzical stare then looked down at the box. With purposeful movements, he flipped the lid open. His eyes narrowed again. "Is this a spool of thread?" he asked, confused.

In his puzzlement, I rose to a sitting position and took the ring and pre-readied thread from underneath my pillow. My anxiety caused my heart to race, and my voice to crack as I spoke. "I'm not sure I was ever given the option to love you. It was from our first meeting that I began planning our long lives together."

My fingers trembled slightly as I added the loop at the end of my piece of thread onto Beau's ring finger. "We've been through hard times. The complete destruction of ourselves and our families. Through it all, we stayed committed if only by a thread." I grinned as I changed my prepared proposal spontaneously. "A text message thread."

I let the heavy ring slide down the string to land on the tip of his finger.

"Will you marry me?" The tears that had stayed just under the surface spilled from my eyes. Not a flood, only a slip here or there.

"Baby, you know we can't do that," Beau whispered, his eyes riveted on the ring stuck right above the knuckle.

"I refuse to be excluded from anything straight people can have. We'll have a commitment ceremony, and I'll take care of..."

Beau's brawny frame shifted, toppling me over as he extended his arm for a small sack on his nightstand. I hadn't noticed it before. With flourish, he settled into a full sitting position, back against the headboard, a pillow crammed behind him. A small gift bag was presented to me.

Oh wow. I loved my guy. So much love, but where did my proposal land? I rifled through the crumpled tissue paper and matching ribbons that kept the treasure securely inside. Finally, I made it to the bottom and saw a ring box. My eyes shot up to Beau as I dropped the small gift into my palm. With seriously bated breath, I opened the lid. My bottom lip tucked between my teeth.

A ring, made in the same fashion as the bracelet from yesterday. "Is it from the same place? The wood comes from Sea Springs?"

"Yeah. You can wear it until we can get you something else," Beau said. In my periphery, I caught him sliding on the ring I'd given him.

"We're supposed to wait until our commitment ceremony to wear them," I said, letting the weight and texture of the antique silver and smooth shaving of the oak tree caress across the pad of my thumb.

"We're giving our pledge right now," Beau said. He lifted a hand to cup my neck, drawing me forward for a sweet sampling of our lips. I loved the way he touched me, giving me meaning and depth. He filled my soul with joy and purpose. He moved away too soon, but only by inches, staying close to my face. "I pledge my life to you. Now say it back."

"Are you sure you want to do it this way? We could dress up and exchange vows. Have a party..."

Beau literally laughed in my face. "With who there? My mom?"

"Good point. She might want to see what we're doing," I offered, trying to be forward thinking, but a bit of sweet sex might be a better idea.

"She'll be fine. We'll tell her before we leave this morning," Beau said as I began to move closer to my nightstand.

Before I managed a single inch away, Beau's strong palm landed on my thigh, locking me in place.

"What do you need?" Beau asked as he rolled on top of me, extending his hand to the nightstand. "In the drawer?" I was forced to lie underneath him as he opened the drawer and felt around. "You need this box?"

"Yes and get up. You're making me into a taco," I said, pushing at his chest until his back was against the headboard again, his palm extended for me to take the box. Sometimes, I had to remind myself how much I loved that bulldozer of a man. I swiped the box, tamped down my frustration, and opened the lid. It held a matching ring, a duplicate of Beau's.

"I felt like this might go down this way," I said, turning the box to him. After a month of shopping for wedding bands, the design of these rings, with a unique script pattern and beveled edges, had me buying both on the spot. I regretted it only because I loved the idea of Beau buying me the ring. "I bought one for me, but I'll return it."

"No," Beau said, his calloused palm resting on my hand, covering my attempt to close the ring box. "Match mine. I don't know how long the other ring will last." As suddenly as he had placed his hand on mine, he did a fluid move of untangling from me and left the bed.

How hadn't he figured out that he was my anchor, keeping me in place. I tumbled into his spot. Both rings fell from my grip.

"Don't put the ring on. Let's tell my mom and slide them on in front of her. Since we're all we have, it'll be done."

I gathered myself, moving up on all fours, looking for what I lost. "They're by my pillow," Beau said, going for the closet. "And quit flirting with me. We'll do that later." I didn't immediately understand until I realized I was positioned for doggy-style sex.

Beau seriously had a one-track mind—food then sexy time, or sex then a multi-course meal. I tumbled from the bed, not nearly as gracefully as Beau, and made a beeline for the closet.

Beau was already slipping on some athletic shorts that hugged his muscular frame. I took credit for how well the shorts framed his strong legs. It took me forever to get him to agree to a shorter inseam, remaining oblivious to the eye-fucking I regularly did, admiring his hard body.

Suddenly, fabric hit my face. You'd think with as much staring as I was doing, a person would've seen my shorts flying at me. More importantly, since his mom had been here for over a month, I'd relaxed my appearance standards. Still, I couldn't just go there willy-nilly. I needed a brush on my teeth and hair, and most likely a quick shave. I quickly changed direction, pivoting toward the bathroom.

"Don't take too long," Beau said, shoving his hair off his face. "I'm gonna get her up. Let her get her coffee. Put the rings in your pocket."

I gave the wall separating us a critical stare. This was my proposal, and Mister Bossy needed to give me back the control. My mind had conjured a meaningful proposal, then anniversary sex, then planning an intimate, cozy ceremony, something special for the three of us.

Not how it turned out at all. I did as he requested and put the rings in my pocket. I gave myself a moment, staring into the mirror. Overall, my life was coming along just the way I'd always hoped it would.

12: The Climb
Beau/Dash

Beau

My palms itched with anticipation of getting my ass back into the volleyball game. Unfortunately, none of Dash's friends possessed a single athletic bone in their bodies. What a seriously dumb choice to leave the game in order to let another player take my spot on the team, considering I *was* the team.

When I left the court, we were up by ten, and my side hadn't scored another point since then. With me out, Dash, who played on the opposing side, had taken control of the game. His relentless competitive spirit never allowed him to back down. He and I faced off one-on-one several times, and despite his earlier instructions about only playing for fun, each time I bested him, I playfully mouthed *I win*. He reciprocated the sentiment the few times he managed to score against me.

"Beau." My mom's soft voice was the only interruption to penetrate the humming of my unyielding competitive nature. I missed playing sports. I had no desire to return to a university team, but I needed a better outlet to channel the drive inside me. Law students on a beach volleyball afternoon didn't cut it. Neither did my work at FedEx. Regardless of how quickly

I completed my tasks, and generally outperformed everyone else, no other driver cared, making the win not nearly as fun.

I cut a glance back over my shoulder, first at my mom, then beyond. The outdoor, city owned, recreational sports park had several choices to play other than beach volleyball, positioned right off the lake. There was a basketball court, a tennis court, and a jogging trail. Times were reserved online. We still had at least an hour blocked to play volleyball. Weaved throughout the entire park were places to throw out a blanket or chair, and enjoy the sun, or a game, but the rock climbing walls pulled my attention there. Although I'd never officially climbed a rock, I felt I could easily conquer those walls. The highest point couldn't be more than four stories. With no fear of heights, my challenge would be against myself as I aimed to scale the wall faster and faster.

"You're not paying attention to me," she said, resting a hand on my forearm. My thoughts shifted to the unconditional bond we shared. We were also evolving into friendship, causing the lines between parent and child to blur. Since I'd commandeered a decent-size section of the blanket she'd brought to sit on to watch us play, I made a deliberate effort to listen this time—at least after I voiced what I wanted to say.

"You're pretty, Mom. I like that you're able to take better care of yourself."

She squeezed my forearm where her hand still rested, beaming under my praise.

"It's been easier to take care of myself since we're no longer living under such an oppressive life." Over the last six months, she had immersed herself in a bohemian style of life. It fit her new personality like a glove. My mom was tallish, sort of, and wore flowing, loose clothes that somehow still fit her frame while giving off a breezy, delicate vibe.

"You're still young," I murmured, not even understanding why I said it.

"Every year you get older, I get older." Her laughter drew a smile from me. She lifted a finger, pointing toward a man on the other side of the volleyball court. He had arrived several minutes ago. He was older, but not that old, fit, and appeared to come from money based on how he wore his clothes. "Who's that, son?"

"Dash mentioned Carter was stopping by today to meet everyone. It might be him," I said, unsure. Just then, this game concluded, my team was defeated, and a sweaty, disheveled Dash hurried toward the man my mom had noticed. She and I watched their interaction as my guy turned and pointed toward us. I raised my hand, feeling uncertain what to do.

"You don't see someone like him in Southern Alabama." I agreed with that. His walking shorts were perfectly tailored to his body. The tasteful Hawaiian style shirt hung from his shoulders in a way that accentuated a broad chest. His sun-kissed tan and blond highlights in his chestnut hair appeared naturally acquired. I had discovered my new fashion mentor. I suddenly aspired to exude the same polished yet relaxed style.

"Everyone around here is a different breed than me. Their priorities are different," I finally blurted out my biggest concerns about living here. "The way they see life is different. The food they eat, the beer they drink, the conversations at dinner are all different. Dash's different, too, when he's around them."

"I wondered if you noticed that," my mom said. The hand on my forearm swiped downward in a caress. "But he only has eyes for you. I worried that he was too controlling but seeing you two together has ended that concern. He really tries to care for you. You don't make it easy on him."

I laughed and tilted my chin to glance at her. "I don't need anyone to take care of me. I want him to be my partner." The wedding ring on my finger seemed to have a direct line to my emotional well-being. My belly did a little flip-flop as the tip of my finger skimmed the band. Maybe I rushed us into wearing these rings too soon. I just liked it, and what it stood for. "Since we moved here, he's been a better equal to me. He doesn't try to take care of all our expenses alone. We do it together now."

"You know, he still hasn't cashed the check for the truck," my mom said.

"I know, but keep the money ready. I think we're headed into some hard times," I said, but that was only a fifty/fifty bet. Dash had somehow orchestrated life in a way that he wasn't doing without. I was concerned about his strong ties to his family, and what it might mean losing his foundation so dramatically, but he hadn't had a landslide yet.

"I appreciate the way you've started adding the g's to the ends of your words."

"It wasn't intentional," I said, dryly. For the entirety of my life, she'd been on me about the way I spoke. I'd never give in. Probably even dug my resistant heels in harder. Now, I had another thing to add to the list of cons about Chicago: involuntary accent change.

"He's headed this way," she said.

"Invite him to sit with us," I suggested. "If it's Carter, he's been really good to us."

"Of course I will, I'm a southern woman. Manners before God, country, and family." She grinned at me, but she wasn't wrong. I laughed, if only on the inside, staring into her round sunglasses. Her cheek leaned against my bicep as we watched Carter's approach. He grinned broadly when my mom loved on me.

"I'm Wesley Carter," he said, still a few feet away. I made myself rise, stretching out a hand, instantly intimidated by the man. Carter was lean and fit. As he came to me, he removed his sunglasses. I did too, only because he did.

"I'm Beau. This is my mom," I said, hooking a casual thumb to the side. "Linda."

All his attention landed on my mom.

"Dash told me this was your mother, but I doubted him. You must have been very young when you had him," he said, causing my mom to beam under the compliment. On the other hand, I furrowed my brows. Since Carter didn't linger, I let it go. "I understand congratulations are in order. You three had a big morning."

My eyes dropped to my commitment ring. The tip of my finger ran again reverently over the band, a symbol of everything Dash and I shared. I had to put the doubt away.

"You two have the same rings," he said, bending to peer closely at mine. I appreciated his genuine interest and attention to detail.

"Dash surprised me this morning. It's his birthday today, and now the day holds even more significance," I said. "I don't know how much more the day can handle. Better for me though, I knock out all the sentiment in one twenty-four-hour period."

He chuckled. I did too because I was damned funny, and it was true. I bent, starting to take my seat. "Join us. We're waiting for Dash to take a break. He's kicking these people's butts. It has to be exciting for him."

Carter didn't immediately sit. Instead, all his attention focused on my mom again. "And you're the mother figure I've heard so much about."

"I am. Have a seat, Wesley." She patted the blanket beside her.

"I don't want to intrude, but it'd be nice to have some company," he said. I was regularly baffled by how she effortlessly engaged in conversation with anyone around her. A talent I didn't possess. "Most call me Carter, but you can call me Wesley, and you're beautiful."

My brows instantly snapped together. Apparently that particular muscular contraction was my newest superpower. I jerked my head toward my mom. A blush creeped up her cheeks. She seemed to melt right in front of my eyes.

"Not true but thank you." He settled comfortably beside her, both of them ignoring my very direct stare. Oh no, I wasn't sitting here on this gorgeous day with not a cloud in the sky to watch my mom be flattered.

"I'm gonna go rock climb," I said with irritation in my voice and hooked a thumb behind me.

At least they both glanced behind them, rather than staring so intently at one another. "That's awful high," my mom said.

"Yep. That's the cool part," I said, letting her chew on that as I started toward the attendant manning the wall. "He isn't afraid of heights, but I don't know if he's ever climbed something so tall," she explained to Carter. I heard the concern in her voice, which was silly. I'd be harnessed in if anything went south.

Hours later, I was hot, sweaty, probably sunburned, and out of money. I also had scored mad respect from the attendant.

"I doubted you," he said while helping release me from the harness. "Not too many guys your size have the strength-to-weight ratio needed to be a contender, but you held your own. With proper training to perfect your technique, you could compete."

Even with the words tickling the competitive part of my being, I shook my head. "Nah, I don't want to be on the competitive level of anything anymore, but I'd like to learn how to mountain climb properly." I glanced up at the wall and smiled. "I really enjoyed this today. How're you involved here? Is this your business?"

"No. This is owned by the city, but I'm here every weekend and holidays to earn extra cash." As I stepped away from all the safety gear, he handed over a business card. "The money I make goes back into rock climbing. I'm addicted." His good-natured grin showed how happy he was to be hooked on the sport. That said a lot. "I suggest you go with Spider-Dan's local group, Clutch. Here's the number on the back. They'll teach you what you need to know and give you real time experience."

With my forearm, I brushed away the sweat collecting on my forehead. I tossed my shirt to the side about an hour ago when the warm sun and high humidity caused it to cling to me. My adrenaline had surged as the attendant had taught me the process for climbing the wall then again when I'd tossed to the top. I'd broken records for the wall, then broke my own time when I went again.

For the first time since the beginning of the climb, I searched Dash out. I found him in the crescent-shaped clique of his friends. My mom, Carter, and everyone else were all now facing me. My guy stood from the beach-style lawn chair and whistled loudly, clapping his hands. The others followed suit.

The irritation I had harbored while being so completely ignored by Dash was now fully resolved. I swiped my hand through the air, downplaying my accomplishment, but my joy was impossible to hide. The attendant playfully knocked me in the back when I started toward Dash.

"I forgot to add, rock climbing brings the ladies out of the woodwork."

Not the incentive it might have seemed. Dash jogged through the sand toward me. I grabbed my shirt and started in his direction while pulling my ring out of my pants pocket where I'd tucked it for safety and sliding it back in place. I swore the energy of the gold band liberated me. A material symbol of what we shared that gave me the same feelings as if Dash were right there with me, whispering all his reassuring words of love that scooped up my doubt and tossed it away.

"My guy's such a badass," Dash said and extended a cold Gatorade, condensation dripping down the outside. He slowed a couple of feet from me and walked the final steps, a giant grin on his face. "We ended the game, and I spotted what you were doing. We've all been watching you climb, shocked that it was your first time."

Dash came straight in, chest to chest, and kissed my lips. He never backed away or worried how others might react, he just loved me through and through.

"We should go home and get cleaned up," he said, staring me straight in the eyes, his face only inches from mine. My arms circled around him and squeezed tightly before I let him go, turning in the direction of my mom. "We have dinner reservations in two hours," Dash called to my mom. "Carter, you're welcome to join us."

Dash's hand intertwined with mine. Life was back to right as rain.

Dash

One iPod, one set of earbuds split between two ears, his and mine, while slow dancing, locked in Beau's strong embrace... My belly was full from a delicious dinner. Life was so good.

I had my face resting in the crook of Beau's neck, breathing in the spicy, erotic scent of his cologne. Our bodies did a slow sway to the sounds of "Better Together" by Jack Johnson. Our shoes were kicked off, our bare feet sifting through the sand as we moved together, with a darkened Lake Michigan churning in the background. The full moon helped set the romantic scene. We were somewhere between the parked truck and a section of the beach we claimed as our own a couple of hours ago. Booming pops of fireworks sounded off in the distance from the shows in the suburbs.

"I dreamed of this day," I said quietly, my eyes closed while breathing in another long inhale of his scent. "In my wildest imagination, I never thought we'd be this good."

Beau chuckled, gently tousling me with the movement of his chest. "I did. It scared me. You're so out of my league."

Reluctantly, I angled my head to better see his face. He tilted his head in the other direction. His earbud slipped from his ear. "Where's that coming from? I think we're very compatible."

"Huh," he said. He cupped his palm against the back of my head, trying to lower my head back to his shoulder with a solid push. It was a playful gesture he frequently used when he wanted to avoid a conversation. He furrowed his brows at me when I resisted, prompting him to push a bit harder.

"Not happening until you answer." I stopped moving as I continued to stare at him. The romance of moments ago took a backseat as I worked through all the possibilities of what I'd done to cause him to feel that way. "You're going to have to tell me what I've done. It wasn't on purpose."

"Then lay your head down or let's go and finish the conversation in bed." His easy grin caused one of my own, even understanding this was another attempted diversion by Beau. It also assured me that whatever caused the words wasn't going to ruin our night. I tugged the earbud from my ear, letting it hang from my hand.

Beau's smoldering stare held my attention as he stepped into me, his fingertips caressing down the length of my arms until his hands took mine. "Let it go. I shouldn't have said it. Especially today. It's been a great day."

"Tell me now," I murmured, clasping his hands. With him standing so sexy before me, I knew this needed to be finished before we took it into our home.

Since I stared intently at him, I saw the moment his expression turned to resignation, which meant I'd won. I wasn't going to declare my victory now, but he'd know before we went to bed. "I don't get along with your friends here as well as I did back home. They're different. Here, it's all so intellectual. They come off as better than me."

"And I spent so much time with them today. Did I make you feel ignored?" I asked, releasing him as he walked away, moving toward our shoes.

"Come on. I'm not upset, I shouldn't have said anything. I'm happy that you have friends. You haven't had many in your life," he said. The full moon cast Beau beautifully. I wished I had a camera to capture the moment. When he turned back toward me, he knocked the shoes together to remove the sand and tilted his head toward the truck. "Let's go. I've always considered you out of my league. You're just so personable. You don't see class differences. And honestly, all those qualities gave me a chance to bag a guy like you." With a playful glint in his eye, he lifted his left hand, wiggling his fingers. "I can feel it on my finger all the time. How long do you think it'll last?"

"I considered you might be feeling left out today," I said, walking toward my side of the truck. "Then I saw you rock climbing, well everybody saw you climbing like a spider monkey, and I left the game to watch you."

"No explanation needed," Beau said. "I want you to have friends to help get you through the next few years. I just don't vibe with them." All the while, he also went to his side of the truck— the driver's side—tracking me as I went. He was nervous. The locks released with a click.

Since I'd studied his face all day and night, I knew his little signs of fibbing and saw none were present. "Well, I want to know your friends," I said and climbed into the truck. "You haven't introduced any to me."

"Middle of the seat," he said, climbing into his side.

I followed his instructions. It was growing late, as we drove along Lake Shore Drive. The streets were unusually quiet, a stark contrast to the noise we heard twenty-four seven. About five minutes from the parking garage, I grazed my hand down his thigh.

"You really were in your element while rock climbing," I said. "How did it feel?"

"Good, natural. I've always enjoyed climbing, you know that." He smiled at me while I pressed the gate button. It slid open smoothly as we pulled into the garage. "If it's not too expensive, I'll probably pursue it. My belly's getting flabby."

Oh lord, that was a far cry from reality. Beau rounded the floors like a pro until he parked next to Carter's vehicle. A wave of melancholy washed over me. Our day was almost over. We went hand in hand up the elevator then down the hall to the front door. Beau, ever the gentleman, swung the door open for me, ushering me inside first. Something from the right side of the penthouse caught my attention. I was stunned speechless, which was a good thing. Carter and Linda were walking into the guest bedroom suite entrance, holding hands. Carter saw me when he turned back to the door. He looked me straight in the eyes before closing the door behind them.

What on earth was happening? Reacting instinctively, I flipped around, pressing both palms firmly on Beau's chest, catching him off guard enough to shove him back several feet. My thoughts raced as I blurted, "Close your eyes."

The sudden spark flickered in his amber gaze, causing a mischievous smile to tug at one corner of his lips. A look I typically found quite endearing, often leading to sexy time. "Seriously, I forgot something to give to you."

"You gave me enough, Dash. We can't spend all this extra money," he lectured, but closed his eyes as I'd requested. I took his hand and walked carefully through the entry into our side of the penthouse. I quickly glanced around and didn't see anything out of place and let go of a breath I didn't know I'd been holding.

"Oh wait, I decided to give that to you for Christmas."

Beau instantly stopped and popped his eyelids open, looking around. "Are you lying? Am I missing something?"

I left him standing there and started for the stairs. "Of course not. I just forgot. I was lost in all your sexy cologne." I prattled on until we were up the stairs, in the bedroom, with the door shut behind us. Even then I still continued to talk. Beau would tune me out eventually, he always did.

13: The Surprise
Beau/Dash

Beau

December 2006

"I'm so cold," my mom said, giving a full body shiver for the third time in a matter of minutes. I flipped the heater on the highest option then adjusted all the vents in my truck in her direction. She had worn her normal, Alabama type cold weather clothes with a fleece jacket as her outerwear. I'd tried to explain the low temperatures and how the wind blowing off the lake made it brutally cold. These people in Chicago wore their cold weather clothes virtually year-round. Dash and I had purchased new clothing, because we were ill-prepared for the elements when moving here. Apparently, the thin zip-up was her way to embrace the cold weather.

"Mom, put my coat on properly." I'd said the same words many times since picking her up inside the airport, then through the parking garage, until right now as she sat with her hands close to the vent, her body tilted forward to get closer to the warmth.

She was unnecessarily hardheaded, refusing to take my coat until we were outside, with snow on the ground, and I finally shrugged off my Carhartt and placed it over her shoulders. Still she fought me, trying to give it back, then purposefully wearing it draped over her shoulders refusing to commit to using it fully. Mothers were a different breed. They were weird about their children no matter the age. She still put me before everything else.

"I thought the leggings might be an extra barrier against the cold. Instead, they make me colder." Her last word came with another solid shiver. "I've got to go shopping."

"Yeah, I'll take you tomorrow. The weatherman says it will get colder for the next week or so, then it chills out and we'll be in the seventies. They're forecasting a chance of snow for the holidays," I said and started the slow descent out of the airport parking garage.

"They know that already?" she asked, amazed. "We still have weeks to go."

"Yeah, I guess." The way I drove was different these days, driving my personal vehicle with the same assertiveness I did my FedEx truck. I could edge my truck into traffic when there was little room to do so. The frustrated honks ensued when I did that now. Chaos was the only way to describe the exit out of O'Hare airport. "You're gonna have to babysit Dash. He's in freak-out mode, trying to get everything finished to graduate in a few weeks. Then he goes straight into preparing for the bar. He's working for a law firm on weekends, and some nights... You know that I'm slammed at work." I gave her a little sideways glance to make sure she was paying attention to me. "So take care of him."

"I know, and I will. He and I text all the time. I can read the stress even without his voice," she said, humor in her tone. "It's why I'm here so early. I gotta help my boys. Don't stress about it. He's just as worried about your workload. It's sweet how you look out for each other."

Her words relieved some of my worries. Dash and I had been going in different directions for the last few weeks. No amount of preparation had us ready for the holiday rush, and we still had weeks before the final push, the busy days leading up to the actual holiday. Between the overwhelming number of packages to be delivered and the weather conditions outside, Dash and I only saw each other in bed. And that wasn't for long. My day started at three in the morning, while his lasted until ten, or eleven, or even later some nights.

Maybe this was just adulting, except we weren't paying rent or utilities. My cash went for the groceries and eating out. The rest was saved. The law firm paid Dash twenty-five dollars an hour. His money went toward professional grooming. Jumping headfirst into his expensive haircuts and highlights, buying high-dollar hair products and facial soaps and lotions that supposedly made his skin soft and youthful. He made me use the products too. I couldn't tell the difference, but he swore they helped.

"I have the Christmas dinner menu planned. Wanna hear it?" she asked, rifling through the purse she had hanging over her body. "Actually, it's a lead-up menu, starting a couple days before the big day. The meal takes time, so I created a three-day celebration. Dash told me he'd be off through the holidays, then start with the firm full time in January. I figured you'd have to work through Christmas Eve."

I nodded, fearful that I might have to work Christmas Day. My mother continued telling me about her menu without so much as a grunted response from me. "I plan to have an appetizer party, celebrating Dash's graduation. Dash asked to have friends over. People who're displaced for the holidays." Well, that was new information for me. The distraction had me barreling up on a small car. I had to focus on the road. It wasn't easy. Nothing had changed for me. I didn't like his friends, more so now. They were like Dash's family. Pretentious and believing they were on a higher plane than everyone else, but Dash really enjoyed them, so I suffered through.

"Of course, I'll have the cheese dip you like and your favorite chips. Then I thought we'd change it up. Have individual caprese appetizers." She looked over at me, or at least I felt her eyes on me. "They're easy, and Dash likes them. They're a grape tomato and a small cube of mozzarella. Then basil and olive oil. I'll add olives and sliced meat to the tray."

In the silence, I realized she was waiting for me to respond. I nodded, and she turned back to her list. "I planned for warm brie and pear tartlets. Bacon wrapped figs. Cranberry, pecan, goat cheese individual balls. I'll probably go half cream cheese and half goat cheese. And the best tasting Gruyère and thyme stacked potatoes—small bite-size potatoes. All of that can be made ahead of time. I also found several cocktail recipes I want to try. I thought you could take leftovers the next day for lunch. They may be easier to eat throughout the day. Sound good?"

I nodded again but had my apprehensions. It sounded fancy, which wasn't her normal style. "Christmas Eve, we'll have the ham that you like so much, cheesy potatoes au gratin, and fresh green beans. Your favorite meal."

I nodded this time in appreciation. A honey-baked ham and green beans were the best food out there.

"Then prime rib, leftover ham, a new dressing recipe that I found, seared broccoli rabe with toasted almonds and homemade croutons—my favorite—and glazed carrots, roasted sweet potatoes, and I found a shaved brussels sprout salad. It looks amazing."

Huh. That was a far different meal than she'd ever made before. I scrunched my nose at brussels sprout anything, but the rest sounded pretty good. "What about bread?"

"Yep, got it down. I think yeast rolls are a good choice."

Yum. My favorite. "Amelia's coming to stay for a few days, she's making tamales in bulk for some guys at work. They're paying her. I'll help you however I can. I'll chop anything and do the prep work when I get home at night," I offered, breathing a sigh of relief when I finally merged onto the right freeway to take us home.

"That'll help a lot. I feel like this is a big undertaking, but I like to cook, and we've been so poor..." Her words trailed off as the freeway opened at least enough to pick up speed. "No, I'm not going backward, only forward. I have a decent budget for decorating."

"Mom," I started. We talked about this. No over-the-top decorations. Maybe a tree but nothing more.

"But I want to, Beau. The lights are colorful and bring joy. We can run lighted garland up the banister and over the windows and doorways. Of course we'll do the tree."

"Where am I gonna put all that stuff when the season's over?" I asked.

"Half the condo isn't being used, or we can get a small rental unit. We'll figure it out," she said. "Let me do this. You two are carrying a load and I'm proud of you." Oh man, mom guilt was the worst kind of guilt.

I finally nodded because I knew her better than anyone. She'd argue all the way to actually putting the decorations up.

Weirdly, I was developing a new set of insecurities that I needed to figure out. Dash was diving headfirst into his career path, which I was so proud of him for. He deserved only good experiences from life. But something about the long relentless hours he put in, followed by lots of gatherings with his peers, was running my guy ragged. Maybe I was jealous. Dash had loved me so good that it was hard to lose his undivided attention. Yeah sure, he always included me in his outings, but Dash rarely slept. I needed rest. And our sex was lackluster at best.

"What's got you so quiet?" she asked, pulling me from my downward spiraling thoughts.

"Nothing, really," I said, keeping my eye on the road. We'd traveled farther than I'd realized so I moved into the exit lanes. "Dash's burning it at both ends. I get that it'll work out better once he graduates. It's good that you're here."

"I wouldn't miss this time with both of you. He's done such great things," she said, and turned back to stare out the front window. "And he's so smart. Did you always know how smart he was?"

A grin took my worries away. She was funny. "Remember, he graduated early from high school and had his associates degree. College lasted about a year. He's taken his time with law school to get some age under his belt."

"That's right. Have you thought about going back to school?"

Oh lord, here we went again. A conversation she wanted to have all the time. I rolled my eyes and followed the road as she started in on the value of a college education. She wasn't wrong. I just had too much energy to sit and study for so long. I was happy with my job. It was good enough for me.

Dash

Christmas Party

A tipsy Beau was a beautiful guy. No matter the number of people at our party, or even the late hour, his attention was only on me. Right there in my face, I noticed the worry lines and semi-permanent frowns we had been living with for well over a month were now gone. Maybe due to us never leaving our spot, in the corner, with the window of the view of the lake against our side. Beau loved everything about the lake. He'd been fishing there several times over the last few months.

His mom had been working herself into the ground to put on the perfect holiday party. The entire home twinkled under the thousands—I might be exaggerating a little—of small lights in every piece of garland hung just about everywhere.

Helping with the decorating had become a way for me to put aside my stresses and help his mom work on the house. I'd always loved the season and taken it upon myself to decorate, if only just for me and Amelia.

"Did you try a tamale?" I asked Beau.

"I've tried everything at least twice. I'm just biding my time for a third round," he said, sliding one of his hands underneath my shirt to skim to the back. The skin-on-skin contact was everything for me, him too.

"Incoming," Amelia said behind my back. Beau started to look away to see what was coming, and I quickly cupped the back of his head, keeping him in my face.

"I want you to promise that you'll be open-minded."

Beau nodded, but I saw confusion in his gaze. My guy was nothing if not open-minded.

I nodded, then he nodded and turned to a fast-approaching Carter, walking side-by-side with Beau's mom.

"You made it," I started. Instead of shaking his hand, I leaned back against Beau, holding his arms that automatically circled around him.

"I did. We had some problems with the plane. I was afraid I wouldn't get here in time," Carter said, wrapping an arm around Linda to draw her closer to him. I felt the second Beau realized Carter was touching his mother in such an intimate way. His body tensed like steel and heat ran through him and into me.

"Beau, honey. Can we talk to you?" his mom asked. "Privately." No matter how tightly I held on to him, he broke free. I suspected he sensed what was coming next.

"What's going on?" Beau said, his tone harsh and strong. So much for my tipsy theory. "Just tell me."

"Your mom and I have been dating, and we've fallen in love," Carter explained. He also spoke confidently, but I saw the moment he swallowed his fear and stopped speaking. My guy must look like the thing from the black lagoon to have Carter halting his words.

"Beau, get that look off your face," Linda said, confirming my theory. "I waited to tell you until I knew more about where we were headed, but we've decided to be a couple. We also decided to tell you together."

"Well, I think that's great news," I said, maybe laying it on too thick, but I went with it, reaching out to hug Linda then shake Carter's hand. "He's always been protective of his mom. Watching out for her."

"I've heard," Carter said, extending a hand to Beau. Beau looked at him and then over to me.

"You knew about this already, I can tell," he said, shifting that hard stare to me.

"Who me?" I asked in feigned confusion.

He didn't buy it. "Yeah you. Don't do it again." he said. That mean stare shifted back to Carter. "Don't fuck with my mother. Her life hasn't been easy," Beau said.

"It's the last thing I want to do," Carter said, lowering his hand. It was incredible to watch how humble he stayed to make this news easier on Beau. My father would have never acted that way. Finally, Beau extended his hand to shake Carter's, who lifted his hand again.

"We waited to tell you until we knew what was happening between us," his mom said again. "Let go of his hand, Beau."

When Beau immediately released his grip, I realized I'd gained a secret weapon. In order to get him to comply, involve his mother. He shaped right up.

"Carter's going to stay with us through Christmas. Then we'll traveling for New Years. I'll be back to help put everything away," Linda said.

"Is it too soon to be calling you my sons?" Carter asked teasingly. Everyone but Beau thought it was funny.

"Come on, Beau," I said to my guy. "I'll get you a new drink to help swallow all this down."

I ignored his bluster, drawing him to the bar with me. We still had days to go with Carter under the roof, but I called this a win for tonight.

Part 2

14: The Fit
Beau/Dash

Beau

Late Spring, 2011
Chicago, Illinois

As I navigated through the obstacle course I'd created in my living room, I meticulously assessed the angles of the various inverted pots and pans strategically placed from my sofa to the large windows overlooking Lake Michigan. Since this game was classified as an "I win" challenge, every placement was crucial. I couldn't fail. I knelt on the floor, becoming one with an imaginary ping-pong ball as it bounced off each pan's bottom until the path concluded in the red Solo Cup at the end. I added another magazine to the first upside-down skillet to tilt it closer to the second pot. With a breath, I crossed my fingers that I'd arranged a perfect course.

"Brooks, you ready?" Scott asked impatiently. He had arranged a similar course in his living room in Alabama. We'd positioned our laptops, webcams active, to the side of the game to give us an unobstructed view of our opponents playing field. At the end of the course, each of us had a video recorder precariously placed on a step stool. If everything went as well as I hoped, I'd toss the ball at the start and it'd bounce off each cooking device until it landed in the cup. The first one to make it to the end won the game.

Scott and I had dived headfirst into many different challenges starting a few weeks ago for a new YouTube channel he wanted to create. Turned out, Lauren, his wife, knew about editing videos. And since I was nothing if not ready to one-up Scott at any given moment, I'd happily joined in the fun.

I took my seat at the front of the course and wiggled around until I found the best launching point. The fall colors and natural sunlight from the floor-to-ceiling windows behind the camera allowed just the right amount of light to make my portion of the video look normal, or so Lauren explained.

"Hang on. I need to hydrate," I said, grabbing a Powerade set strategically to the side. I took a long swig then grabbed my bucket of ping pong balls, placing them between my crisscrossed legs. As if I were about to play the toughest of sports, I stretched my arms and back while swiveling my neck around both directions.

The first one to successfully land a ball in the red Solo Cup was the winner.

"Start on *go*," Scott instructed. "No cheating."

"Zip it and say *go*," I shot back, mentally gearing up for the ultimate cup-sinking showdown.

"One, two, go!" Of course, Scott played unfairly, but this wasn't our first contest. I was prepared and tossed the first ball, watching it ricochet from one pot or pan to the next until it fell flat three-quarters of the way down the path. I recalculated the position and strength of the throw then made a slight adjustment. With my new trajectory established, the second ball was tossed. I kept going just that way, one right after another.

"Oh man," Scott called out.

"What?" I asked, keeping my gaze locked on the ball. My effort to engage him in conversation was primarily intended to distract him from his focus.

"I *just* missed the cup."

I did not expect to hear that. My vision narrowed, my focus sharpened, and I continued sending the balls bouncing down the course. A slow trickle of sweat ran down my cheek. The world around me disappeared. The only sound that registered was the ping of the ball striking the bottom of the various pans. Less than halfway through my bucket, I could feel and hear exactly where the balls needed to land to make it to the cup. It was time to buckle down and get serious.

I leaned into the throw and let the ball go. I watched the zigzag the ball made all the way to the end. Driven more by instinct than careful thought, I made a small adjustment and released another ball with a little less force than before. My gaze darted back and forth until the ball landed in the cup.

"Yeah!" I exploded, shooting to my feet, jumping up and down. The remaining balls in the bucket scattered everywhere as I reveled my win. Out of the corner of my eye, I noticed Scott hollering and hooping in celebration with me. I was so damned proud of myself I brought forward the old dances from my youth. First, the running man. Second, the cabbage patch.

"I win, I win, I win," I chanted as if it were my own special song. Though, I'd easily admit I wasn't a lyrical genius, I did get my point across.

On the turn of an exaggerated swivel of my hips, I spotted Dash and his mentor and hot, older boss, Lon Blackman, standing in the entry of our living room, looking very much like an advertisement for Dolce & Gabbana. Where Dash was blond haired, and blue eyed, Lon was dark headed, dark eyed, with a perfectly tanned complexion. They appeared like the type of lawyers that seemed ready to walk into a courtroom, and kick ass at any given moment.

In contrast, I wore my normal weekend attire, vintage athletic shorts from my college days and a well-worn T-shirt. Since I'd had Friday off, two days worth of facial hair caused an itch at my chin, and my prized Texas Rangers ball cap turned backward on my head completed my ensemble. The cap didn't really fit properly due to the shoulder-length disheveled hair that I hadn't cut in years.

No question, if I didn't look like an ass, I felt like one. Which wasn't an unusual feeling with ninety percent of my interactions with Dash's colleagues. I halted dead in my tracks, the happiness of moments ago drained off me at the same time as my hands fell to my sides. Scott must have taken in the scene. His laughter came louder.

"We're creating a video for YouTube," I said, not sure I'd even told Dash about Scott's new channel. I gestured to my obstacle course as if that would help clarify the situation. The brief moment of embarrassment that crossed Dash's brow had my shoulders drooping. "Scott, I'll send you the video."

"No, don't break the connection. I wanna see how this plays out," Scott shot out seconds before I shut the lid.

"I wasn't able to reach you," Dash said. "Lon and I are having lunch with clients and their significant others. We'd like you to join us." His hands were clasped together, the grip tight, another sign that I had let him down again.

"What's all this, Beau?" Lon asked in the cultured way he spoke, shrugging off his suit coat, stepping farther into the living room. With a toss, the jacket landed over the back of an armchair. The entire time he surveyed the course, undoing his buttons to roll each sleeve up. I quickly lifted my hands in surrender and mouthed *I'm sorry* to Dash.

"The goal is to get a ball into the cup at the end. You toss from here," I explained, pointing to the start position. As if I thought he was too dumb to understand, I scooped up a ball and sent it bouncing its way down. This time it came close to the cup but missed. Lon came to my side, lifting the material of his slacks to squat and survey the course.

"Fascinating," he remarked earnestly, casually tossing his tie over his shoulder. He gathered a few nearby balls and sat on the couch in front of the course. My gaze darted to Dash. His stare fixed on me, the disappointment easy to read. Dash had worked so damned hard and climbed the firm's ranks so swiftly that now he was an associate to a senior partner: Lon. If Dash continued this momentum, he would likely make junior partner before too much longer. Apparently, it was a meteoric rise, unprecedented in Dash's circles. Yet, he'd managed to do it.

I felt a sense of pride for him and tried my damnedest to be a suitable partner, but he and I both knew I was failing. I was never able to truly settle into the fancy places he took me, or be ready at a moment's notice to join him. Dash worked tirelessly from morning until late at night, seven days a week, while I found myself in bed these days at about eight o'clock. Many times, my day began when Dash's day was winding down.

Dash's level of ambition was a foreign concept to me. I would never understand the way Dash's "work buddies" constantly undercut each other on their climb up the ranks, yet, somehow, they still remained friends. I was regularly ready to knock their lights out for putting Dash in various risky situations. However, he only brushed off my irritation, assuring me it was nothing more than good-natured ribbing.

"Give me a minute to change clothes," I said, pushing my palms down the front of my T-shirt. I was damned nervous and needed to remove myself as Lon let go of his first throw.

"Beau," Lon said. "Is the camera set up at the end still on?"

"Yes, I can switch it off," I said and started that direction.

"No, no. When I master this, I want the video." Again, my unsteady gaze skidded to Dash's face, who had gone blank as he walked across the living room to the stairs leading to our bedroom. His head cocked toward the staircase, directing me to go with him, before he turned and trotted up.

Dash

My thoughts raced ferociously, which said something given the fact I typically processed information at lightning speed. I'd made a mistake, but dammit, there was no escaping Lon's decision to stop by the house to gather Beau up. I walked fully inside our bedroom and pivoted around to face Beau as he slipped inside. My hands splayed in front of me as he quickly shut the door behind him.

"Beau, babe, we talked about this," I hissed.

"I know."

I'd have to give it to him, he looked remorseful.

"Why didn't you call first?" he asked, finally heading to the bathroom to get dressed.

"I tried to call you multiple times," I said, trailing behind him. I headed straight for his closet to pull appropriate clothing for him to wear. "He'd like you to join us to keep the women occupied. Lon wants to sign a large construction company to the firm. They want to meet Carter for some investment opportunities. Lon's shooting for sole representation and wants a commitment before we leave tonight. It'll be my account to handle and will count toward my billable hours. Hurry and get dressed."

Beau paused while shaving, casting a glance at me through the mirror. "I've already told you that I'm not involving Carter in anything."

I shook my head in frustration. We'd discussed this countless times. No one understood Beau's position better than me. He wanted nothing to do with his new stepfather, whether it be with his business, his money, or the man himself.

"Nothing's changed. I handle Carter," I snapped, unable to hide the irritation in my voice. "I thought you were getting a haircut this morning."

A primal battle cry echoed from downstairs, sparing me from waiting for whatever excuse Beau gave. We both turned our attention in that direction.

"He probably landed a ball in the cup. It's thrilling. You wouldn't understand unless you've done it."

Okay, he was poking at me about doing nothing more than working anymore. Before an argument ruined our afternoon, I left the bathroom.

"We have a car waiting, please hurry."

Just beyond the closed bedroom door, I pressed my fingers against my eyelids. I asked so little of Beau, and only that small amount of interaction to avoid my company's judgment. Not that I'd ever said those exact words to my guy. Regardless of how much I tried to refine his image, my firm had a specific type and wanted nothing beyond that. Representation was everything, and spouses and significant others mattered. Most of the partners at the firm considered Beau a step above a hillbilly.

The only reason they tolerated his unkempt appearance and rural demeanor was due to his intimate connection to Carter. If they discovered Beau had no intention of ever speaking to Carter again, they'd sideline my guy from any other company sponsored events, leaving me to make decisions about him I wasn't ready to face.

If I could maintain my balance while handling the firm, my clients, and Beau's needs and emotions for a few more years, I'd land a senior partnership position.

But then what?

No, I wasn't going there. I summoned all my mental strength to shove the uncertainty aside and steel my resolve. Within moments, I was trotting down the stairs as if I hadn't been on the brink of a nervous breakdown.

"Well, that was great fun. It brought back all those good youthful times," Lon said spiritedly, shrugging on his suit coat. "I was surprised at the level of precision involved. I felt exhilarated. A true sense of accomplishment when the ball landed in the cup."

"Beau and his childhood friend enjoy these games together. Beau's also an avid fisherman. We have a boat moored at the dock. He and his friend often go fishing together while online. They're always competing," I explained, trying to find the words to make the scene we'd walked into okay. "Can I get you a drink?" I asked, maintaining my pace until I reached the small bar in the kitchen. I sensed him trailing behind me. I poured myself a shot and downed it as I felt Lon's hand gently squeezed my shoulder.

"I understand that you face challenges due to him. Lawyers can be ruthless. We exploit people's vulnerabilities then pounce, especially when you're climbing the ladder as fast as you are. In your case, your weakness is Beau. Naturally, the vultures will try to undermine him to provoke you. Don't allow them to create issues for you. You work for me, no one else."

"Thank you." I nodded, craving the comfort of those words. What Lon didn't know was my growing ire with Beau's complete unwillingness to help me navigate our lives. While I had grown into a man with duties and responsibilities, always fighting to be seen older than my years. Beau remained determined to live the life of a younger man. And since I loved my guy more than life itself, I hadn't said these words to him. Instead, resentment was building for me. "What would you like to drink?"

"A vodka tonic," he requested and pointed past me toward the bottle of Grey Goose I had purchased for occasions like this. As I poured the drink, Lon browsed through the pictures we had on display to give our home a personal touch. Most of those photos were of Beau, highlighting his rock-climbing escapades and moments when he proudly held a big catch before releasing it back into the lake. He was living his best life. The only photo of me showed me toiling away in my new office. A picture Beau had snapped after I received my junior partner position, and then missed our celebratory dinner. He'd come to my office late one night, surprising me with a meal, and his company.

I gave my head a slight shake to dispel the special memory. I heard Beau's approach. He clomped around like a yeti in dress shoes.

Stop. I reached for Beau's preferred IPA and popped the cap. I offered the beer to Beau as he walked into the room and handed over Lon's vodka with a splash of soda as he tapped on a frame.

"Where's that?" Lon asked Beau.

Beau leaned in for a closer inspection. "Curacao. Great island. I could live there easily."

"A tad too humid for me," I added about the only climb I'd ever been on with Beau before sipping my drink. "The next one's Pike's Peak. It was his first 14er climb," I added, pride again in my guy easily surfacing in my tone.

"Fascinating," Lon replied. "Meaning fourteen thousand feet in elevation, correct?"

"Exactly," Beau answered, tilting back the long-neck bottle for a nice-size swig. It was then that I truly noticed him for the first time since entering the room. I had commissioned the suit for Beau after seeing how the fabric matched the amber of his eyes. His sun-kissed skin stood out brilliantly. It didn't matter how many years passed, I still thought Beau was simply stunning.

"And here," Lon said, redirecting my wayward attention by pointing at a picture to the right of the previous one.

"Mount. Rainer. That was my first time going solo," Beau explained.

"The volcano?" Lon asked, surprised.

Beau nodded in confirmation.

"How do you manage such heights?" Lon asked, studying the photo. Before he could respond, he turned to me. "Are you snapping these pictures?"

Beau chuckled at what he thought was a joke. "He's always working these days. He'd never take a day off, let alone a full week."

"That's untrue," I replied, grinning, shaking my head at the absurdity. Except it was the truth. "I get two weeks off for the holidays."

"And you spend that time catching up." My guy's sweet smile shone brightly at me, pulling me solidly back under his spell. I'd make sure we had sexy time tonight. "Let's head out."

"You have a fascinating life," Lon said, clasping my shoulder, leading the way out first.

15: The Sheets
Beau

The buzz of fluorescent lights followed us through the parking garage then to the elevator. I stifled a yawn, grateful tomorrow was Sunday, and I could sleep in. Dash's meetings over drinks and dinner tended to last well into the night, which would be fine, but I typically had to rise early for work the next morning. That lack of sleep made the following day feel so much longer.

The elevator doors parted at the press of the call button. As we ascended, Dash extended his hand toward mine. I grasped it, interlocking our fingers. The weight and grip brought back memories of a time when we'd held hands everywhere we went.

As if Dash read my mind, he said, "Not too long ago, I couldn't have made it five seconds without touching you."

"We used to spend more time together than apart." I leaned my ass against the railing in the back of the car. Moments later, the doors spread open.

"I never imagined I'd work this hard," Dash murmured, holding my hand as we exited the elevator and started down the hall toward our home.

"Me either," I replied with a sincere chuckle. Dash left the house after me, but always by seven in the morning, and most nights he didn't return home until after I had gone to bed. The weekend used to be our time together, but those days were only a good memory. Dash now worked seven days a week. I missed our lives together. Tightening my hand holding his, I forced myself out of my head before my thoughts turned darker.

"You're being quiet," Dash said while entering the code to unlock the front door.

When I didn't respond quickly enough, he cast a questioning glance over his shoulder. My gaze was instantly drawn to him, and it was still overwhelming for me. He had always been a handsome guy, but with age and a well-tailored suit, Dash looked genuinely GQ-ready.

"I tend to be the quiet one," I reminded him.

"Not usually with me." He fixed his gaze on me, using his butt to hold open the door to allow me to get ahead of him. Once inside, he tossed his key fob on the entry table. A habit he'd had since we moved here. He tightened his grip around my hand. "You've been preoccupied all evening."

"I understand that you find a way to make it work a certain way, but it bugs me to have Carter mentioned so much around me. I don't like him. I feel like my mom made a bad decision in marrying him," I said, releasing Dash's hand to shrug off my suit coat. Thankfully, I didn't have to wear a tie today. They were so annoying and dumb to wear.

The quiet in the house always made it feel cold. The game that I left out in the living room was picked up, no sign that it was ever there. Apparently we had housekeepers that I never saw, but miraculously kept the house uber clean.

As I trudged up the stairs for the bedroom, an instrumental piece started to play throughout the house. Sometimes, I turned on Dash's playlist because it always reminded me of him. Once I realized he hadn't followed me up, I searched him out. I found him still on the first floor, moving toward the staircase at a snail's pace as he removed his clothes. My steps up became slower as I watched his suit coat be draped over his arm. His knotted tie hung loose as he worked his cufflinks free. I don't know why I found that such a sexy move, but I did. My cock plumped, growing firm on my final step up.

"Beau, baby, Carter admires your determination to be a self-sufficient man, and he deeply loves his family, which includes you," Dash explained, oblivious to all the sexy time pheromones I was throwing down.

"I wish you'd use my income to help pay our bills. I liked it better when we combined our paychecks," I said, bringing up a topic sure to divert Dash from any more talk of Carter.

"I keep forgetting to tell you that the Dallas house is ours. We won," Dash said in his own diversionary countermove, finally making it to the top step with me. We were now eye to eye, Dash's smile spreading.

"Congratulations," I said, falling in step with him as we moved toward the bedroom.

"Joy reached out to me. My father had a meltdown with the news and fired his lead council."

"I bet," I said. Whether Dash showed it or not, he was joyful about beating his father. I was too. "And you haven't heard from your mom or any other family?"

"No. Thankfully." We were in a lifestyle reminiscent of an old married couple. Instead of tugging off each other's clothing to throw down in bed, I headed for the closet, and he followed. The overhead lights flipped on as we entered. "I saw Scott's YouTube channel. I was surprised he posted both his and your shared videos. Has he noticed that you beat him every time? It's funny. The comments bust on Scott."

"He's got baby brain," I said, letting that be enough to explain where Scott's head was anymore. I toed off my shoes and worked the buttons from the front of my dress shirt.

"With three children in four years, I bet he's always going to have baby brain," Dash said. We shared a look that meant no truer words had ever been spoken, then continued to undress.

"We're godparents to four energetic young girls. I'm not gonna lie, they're pretty special," I said. By mentioning my tiny baby sister Kailey, one of the four young girls in our lives, caused me to worry. I wasn't sure almost five years was enough time to truly vet Carter as a stable guy. What if there was a hidden alcohol problem, or something more devastating that put my mom and baby sister in a bad way?

I headed off to brush my teeth, and Dash trailed behind me. "I've been thinking about the Dallas property. What're your feelings about putting it up for sale and having Amelia relocate here with us?"

"Oh joy. A light, witty conversation," I said. The next few minutes were quiet, I didn't like talking while brushing my teeth. When I was done, I reached for a hand towel and continued, "Has something happened? You playing hero again?"

"Let's not go overboard with the praise. I'm not in a virtuous mood," Dash said, turning me to where my ass hit the bathroom counter.

He slid his palms down my back then over the swells of my ass. He squeezed both cheeks as he pressed a kiss on my lips. Where I was ready to tongue and teeth the kiss, he backed off.

"I apologize for all the challenges I'm creating for you. I didn't fully grasp the time and effort involved in this career choice. Stick with me. You're perfect the way you are. Every part of you still stuns me." Dash pushed his hands inside the waistband of my underwear and caressed his way to the front. "Why wear underwear?" He curled a hand around my shaft. His other had shoved my underwear down until it pooled at my feet.

I arched into his touch. My hips pitched forward, driving into Dash's fist. Extreme desire drove all the feels inside my body, but my head wrapped around Dash's words. "What've I done really wrong? Why am I good the way I am?"

"Nothing," Dash murmured, lowering to his knees. He darted his tongue forward, swiping at my already beading tip. My vision zeroed in on my guy swallowing me directly into his mouth. Jeez, he knew how to blow me, doing everything to drive me crazy. Dash sucked me straight into his mouth, deep diving down my cock until my tip hit the back of his throat.

From the go, I whimpered unintelligible words while I gripped the edge of the countertop, digging in before my desire spun me out of control. Dash bobbed and licked his way around the entirety of my cock. It had been too long, maybe three weeks, since we were together in this way. I loved Dash on me. My orgasm already brimming, ready to release at any given swipe. At the same time, I gripped the base of my shaft with my rough palm, pushing my cock farther down his throat. Dash took it with ease, trailing his fingertips lovingly up the inside of my thigh.

The caress tickled until my balls landed in his palm. He gave a solid tug. Man, I liked that move. His talented hand and sinful mouth worked in unison. What a heady mix of love and pleasure. My guy knew me so well.

The thrust of my hips couldn't be helped. My free hand went to Dash's jaw and chin, holding him in place while I fucked his mouth. I liked it rough, but he craved domination, wanting me to cut off air. He gagged around my cock. His eyes were screwed closed as his hand stroked his own dick. The sight had my balls drawing up tight into my body.

"Bed," I panted, not a hundred percent sure that I said that word aloud. I recovered quickly, though. I was good for a couple of back-to-back orgasms.

Dash was reluctant to let me go, only pausing due to the shove I gave against his jaw. That sexy mouth released me with an audible pop. Instinct, more than any real plan I had developed, moved me away from Dash where he remained on his knees, tracking me as I went into our bedroom. He followed in that stealthy, tracking of prey kind of way. Oh man, his desire turned me the fuck on.

I carelessly tossed the comforter off the mattress to the floor and slid onto the freshly changed sheets. Splayed across the bed, I bent my muscular legs at the knees, butterflying my thighs open. Heat rushed through my body at the sight of my beautiful guy crawling between my legs. My cock jutted in Dash's direction like a heat-seeking missile, knowing exactly where it wanted to be.

"You're gorgeous," Dash whispered, pressing his lips to the inside of my thigh. "It turns me on to see you this way."

Need churned within me, my slit leaking as he crawled all the way up my body to press those full lips against mine. He didn't deepen the kiss or linger. Instead, he rose inches above me, his hard as steel cock settling in next to mine.

"Never doubt your significance in my life. Our bond's strong and forever. Tell me you agree." The solemn tone didn't match the sweet longing in his eyes.

Even with the complexities of his world, my mate was still devoted to me. I lifted a palm to his cheek, my thumb sweeping light caresses anywhere it could reach. The other hand sought his ass, kneading the flesh there. "Absolutely. I get what's happening, why you're working so hard. It won't last forever. I'm proud of you."

His lips again descended, his tongue swiping directly into my mouth. I tasted my essence as he lavished me, leaving me breathless and eager for more. His skilled lips sucked and nipped their way down my chest, certain to leave small marks down the path he took. My fingers tangled into his silky strands as he took his time delving into the ridges between my stomach muscles.

At my obliques, he licked a wet path over to my needy cock, twitching for his touch. But he denied me. His nose tickled and nuzzled the hair there until his mouth reached my sac. Oh fuck, he was wicked, drawing each ball into his mouth, melding and molding them until my world centered right there between my legs.

I gripped the sheets, fisting the fabric as my ass pitched forward, wanting Dash's undivided attention there. Jeez, I'd been with Dash so many times, but somehow, he played my body like his own personal instrument, taking me to the brink over and over again. I was still head over heels in love with my guy.

"Dashing," I whispered the loving nickname that finally stuck. "It's been too long. I need to come. Take me there." The words came with a hint of a warning to help keep him focused.

With a sigh, Dash sat up and reached for the lube on the nightstand, getting to his knees. He scooted between my parted thighs. Then he drizzled the slick on his fingers before tossing the bottle aside. He stared at me the entire time. His movements sure, his need evident in his darkening blue gaze.

Dash massaged his slick fingers over my perineum, sending waves of tingles racing along my entire body. His cool breath puffed over my heated skin. I gripped the back of my thighs, my body tensing as a guttural moan escaped. Dash, though, was the conductor, guiding my body to play the symphony he created. A cool slickness swiped over my hole, the tender flesh took his thumb like it was meant to be there. With a quick intake of breath, I rolled my hips, my body vibrating with urgency. The hold I had on my orgasm was slipping.

He used his fingers and tongue to relax my hole. My feet dug into the mattress as he added two fingers, pumping them in and out of me. My body gripped his digits, easily drawing them inside. He curled the tips of his fingers to rub against the sensitive bundle of nerves. Fuck, man, he did it for me in every way. My cock leaked in earnest.

"Baby, please." My plea came out breathless and needy.

"I wanna make this good for you," Dash said, drizzling more lube at my hole, adding a third or fourth finger.

"It is," I hissed. "I'm ready."

"Look at me, Beau. Watch me enter you." Situating himself as he gripped his own cock, Dash's eyes locked with mine. He panted as he pushed the tip of his cock past the tight ring of muscle he'd worked to relax.

The sweet way he had about making love to me had my eyes rolling into the back of my head. Ecstasy sent fireworks shooting off behind my lids when Dash fully seated inside me.

Home. My world came together. We were finally home again.

Dash's pleasure-filled moan sent goose bumps shimmering along my nerve endings.

Dash pushed my thighs to my chest. I gripped my hamstrings to keep them in place. His body came over mine, his hand locking on my shoulder, keeping me right where he wanted me. My vision dimmed. His breath rushed out of him as he sank back and forth into me. Heat engulfed me into all that scorching, mind-numbing pleasure.

"God, you feel good," Dash murmured, pushing through my legs to drop his forehead to my chest. My ankles crossed at his ass. He fit so perfectly as if I was made just for him.

"Fuck me, Dash." Those blue eyes were almost a steel color now. Dash was my foundation. He kept me grounded. I grasped Dash's head as I wrapped a leg around his body. My heel dug into the fleshy rounds of his ass, pushing Dash to move faster.

"I love you," Dash whispered, his head lifted to stare me in the eyes. His hand reverently gripped my cock. I tangled my fingers into his hair, tugging him fully down to me, welding our mouths together in a rough, satisfying kiss. A tongue-tangling, teeth-clashing kiss that urged him to pump faster into me.

I clenched around his body, the strain becoming too much to bear. Fuck, Dash canted his hips, his hand pumping my cock to the rhythm he created. He thrust harder as he plundered my ass.

Dash's throaty moans were addictive. I loved drawing the guttural, wild sounds from my guy. His gaze met mine. Something deep exchanged in our stare. Dash's hips faltered. "My love..."

Dash pulled out then slammed back into me over and over again. My body trembled, and I took over the stroking of my cock. My legs trembled from exertion. Fuck, I was close. My balls ached to be emptied. Liquid fire raced through my veins, sweat beaded my brow, my hips lifted to meet each thrust...

Nothing had ever felt as good as having Dash balls deep inside my ass. For these moments, we were one.

"Ahh fuck yes! I'm coming." The husky and ragged words rumbled through our room.

"Together," Dash commanded. He slammed into me one last time. My ass clamped down around his cock. I shook with pleasure as he rode out his orgasm. I traced the indentations on my stomach. Dash collapsed face down on top of me, absolutely still. That was just fine with me. We could stay just like this together for a lifetime.

Dash's cock slipped from me, and he lifted his head, pushing himself up enough to press his lips against mine.

"Mind-blowing. Thank you," he whispered with puffs of breath given in irregular intervals. He was coasting on the afterglow.

"It's always that way." A secure sleep pulled me under.

16: The Next Morning
Dash

Eggs, check. I placed those on the counter. Bacon, check, check. That unopened package landed beside the eggs. Biscuits, butter, and milk followed, though more gently. I shut the refrigerator door only to tug it open again. Beau liked shredded cheddar cheese on his eggs. That bag slid next to the bacon.

Staring at the bounty, I realized two things: First, it had been years since I'd been to the grocery store, and second, I hadn't had a home-cooked meal in about that same time. *Huh.* I surveyed the items and decided to start with the bacon. Beau's favorite artery-clogging meat. After that, I'd tackle the biscuits, scramble the eggs, then make the pepper country gravy from scratch. Beau had introduced me to the delights of well-made biscuits and gravy.

I tightened the belt to my robe and swiped my freshly filled coffee mug from the base of the Keurig. My quest was to make my guy breakfast in bed. With the press of the bake button, I set the oven to preheat and readied the skillet for the bacon.

So far, so good until I got twisted up searching for the sheet pans. I opened and closed all the cabinet doors and drawers, pulling out all the cookware I thought I needed, and found the pan in the last cabinet. Why did anyone need so much storage space?

My cell phone buzzed and vibrated on the counter. It couldn't be much earlier than six in the morning, but phone etiquette was tossed out the window since working directly for Lon. I glanced at the screen, set the coffee cup on the counter, and answered the phone while adjusting the heat for the bacon.

"Good morning."

"Hey, Dash," Penny said. Lon's pretty, smart as a whip assistant sounded ready to tackle the day this Sunday morning. Lon and Penny had worked side-by-side for more years than I knew. She technically worked for me as well, but what did you call an assistant who regularly had the answers before you knew to ask the question? I'd learned a lot from her as well.

"Hey," I said, wedging the cell between my shoulder and chin while popping open the biscuit container and arranging the dough on the sheet pan.

"Lon's curious if you genuinely intend to take the day off, and if so, are you prepared for court tomorrow morning?" she asked, referencing the case Lon dumped on me last week.

"Yes to both questions. If Beau has plans for today, you might catch me for a couple of hours this afternoon."

"Lon wants me to emphasize that this is your vacation for this year."

I chuckled, fully aware of his seriousness. "Got it."

"This part's from me: Taking off to be with your guy? I'm really proud of you," she said. "He's awfully patient with you." I turned the bacon, appreciating her words and all her help with birthdays, anniversaries, and holiday gifts. She spoke Beau's love language so well, making me look great during those events.

"Yeah. He needs some love and convincing to stay with me. I'm having to refresh my breakfast-making skills. I probably should've ordered in. I feel like I'm fucking this up."

The laughter she gave was definitely humor at my expense. "Concentrate, I'll let Lon know. Bye."

I tossed the phone on the counter and flipped the bacon pieces sizzling in the pan. Once I felt confident that we were on the way to perfectly cooked bacon, I started cracking open the eggs. Beau liked them scrambled, or at least he used to. The whisking part of the eggs took a minute before I dumped them into another skillet.

"What're you doing?" Beau asked huskily, startling the shit out of me at a crucial moment of keeping the eggs moving in the pan while flexing my ambidextrous skills to remove the bacon. Even with everything I had going, I managed to push the Keurig start button to begin Beau's morning cup of coffee.

"I took the day off with the hope of spending it with you. My plan was to surprise you with breakfast in bed. But my culinary skills are rusty. We'll see how it turns out," I said, only then remembering the cheese. Dammit.

"Let me help. I'm in here all the time," Beau said, giving a long jaw-cracking yawn. I didn't deny his help. The biscuits weren't even in the oven yet. He took care of that oversight first thing.

"This is your coffee."

Beau reached around, placing a kiss on my cheek. "Is the milk out to make gravy?"

"Yes, but that might be a more significant challenge than I'm ready for."

Beau's mom had spent time with us years ago, teaching Beau and I how to make the homemade country gravy that Beau enjoyed. I hadn't made it since.

"Let me." Like a pro, he went through the steps, eyeing how much flour and milk to use rather than using any measuring device. I picked up my cup and leaned against the counter, sipping and watching Beau work. Of course, I noticed a difference in our relationship. Neither one of us depended on the other to get through the days. I attributed that to growth and maturity. But right now, I sensed our old bond sliding back in place.

I chided myself for not making more time for my guy since he was better than all the ice cream in the world. I smiled and sipped my coffee as I decided to take more ice cream breaks too. Ice cream on top of Beau's sculpted body... Now, that was a treat that deserved all my attention. My gaze locked on his profile. With age and relationship time under our belts, Beau had grown more reserved, quieter. It took effort to extract his thoughts. He'd always been my toughest challenge.

"Do you have plans today?"

"No, not exactly. I had fishing in mind, but the weather isn't great for it." While he spoke, he continued stirring the gravy, never glancing at me. I wasn't thrilled about that. "But we can go anywhere. I'm in."

His enthusiasm bordered coma levels. "With as thrilled as you are, I must be lagging in my partner duties," I said teasingly, taking another longer drink of my coffee and scooting closer to Beau.

"I'm barely awake and making the most delicious peppered country gravy you'll ever eat in your life. Get the pepper grinder and keep grinding until I tell you to stop. Hurry, it's beginning to thicken up." Following his instruction, I felt like I added more pepper than there was gravy before Beau told me to stop. He removed the sauce from the heat and continued stirring. "I think the biscuits are done. Can you pull them out?"

We had switched roles. I'd been making breakfast for him. Now, he was preparing mine. I opened the oven door to see Beau's sniffer was on point and pulled the sheet pan out. He held out a plate for me, and filled his own, right down to tearing the biscuits apart to top with a good helping of the pepper gravy.

"Where're we eating?" Beau asked, grabbing the silverware then picking up his coffee cup.

"I thought we'd eat in bed, but how about by the window to watch the sunrise?"

"Perfect." A few years ago, Beau purchased a small dinette and placed it by the large windows. I envisioned him sitting there for any meal eaten in the house. He placed his plate and coffee down and went back to the kitchen to pour two small orange juices.

For the first few minutes, we sat in awkward silence. Him staring at me through the bites, then vice versa until I finally said, "I need to treat you better."

That declaration seemed to catch Beau's full attention. "What do you mean?"

"I've failed at reminding you how much I care for you. How I want to know more about your work and your hobbies," I explained, then dug into the biscuits and bacon, taking my first bite. It reminded me of southern living and better times.

"What makes you say that?" Beau asked between bites, dropping a pretty decent size of bacon into his mouth.

"You're quiet," I said, restating the obvious feeling of distance between us.

"I've been quiet lately. There's not much to say that you don't already know," Beau said, distracted by eating. "Best reason to climb. I'm virtually alone. The meal's excellent."

When did being a loner become his thing? We ate the rest of our meal in silence. As the sun rose over the lake, it drew Beau's attention in that direction. He was such an outdoorsman. Nature fueled him in every way. I suspected the sunrise set his mood for the day.

The constant calculations and arguments that occupied my mind were as foreign to him as relishing a sunrise was to me.

"I'm probably going for seconds," Beau said, pushing his chair back and lifting his coffee mug to his lips. He lifted his brows and looked at me. I translated the look to a question about whether I wanted him to bring me more. I shook my head no.

A great feature of the home was how the window tinting increased with the brightness of the sun. I'd always appreciated how that kept our energy costs down.

When Beau remained seated, staring at me, I stood with my coffee cup in hand. I rounded the table to approach him, hoping like hell the chair was strong enough to hold us both. I sat on top of his thighs, catching him off guard.

"Hey now," Beau teased, setting his coffee cup on the table before it spilled over. I wasn't small in either stature or weight, but his arms wrapped easily around me as mine circled his neck.

"Your body's changed. You're leaner," I said, less than six inches from his face. My coffee had cooled, but I sipped it anyway.

"My workouts are different these days," he said, staring out the window at the lake.

"You know nothing's changed for me. The number of hours I work are so I can climb the partnership ladder faster," I explained. I'd said those words so many times before. His captivating amber gaze landed on mine.

"I'm sorry I'm so basic. I don't fit well in your work life, but I try." He leaned in to kiss the side of my neck, just below my jaw.

"You fit anywhere I'm at." I told the lie as evenly as I could. "Lon likes you."

Beau nodded, but I didn't get the sense that he believed me completely, then he turned back to the lake, saying nothing more.

I continued staring at him and his perfect profile. Beau and I were still somewhat young men, regardless of my responsibilities. I felt our bond, but it needed to be nurtured. I ran my fingers through his shaggy hair, wishing he and I were back to where we started. The guy that drew me to him with just the sparkle in his eyes. I kissed his cheek. "I wish I knew what you were thinking. I'm afraid you're hiding from me, and I'm lost to your pretty face so I can't figure it out."

His serious gaze shifted back to me, telling me I'd finally cracked his facade. "You have to know that I spend a lot of time alone. I try to be supportive and understanding. But you've become something I don't get. I try but can't figure you out."

"We have drinks and dinner a couple of times a week," I said, not truly answering his statements.

"With whatever client you're trying to woo or show appreciation to," Beau answered. "I get what you're doing. Truly. Other couples go in different directions too. We're maturing. I'm good. I probably need more sex; we can work that out." Beau tightened his hold around me and kissed my lips with a quick peck. "I'll keep working on how to fit in better. Something's got to stick."

I had immediate remorse for the pain in his voice. I furrowed my brows and placed my head on his shoulder.

Through my niece, Joy, I knew my father was following my career. I loved getting under his skin. Now, I was handling all Carter's overflow from his legal department. My father had eyes, or spies, everywhere, and had to be trying to find my weaknesses.

"Hang on for a little longer. I'll do better by you."

Beau laughed at my sincerity. His strong arms tightened around my waist.

"Seriously, stop," Beau said, grinning cheekily, pressing a kiss on my lips again. "What're we doing today?"

I perked right up. "Wanna get a haircut?"

"I feel like they're bad luck," Beau said, causing me to laugh with him. "I'm serious. It's the truth."

When I didn't stop with the humor, his hold and hands threatened to dump me onto the floor. In a quick grab, I tightened my arms around his neck. If I was going down, so was he. Then he did something more surprising. He scooped me up in his arms and started for the stairs. I had no idea he could carry me this way, and if he didn't tire out before the top step, I felt sure he'd be dominating me in the sack in a short time.

"I'm not sure *Avatar* lived up to the hype," Beau remarked as the credits rolled. He reached over for another handful of popcorn, tossing several pieces into his mouth. I patted the top of the blanket I'd used to stay cozy warm, looking for the remote. As far as I was concerned, with my head resting half on a pillow and half on Beau's thigh, his fingers brushing through my hair, I could lie here forever.

"I can't find the remote." I started to rise when Beau slid his hand between me and the couch then handed me the remote. "More pizza?" I asked.

"Yeah, sure." While I was dislodged from my comfy spot, I reached for the pizza box on top of the coffee table, picking up a thin slice of pepperoni pizza.

"That might be the longest movie I've ever seen," I said, just as I heard the faint sound of a ringtone. I reached for my phone at the same time Beau bumped my head up, taking his phone from his back pocket. It turned out it was his phone ringing. "It's my mom. She video-calls every Sunday evening."

That jackknifed me straight up, and I immediately tossed the pizza back on the box and pushed my hair back into place. I wasn't sure that I knew she called every Sunday since she texted both of us all the time.

"Hey, Mom," Beau said to the video call. Kailey, Beau's baby sister, played with a toy in his mom's lap.

"Hi, babe. Kailey, say hi to Beau. Is that Dash there with you?"

"Hi, Linda," I chimed in, but Kailey held my full attention. I waved, giving her my brightest smile. Every time I saw the almost one year old, she looked more like Beau to me and seemed to grow inches between visits.

"Hi, Dash. Are you off tonight?"

"I took the day off. We just finished watching *Avatar*," I replied as Kailey's nanny came into the frame and lifted Kailey into her arms.

"I'll be up in a few minutes," Linda said to the nanny. "Don't start her bath until I'm there." Words I'd never heard my mom say to my nannies.

His mom's transformation was truly remarkable. Her chestnut hair was elegantly swept up. She looked as youthful as Beau and effortlessly beautiful, happy, and content. I envied those feelings. My parents, particularly my father, still had a strong hold on me. I wanted him to regret what he'd done to us. A focus on vendetta was taking over that place inside me where my reasonableness used to reside. And my guy was in sync with everything about his family. Well, except Carter himself, who Beau obviously hadn't accepted.

"Dash, Wesley asked you to call him in the morning, early. He's sorry he missed your call last night," she said. "I was going to text you. He and I just hung up the phone."

Beau turned to look at me—more like a glare—but I didn't look at him to know for sure. That silent stare spoke volumes, asking when I'd had time to call Carter while I was with Beau last night. And ultimately what he wanted to know was why I was calling Carter at all.

"How's Kailey doing? She seems to grow every time I see her," I asked, trying to steer the conversation in any other direction at least for now.

"She's good. Beginning to walk. Wesley's upset he's missing her first steps," Linda said. I, of course, grinned broadly, but Beau stayed awkwardly silent and stone-faced. "When she can't stand on her own, she gets angry. Has Beau shown you the videos?"

Well, no he hadn't but that was where Linda shined. She included Beau in everything, making sure he felt secure in their new family.

"Kailey's gonna be a handful," Beau said proudly.

"Honey," his mom hedged, trying to form her words. "The reason why Wesley's trying to get ahold of Dash is that he wants us to designate you as Kailey's guardian if something happens to us."

"Mom, nothing's going to happen to you," Beau interjected as if that was the dumbest thing he'd ever heard.

"No, Beau, this is important to us," Linda said. "Wesley has a big extended family, so these decisions have to be made and documented. Wesley has named Dash as his executor to the trust we have for both you and Kailey."

Beau swiveled his head in my direction again. This time there was no denying his accusatory expression. My explanation of attorney/client privilege wasn't going to go over as well as I'd hoped it might.

"Dash named executor?" Beau asked. "He probably should have told me before making that commitment."

"I felt it was better to let the information ride until you found out," I whispered. "I know how you feel about him."

"I don't feel anything about him," Beau scoffed, dismissing the claim.

"Save such a lie. We three know that's untrue," Linda said. "Son, I'm safe and secure, as is Kailey. Wesley's a wonderful husband and great father. I'm truly very happy. Wesley feels the same way I do. We love each other."

Beau stared at the screen, his face morphing into a passive expression.

"He's no longer pouting," I said to her when he didn't speak. She and I both knew Beau wasn't pondering her words. Instead, he turned his dislike into himself, handling it privately.

"Go give Kailey a bath," he finally said. "Dash took the day off to spend time together."

"Shocking," his mom teased. Her raised eyebrows spoke even louder than the words as she looked at me.

"Hey now, I was just on your side, and I like Carter," I said teasingly. "Stay mad at Beau, not me."

"I'm not mad at Beau. He's got to work through his issues with Wesley on his own timetable. But you and Beau rarely see each other anymore," she said. Her sweet smile and motherly concern almost made up for throwing me under the bus. "And that's your deal. None of my business." She lifted a hand and waved. "I love you both. I'm going. Beau, call me tomorrow."

"Bye, Mom," Beau said, certainly eager to end the call. My guy. He rarely gave an inch, and that only came when dealing with his mother. Carter didn't ever stand a chance with Beau. His decision was made and set in stone.

"Bye, Linda," I said and waved.

Her warm smile vanished when the screen turned dark.

"Beau, I don't want this to sound wrong," I started, turning to better face him.

"Then don't say it." Beau's hand slashed between us, cutting me off. "My feelings about Carter are mine, not yours to share. So get off me about it."

"We're buying this house from him at a very reduced price—"

"I'm only in a place like this because of you. I'm not this kind of guy." He stood up and straightened our mess on the coffee table. "How about we go for a walk before it gets too late?"

My guy was a seriously hardheaded man. I followed Beau as he carried the remaining pizza and popcorn into the kitchen. "Babe, you're not seeing the bigger picture. We can sell this place for three times more than we'll pay. It's a great investment."

"Leave it alone," Beau said, and dismissed me. He left the room with his hands full of our snacks and glasses.

My heart did a flipflop in my chest. I was a successful attorney, winning cases for a living, but whenever I was with my mister, I eventually reverted to the young man who hung onto every word he said, desperately hoping for a smile or caress along the way.

I wasn't sure which version of me I liked better, the younger man with ideals and dreams, or the new me who no longer wore rose-colored glasses. My life was spent calculating and arguing for a living. I took a deep breath and slowly exhaled, rising to follow Beau. The truth hit me like a ton of bricks, halting me in my tracks. I had new goals for the rest of my life, I wanted to be a man whose reputation instilled fear in his opponents. In order to do that, the rest of my life needed to mature, including my relationship with Beau.

With a spine built with steel, I was determined to be that man. I no longer planned to dress Beau up and pray for the best. My love needed to fill his life with the things he found interesting, and then be waiting here at home for my return.

17: The New Hire
Beau/Dash

Beau

Chicago, 2014
Late Summer

"I'm regretful that I couldn't find time to spend with you before you leave," Dash said, expertly handling his pan fried pork dumplings like a chopstick pro. Years ago, we dedicated several days, maybe even weeks, to mastering the art of chopstick use. Today, his skills were on full display for his entire firm to see, thanks to the glass walls enclosing his office. If he were to mishandle his choice of utensils and drop food on his crisp new business suit, he'd undoubtedly face relentless teasing for the rest of his tenure with the firm—his words.

"I understand." I swallowed my lie down with a pretty decent-sized bite of the cheeseburger I'd brought for me. Technically, today marked the first day of my two-week vacation. We'd planned for Dash to accompany me on the trip. When that fell apart, he wanted us to have lunch then he'd drive me to the airport. Last night, that turned into me bringing lunch to his office, then driving myself to the airport and parking my truck in long-term parking for fourteen days due to another case Lon assigned him.

With great effort, I avoided sighing at the thought of another year, another life led alone.

Honestly, I didn't like a lot of things these days. But, what had become our new normal, had me burying it all inside.

"I mentioned to you about the case I'm arguing. We've found something damning. If everything aligns like I hope, I'll secure my client's acquittal this afternoon. People are funny. They often believe they're above being caught." Dash let out a sudden bark of laughter. He quickly bent forward to ensure nothing landed on his tie or vest. That vest was part of his latest fashion trend of wearing a three-piece suit.

I glanced down at the outfit I'd thrown on for traveling, which I thought was completely normal attire for this time of year, early fall. A flannel button-up layered over a dark tee, a pair of well-loved jeans featuring holes in the knees, made naturally, and a comfortable pair of work boots. Of course, the firm had a strict dress code for everyone inside these offices, including myself. Today, I stood out in the crowd of designer suits and crisp jackets. The same style clothing Dash had laid out for me this morning. I'd been asked by Dash repeatedly to adhere to the firm's silly rules. My frustration and loneliness had pushed me here to have lunch with Dash before I left but fuck the dress code.

Maybe whatever trouble he landed in for my appearance today might help him remember to abide by his promises next time. I'm not sure when I'd become that petty, but I couldn't help myself either. Those broken promises had included more than the ride to the airport. There were also all the rescheduled dinners every night for the last two months, and the missed pledges of blow jobs he'd given to make amends for his breaking our plans.

Yeah. My resentment was coming in hard. I couldn't see where this would change in the future.

"Do you have the girls' gifts?" Dash asked.

"Yeah. The Taylor Swift gear. It was genius." Though I was even more shocked that he'd found the time to think of anyone but himself, and second, that he'd actually ordered the gifts and not farmed it out to Penny.

"Penny came up with it. She steered me to the right things," Dash said, grinning out the glass to where Penny sat. His smile was my favorite one, but it didn't hit me the same way. *Hmm.* I took another hearty bite of my burger.

"Hey, Beau." Time stood still as the recognizable refined voice sent stunned shockwaves through my system. My mind short-circuited. The microscopic particles in the air became vivid details slowly floating by. Turning my head, I saw Chandler, Dash's longtime friend with whom I shared an unfavorable past. He looked immaculate and stylish, blending seamlessly into the surroundings, holding a document of some sort.

I inhaled suddenly, taking the bite and lodging it in my throat. As I choked and coughed, the world sling-shotted back in place. How in the fuck had Chandler gotten hired here?

"Dasham," Chandler continued as if I hadn't just suffered a major medical emergency at his arrival. "Here are the photos printed for court." He came fully into the office without an invitation, interrupting our lunch. Dash popped forward in his chair, getting to his feet. His entire demeanor changed. A calculated, devious joy lit his face. Chandler handed him several eight by ten photos. He sifted through them, his gaze quickly scanned each one.

"Excellent job, Chandler. I knew you'd be a valuable hire." Dash lifted his gaze, sharing a private moment with Chandler. I didn't fucking like it at all. "His wife should have taken the settlement offer. Now, she'll likely have nothing. The prenup will hold. Excellent work."

Chandler's playful, flirty smile raised my hackles. "All in a night's work. It took me staying at the hotel bar from two in the afternoon to two this morning to capture her in a compromising position. Along with the man who compromised her," he teased, laughing at his joke. When Dash gave Chandler an exaggerated wink, steam blew from the top of my head. "Dasham's so fucking clever," Chandler refocused on me for the moment. "I don't think anyone works as many hours as he does. I'm thankful to be his apprentice."

With the napkin at my mouth, I gave a final clear of my throat. "When did you start working here?"

Chandler slapped a hand against Dash's upper arm. Dash, who'd been so lost in the pictures, hadn't been paying attention to our conversation. "You didn't tell him about me?" Chandler asked incredulously. That was the first time I agreed with the son of a bitch, which pissed me off that much more. "I feel like that's a relationship foul."

Dash barely glanced at me before lowering his gaze again to the photos. "Beau knows I've been searching for an associate. We've been burning it at opposite ends for the last few months. We haven't had time for anything more than the important things."

"You and I need to start over," Chandler said. Out of obligation and that was only due to the manners my mother had instilled in me, I rose from my seat and took his extended hand. I didn't want to touch him at all. My gut said the pleasant expression on his dumb face wasn't real and neither was the handshake. I hoped my silence told him I didn't believe his bullshit. And fucking Dash should have told me. If he kept this secret, then what else wasn't he sharing?

Now that Dash had "outstanding support" at his side, why was he spending more time away from home than ever before? Jealousy slashed a painful gash into my heart. The fact that Dash wasn't picking up on any of my tension spoke volumes too.

Dash pivoted around, straightening the photos as he went to his doorway. "Penny, will you take Chandler to Lon's office and let him explain these photos? I'll be finished in a few minutes and join you." He handed the pictures over to his assistant, not Chandler.

"Well, come on, Chandler. It's time to meet the other partners," she said cheekily, twirling around on her high heels. Like everyone employed here, she exuded confidence, strutting away as if she were on a runway. Chandler waggled his eyebrows at me, whatever that meant, and jogged the few steps by her side. Dash shut the door behind him, giving us privacy.

"I can explain," he stated with an air of superiority. That tone made everything worse.

"Don't bother. I got it," I bit out through a clenched jaw. The mix of Dash's elitist tone and seeing Chandler's radiant smile, along with his overall charm, had truly gotten under my skin. My words mirrored my irritation. I dismissed Dash, taking another bite of my burger that tasted like sawdust in my mouth.

"This is the reason I chose not to share this in our texts. I wanted to be in front of you to explain my reasoning."

Then he should have come home and told me not to sneak around, ignoring my feelings. Fuck this. What had I done so wrong to have this be my life these days? "I don't want to hear it," I said, pulling my meal together to dump in the trash can. "We barely talk anymore. You're never home. I'm living my life alone..."

Dash barked out a harsh condescending laugh. "You work from early in the morning until dark. Then pick up extra shifts on top of that. And let's not forget the twenty plus hours a week that you train to climb. When I'm at home, you're never there."

"It's my fault that I found other things to do rather than waiting for you to find time for me? I'm not staying here for this." I rammed the remainder of my burger and fries back into the paper bag, so hard that the bottom gave out, everything inside dropped to the floor. "Goddammit."

"Beau," Dash said with exaggerated patience and carefully pulled up his slacks before bending at the knee to help me gather the trash.

"*No.* Stop," I said, pushing his hands aside. Out of necessity, I had learned to live my life on my own. I refused to be manipulated for a single second more. My feelings and emotions were valid, especially where Chandler was concerned. "If you had ever mentioned you were going to be home, I would've gone straight there. I've only found other things to occupy my time because I'm tired of being in that

over-the-top house by myself. I love you, I do, but this place..."
My hand gestured about the room then splayed further to
include the outside of his office. "Owns you. There's not a
single instance where you'd drop what you were doing here to
be with me. Now you've brought Chandler here. It feels like
you're doing this on purpose."

Dash stood. I followed suit, moving around him to throw
my trash in the bin. Tossing out the garbage seemed symbolic
to the moment.

"I'm going to brush off your insults. We both know they're
untrue," Dash stated in the flat monotone way of speaking that
annoyed me further. It was one of the lawyer voices that he
used to mask his true feelings and thoughts. "The real issue
is Chandler. He reached out about a month ago when he
couldn't find a job. I know him well. He'll push boundaries
to find answers, just like with those photos. I offered him a
temporary position, but I'll mentor him and see how it goes.
If I can shift work over to him, that'll leave more time to spend
with you."

"Right. You'll spend any free time finding new clients to
increase your billable hours," I said sarcastically, doubting
every word he spoke. I should have been made aware of
Chandler when the asshat first contacted Dash. "So he works
directly for you, spending every day with you?"

"So your sole problem's jealousy?" Dash asked, dismissively.

"Of course, I'm jealous," I said, throwing his words back
in his face. "After everything we've been through, it feels like
we've gone full circle. He spends all this time with you, and
I'm left with none." We glared at each other. Great. I'd hit the
nail on the head. At least Dash didn't try to lie his way out of
the truth. "I've got to get to the airport."

"Your flight doesn't leave for hours," Dash countered.

"Then I don't want to be here any longer," I stated with
conviction and started for the door. "Go join Chandler and
celebrate the end of the case. Train him how to celebrate
wherever you go these days to party. Another place I'm no
longer welcome. Whatever."

Dash

"If you walk out of here, I won't chase after you this time," I said, rooting myself in place. I slipped my hands into my slacks pockets as I watched him stride across my office. "Me following you is the story of our relationship. We made a commitment to be all in to my job for ten years. Nothing has changed for me. I'm on the course that we created together. You know how I feel about you. Everything I do revolves around you."

Beau let out a bark of laughter with his hand on the doorknob. "You're lying," he hissed sharply. "And you're being used. Chandler's here to report back to your family about how you're doing." He rolled his eyes so dramatically I feared they might disappear in his skull. "I'll be back in two weeks. During that time, I want you to rethink what you just said to me, because I can assure you that we didn't plan anything together. Our lives have always been on your terms." In Beau's way, he flung open the door and took long, bruting strides out of my office toward the elevators. He ignored the few acknowledgements he received on his way.

I watched him go, feeling the questioning gazes of my colleagues and staff. Once inside the elevator, he fixed his stare on me as the doors closed. I refused to take this on emotionally. Since finishing law school, I'd grown significantly and so had Beau.

Furthermore, Beau understood better than anyone the pressure I placed on myself to provide for him and challenge my father's expectations. Of course, I knew Chandler was here for a nefarious reason. I'd been planting seeds of disinformation, waiting for Chandler to funnel the data to whomever he was working for, most likely my old man.

I finally turned away to tidy up my lunch and give myself a moment to set my resolve. Old habits took a minute to get past. I had to harden my heart against the deep urge to go after him. I discarded my food in the trash can and headed to my en suite bathroom for some solitude. The heels of my palms pressed against my eyes, shutting out everything except my racing thoughts. There was so much I'd kept from Beau, maybe I shouldn't have.

Chandler wasn't just a mole. Without realizing it, he also gave me information I wouldn't otherwise have about my family. He had told me that my mother was doing everything she could to tarnish Linda's reputation in the elite circle they all ran in. Fabricating inappropriate stories about her, and the connections they shared. My father's focus was now on Carter and putting him out of business. If I continued to work with Carter, I was certain there would be a day that I'd go head-to-head with my father's team of attorneys. With my firm at my back, we'd destroy the Richmond legal team.

My vendetta against my father was reaching new heights. It consumed me day and night, pushing me to be better than the day before. As I turned to stare at my reflection in the mirror, I could tell I was chipping away at my father's meticulously crafted facade.

In the coming two weeks, I needed to find the right words to sit Beau down and buy myself time to allow Chandler to dig his own grave. The seeds I was planting ensured Chandler would suffer mightily.

18: The Court
Dash/Beau

Dash

The basketball left my hand only to bounce back as I dribbled from the free throw line. Lon was bent over, hands resting on his knees, closer to the net, panting like the old man I teased him about being. At forty years old, that was nothing more than a playful jab. Basketball had never been my forte, but it was Lon's. He insisted we play, likely due to the way he consistently kicked my butt on the court. I was learning though.

Tonight's game was as close as the score ever got. I was just one point behind him. He knew my plays by heart. What he didn't realize was that I had been secretly practicing my three-point shots. This was my one chance to catch him off guard. Did I save it for another time or show off my new skill now?

"Are you just gonna stand there?" Lon asked in a dismissive tone, rising from his ready position.

Yeah. Now was as good a time as any. I positioned and sent the ball flying. The ball flew through the air, arcing in perfect form until it slid through the net. *Yes!* I jerked my gaze to Lon for his reaction. He stayed rooted in his spot, no attempt to rebound, in utter shock.

"The whole reason to play with you is so that I win," Lon shot out as if that was a reasonable thought to share aloud with an opponent. "When did that happen?" He waved toward the net to make his question clearer.

"All that matters is that I win," I responded cockily and left the court, walking with a confident strut across the firm's rooftop gymnasium.

"So you've been working on your game behind my back?" Lon asked. Based on the way his voice faded, Lon was still standing close to the net. "Not very sportsmanlike of you. Did Beau teach you that move?"

Oh, the shit-talking was flying. "Beau probably could have taught me to kick your ass a long time ago, but he didn't teach me that shot," I said, spinning around to walk backward to ensure he heard me. "That was all me."

"Huh," Lon countered. "Now you've played your hand. I'll be better prepared next time."

"If there is a next time. I got more from where that came from." My lie sounded pretty damned convincing even to me.

I pushed through the doors into a room that rivaled any professional sports team's locker room. There were private showers, which I had used many times after a workout before going home or beginning my day in the morning. I regularly used the state-of-the-art sauna, stored a week's worth of my wardrobe in the climate controlled storage "lockers"—another perk properly executed by Penny. There were even bedrooms for when a partner's home life got twisted, much like mine right now, and needed a place to stay.

"Funny, how you've just made the news that I'm about to give you much easier to say," Lon said as he entered with a bang of the door against the wall in the irritation of his loss. I took a terry cloth towel off the stack and scrubbed it down my sweaty face then over the wet ends of my damp hair.

"Bad news?" I asked. My tone reflected the sense of disinterest that Lon had taught me to master. I finally cast a glance at Lon before heading to my locker for my shower kit, a term I'd learned from Beau. That thought shifted my focus back to my guy. He'd only been gone for eight hours. Yet, he'd managed to lodge himself into my thoughts. Images flashed through my mind's eye. Beau nude, grinning, walking toward me. His cock was a thing of beauty, just like the man overall. In this memory, he was flaccid, his length bouncing from one thigh to another as he came at me.

Whatever I had done to cause such a reaction from Beau, I'm sure it would end with me being thoroughly fucked. Tingles rippled over my arms. He knew what I liked and gave it to me every single time. No matter what was happening with me, when we were home together, Beau healed me right up, making sure life looked bearable again. How had our perfect lives gotten so messy and complicated? Beau still mattered more to me than anything else in the world.

"I was prepared to trounce you then give you the blow. You're competitive, you wouldn't care what I said." Lon popped open his locker, managing to gain my full attention.

"Is it about Beau or Chandler?" I asked.

"Chandler. Let's start there. He's locked out of everything with no chance of being hired full time. Why's he here?" Lon asked, agitation entering his tone in seconds flat.

"He stepped up today," I murmured, recalling the lowly tasks Lon had assigned to me when I first started working closely with him. "He's also on a temporary contract. Let me figure out his angle, then I'll send him packing."

Lon turned to face me directly. "You have the firm paying a salary to a guy you suspect is reporting back to your old man?" His incredulous tone with regard to Chandler hadn't changed since the first time we had this conversation.

"I'm paying his salary and leading him on a wild goose chase. My father's getting harmful information from Chandler. Why're we still talking about this?" I asked and slammed shut my locker door to drive home my point.

"My suggestion is to let the vendetta go, along with Chandler. You've won. You're moving to senior partner soon. Whatever your family did doesn't matter." Lon shut his door in a normal way, then followed me into the showers.

"Did we cover the blow you were prepared to give me, or is it about Beau's appearance today and the way he left the office?" Sadness blanketed my heart. I'd been wrong not to stand up for Beau over the last few years. The hurt and anger in Beau's gaze the minute he recognized Chandler might leave a lasting scar across my heart. I hadn't expected Chandler to be in the office until well after Beau had left for the airport. Whatever reprimand Lon was about to throw down was nothing compared to the way I beat myself up for allowing Beau to leave without the full explanation.

But damn, Beau should trust me by now. I'd never do anything to hurt him.

"They're formally sanctioning you," Lon said quietly from behind me. That was a much stronger punishment than I'd ever been given before. I will be on probation for the next year. My senior partnership goals were now in question until I served my time. "This time, you'll be given a discipline mark with a probation time and a substantial fine."

"For Beau," I admitted aloud in defeat. There had been countless discussions regarding Beau's appearance, his demeanor, and how the firm wished to present itself. When I was promoted from associate to junior partner, my agreement dictated that my life revolve around the firm twenty-four seven. This wasn't the first time I faced discipline over my guy, and he and I had talked about what the firm required from him. He'd agreed to try his best, but when I saw him today, looking quite lumberjack-like, I'd gone with it. His wardrobe choices were a bold statement. He'd grown into an incredibly stubborn man. He gave me no choice but to try to enjoy the hour we shared and take the hits when they came. I had sacrificed so much due to him.

Before entering my shower stall, I stopped, my finger and thumb went to my temple, rotating against the stress building there. I had given Beau a pretty good life and he resented me the entire time.

"Have I mentioned to you that I was married to my high school sweetheart?" Lon asked but didn't pause for a response. "She was the love of my life. We managed to make it through college together and law school. But once I started working here, everything changed. She was alone most of the time, while I poured myself into my job, day and night. She left and I never looked back. I've never been certain which path would have been better. Professionally, I've found success, but what would my life have looked like with a pretty, wholesome wife, a pack of children, living the middle class dream"

"I can't see you as a family man," I finally said.

He came forward, his palm clamped on my shoulder. "This place molds you, makes you into a different man. I've never regretted my decision. This place is my life. I'm proud of what I've accomplished." He squeezed before he passed by.

He'd made my predicament even more dire. Naturally, I didn't really want to lose Beau. No matter the differences between us, Beau knew how important this job was to me. After I worked Chandler out of the company, and I became a senior partner, my time commitments would ease, no more late nights, a day off every weekend, Beau would again become my first priority. At least that was how I wanted it to be.

Beau had landed in Northern Virginia a few hours ago, and I hadn't heard a word from him. Lon's life scenario could be a possibility for Beau and me, but I was determined to have Beau meet me halfway. He had to fight for us too, understand that there were two of us no matter how I'd placed him first throughout our lives. We had rocky times ahead of us if he didn't.

I needed food, not a shower, then some rest. Time would lead my decisions. Beau was my soulmate. I was his. He'd make the right choices, allowing me to do so as well. I had faith in us.

Beau

The following morning

"Beau. Beau. Beau. Beau. Beau." My sweet, willful little sister Kailey hopped around the kitchen on both feet, chanting my name with every leap she took. Dressed in a bunny costume she wore with pride, she'd been at it for several minutes, never tiring and promising to leave a trail of candy egg treats behind for me to find. At four years old, she hadn't quite grasped the realities of biology, insisting that in fact, she was a rabbit.

"Kailey, go bounce around in the living room. I'm making breakfast," my mom instructed her.

In response, she burst out with a new chant while jumping out of the room. "Cereal. Cereal. Cereal. Cereal."

I sat at the kitchen table, nursing my cup of coffee, when a pretty significant yawn escaped. I slept restlessly last night as I fought my urge to text or call Dash. Staying off my phone took serious effort until I reasoned that he hadn't made contact with me either. Once I realized that, it became surprisingly easy to set my phone aside and drift off to sleep at about four this morning.

The only problem with that was Kailey sneaking in my room before seven and pouncing on me to wake up. At least someone wanted to spend time with me.

"She's full of energy all the time," my mom said, preparing a Michelin-star-worthy continental breakfast.

On the large farmhouse table she had eggs, meats, cheeses, a variety of cereals, jams, jellies, and so much more. Right now, she was slicing bagels which she placed next to small bowls of different spreads on a silver platter. This was my first visit to her new home on the Potomac River. From this vantage point, they had a beautiful view of the river in a cozy yet modern kitchen. My mom had such a knack of making a house a home. She made me feel like I belonged here. These days the only time I felt that way was with my mom.

"Hey." Carter greeted us as he entered the room with Kailey scooped up into his arms, sitting on his hip. He went to my mom. I watched her beam happiness at him as she whispered a good morning to him before placing a light kiss on his lips.

"Good morning. Good morning. Good morning," Kailey started, bouncing in her father's secure hold. She placed both hands on his cheeks and turned his face toward me. "Daddy, say good morning to Beau."

"Good morning, Beau," Carter said with a smile. I had to give it to him, he loved his girl. The entire scene warmed my

KINDLE ALEXANDER

heart for my mom. She truly deserved to be cherished, and those two did love her as much as I did.

I raised my cup, grinning at my little sister who beamed at me. "She's full of energy."

"Would you like a fresh cup of coffee?" Carter asked, putting Kailey on her feet. "Go to the table and wait for mommy."

She did a full run, climbing into the seat she'd arranged next to mine. Her chair had a bolted booster seat, and she climbed in closer to me. "I wanted to sit next to you. You're my *big* brother. Mommy's sitting on the bench with Daddy."

"Need a refresher?" Carter asked again. I lifted a finger to the carafe on the table. Carter nodded. "I should have known. Your mom thinks of everything."

It had been several years since Carter and my mom had gotten together. They'd tied the knot about eighteen months after that first date. During that time, I'd had ample opportunity to see how well they complemented each other. I wanted my mom to be happy and appreciated for everything she brought to a relationship. Carter shared stories about the lives of the rich and famous and the pretense that accompanied such a lifestyle. He appreciated the way my mom anchored him to the life he had always wanted to live.

Great for them. *Woo-hoo.* However, I still didn't let him off the hook. I couldn't shake my distaste for him.

As I grew older, the more I wanted to become a self-made man. I wanted to live and thrive on my own accomplishments. While I had allowed Dash his taste for luxury, I ensured that I still managed my own path. Since Carter was insecure about his and my relationship, he was always offering some sort of financial help. I didn't want it, and I couldn't make him understand why. In that same vein, I wanted to appear strong and tough so Carter always treated the females in my life with the respect they deserved.

He hadn't lost sight of that one time. Not that I saw. But neither had my father...until he did. Though, that wasn't entirely true either. My distrust of the men in my mom's life naturally put us at odds with one another.

"Here you go." My mom placed the bagels on the table and reached for Kailey's training napkin/bib contraption from behind her chair. "You're really not sitting by your dad this morning?"

"Nope." After my mom snapped the napkin in place, Kailey climbed over her chair onto my lap. I had to be mindful of where her feet landed as I helped her settle down on one thigh. She scooted her bowl over closer to her side.

"Well, I'll be lonely over here," Carter remarked teasingly.

Kailey giggled and twisted until her face lifted to mine. "Mommy's sitting by Daddy. He's not lonely. He's tricking me."

"Got it." I started filling my plate, sinking into the comforting atmosphere my mom created. It brought back memories of my younger days, when I'd lived with the same confidence that Kailey currently had. My father was louder than Carter, and angrier, but my old man was often absent, allowing my mom's warmth to guide my life.

The way Dash had stayed lodged in my head was also fading. I felt like I belonged here, with or without him, that it was my home too. I appreciated Carter for that.

"I had my assistant forward you the confirmation email for the place on Duck Key," Carter said, absently filling his plate. "The keys are in a lockbox on the property. Access information is included in the email. I believe you'll really like this place, Beau. It's a fisherman's dream spot."

"Great," my mom responded, pouring milk into Kailey's cereal bowl. "We're planning to leave here by ten at the latest."

"Beau, are your friends arriving today?" Carter asked, his eyes lifting to me. "Do I need to forward them the entry information?"

"No, Scott's had to push back their arrival by a couple of days. He'll get there around the same time you do," I said, assembling a bagel sandwich out of the eggs, various meats, and cheeses. With a nod, I grabbed another bagel to make one for the road. It looked that good.

"Is Dash coming?" Carter asked.

I chomped into the first bite of the bagel and accidentally nipped my lip. "Ouch," I muttered, tasting blood.

Kailey quickly grabbed her napkin from around her neck, dabbing at my sore lip. Her sweet, concerned gaze stared up at me.

"Let Mama kiss it. She makes it feel better," Kailey said, offering all the help she could.

"Sweetheart," my mom started. She received a pretty thorough update about the state of my and Dash's relationship last night. Thankfully, she headed off any more questions from Carter. "Dash isn't coming this time."

"The guy needs to slow down," Carter said, spreading jam over a biscuit. "He hasn't taken significant time off in years. He's so driven."

I swallowed the bite that made it in my mouth and reached for the pitcher of ice water, pouring a good portion into a glass. When Kailey's big green eyes still stared at me in concern, I tapped my cheek and bent for her to place a kiss there. She did happily.

"I feel better. Thank you," I said. She nodded like she completely understood and went back to tackling her bowl of cereal. "I'm pretty sure he's in trouble with the firm. I wore my blue jeans into the office, which is against the dress code," I explained, turning my bagel, eyeing a good next bite. "I rented a pontoon boat and a couple of jet skis for the length of our stay. The company I rented them from will have them docked outside the place. We don't have to do anything."

I glanced up at the silence, taking a bite of my sandwich. Both my mom and Carter held concerned stares. I had to tick back over what I'd said and came up with nothing that should cause their worry. "What?"

"Son," Carter said, the word sounding like fingernails running down a chalkboard. "Your refusal to abide by his office's dress code causes him problems."

Right. I nodded, confused. Why did it matter to him and how did he even know that? "I'm rarely at his office. Three years ago at a Christmas party, I was dressed in a suit and pretty much stayed quiet the entire night. Since then, they've locked me out of the company pretty solidly."

"Wesley, he and Dash aren't doing well," my mom added, choosing her words carefully.

Carter flipped a confused stare at me. "Who? You and Dash?"

"Daddy, I'm done," Kailey announced proudly, diverting the attention off me. As if materializing from thin air, Jenna appeared beside Kailey to tend to her needs. Mom and Carter had hired the early twentysomething college student as a nanny for Kailey and she'd quickly become like one of the family. Or so my mom had told me.

"Let's get you ready for the drive," Jenna said, gathering her from my arms.

"You're going with us, right?" Kailey asked in the abundance of love she seemed to have for the young girl.

"Yes, I am. We need to get dressed so we can get on the road."

"Yay," Kailey said, clapping as she scurried away.

Since the conversation had diverted, I wanted to keep it that way and swept a hand over all the remaining food. "Are we taking this for the ride?"

My mom chuckled and shook her head. "We can do that. I believe you'll have it eaten before we leave the state," my mom teased.

"I'm off. I'll see you guys this weekend," Carter said as his cell rang. He answered while rising and giving a kiss to my mom. "Hang on," he told the caller and stared down at my mom. "You guys be safe. Let Beau drive. He does it for a living."

"Absolutely," she said in the same playful tone as before. "Beau's doing all the driving." Carter chuckled and waggled his eyebrows at me while lifting the phone to his ear. He left us with long strides out of the room.

"Come on, babe. I'll have this loaded up. Let's be on the road early so we don't hit traffic," my mom said, sliding from the bench seat. I stayed in my spot, finishing my cup of coffee. No matter what she said, it'd take her another hour before we ever managed to load into the SUV and start driving down the road.

19: The Pintail
Dash/Beau

Dash

One week later

The click of the camera's lens drew my attention back to reality. Overwhelmed by the emotions assailing me, I glanced at Chandler to see his phone in his hand and him snapping my photo. He sat in one of the two comfortable chairs that Beau and I used while staring out at Lake Michigan. Those were happier times, when I was home more, and life's joy came from being in the other's company.

Tonight was meant to be a celebration. Chandler was the only one to make time for me after another case ended in my favor. The multi-million dollar gangbuster trial ended in a fizzle before we ever made it to the courtroom. But wins weren't the same without Beau here to listen to me regale him with all the details. Though, honestly, it had been a couple of years since I'd included him in my successes, putting the firm above my guy. Shame closed my eyes for a few long seconds.

"It's a good look on you," Chandler remarked, his finger air tracing the outline of my body. I assumed he meant the black-on-black slacks and turtleneck sweater I wore and not the shame I'd just had coursing through me. I brought my scotch glass to my lips, doing my best to savor the rich flavor as it lingered like the warmth of the alcohol. Too bad I'd never grown to appreciate the drink.

"Be honest with me," I said. "Why're you here?" I stared directly at Chandler. "Are you here on my father's behalf?"

Chandler was in the depths of his drinks, edging on his way toward drunk, and gave a slight pause, confirming what I suspected. At this point, no matter what was said, I knew the truth, but I needed a friend, even if it came by way of a wolf in sheep's clothing.

I stood, my mind swirling with concern and anxiety over Beau. I barely thought of anything more than my man. Beau needed to get back here and stop this ridiculous fighting. I'd be celebrating with him tonight, certainly not Chandler. Never Chandler. I headed for the bottle of scotch to top Chandler's glass off to help his words flow more freely with intoxication.

"Your father suggested I contact you about a position," he said with a slight slur.

"What did he want to know?" I asked as if he'd answered a different way.

"He didn't ask for anything," Chandler said. The bottom of his nose gave the smallest flare revealing his lie. Lessons learned after over twenty-five years of knowing someone. "He was hopeful that you were taking care of yourself and living a happy life."

Yeah, right. My father never cared if any of his children were happy in their lives, only that they toed the family line. "I find that hard to believe. So, what have you told him?"

"That you're a badass and I wasn't going to engage in whatever game he wanted me to play." His tone changed slightly as that explanation rolled off his tongue as if rehearsed.

I nodded, feeling it was time to retreat and reassess.

"Dash, I've never possessed the 'it' factor. But you do. That firm we work for could be yours one day."

"Are you here to stir up trouble for me at the firm?" I asked.

"What? Of course not." Chandler answered, affronted by the insinuation.

I nodded. "Have you betrayed Joy for her help all those years ago? I suspect she's firmly on my father's side now, I haven't heard from her since then."

"No, of course not. I assure you. That would incriminate me as well," Chandler said. "When I arrived in Chicago and saw your success, I was proud of you. I wanted to be a part of it."

"If you provide my father with proprietary information, it'll be traced back to me. I'll lose everything. I'm placing my trust in you." I delivered the lie without a hint of emotion and with no change in my expression. While I wanted Chandler to leave for the night, I also feared the depth of my longing for Beau. How low could I go?

"Understood," Chandler remarked.

I nodded, peering down at the condensation from my cocktail glass. "I don't want to appear rude, but it's time you headed home."

"There's no need to be worried about him..."

"Thank you for your honesty, Chandler." I cut him off and replied firmly. "I need to be alone. It's been a long week."

He didn't utter another word as he rose and left through the front door in my final test of the night. The Chandler I knew was never compliant with anything. His sassy mouth made sure of that. The low level panic I managed to tamp down most days, surged. This time I took a larger drink of my watered down scotch, my face scrunched under the taste.

"Damn, that's a terrible drink." I left the glass behind and went to a side window above the parking garage and entrance to the building. I watched Chandler leave in a waiting taxi. The strong man façade I usually wore was beginning to show its cracks. I'd been in mourning mode. I'd gone seven days without speaking to Beau. My beautiful, unapologetically himself Beau. Regret and doubt replaced the happier memories of our past. Why had I declared that I wouldn't be the one to make contact?

What might my concessions be when he returned? If he returned. I reached for the arm of a side chair, keeping myself on my feet, bowled over at the suggestion Beau might not come home to me. Where had that even come from? Of course Beau was coming home. I swallowed a lump in my throat before going to my cell phone. I hadn't allowed myself to sink into a substantial pity party yet. Instead, I distracted myself by drinking into oblivion every night. I should have gone to the Keys with Beau.

As I picked up my phone, an email notification chirped, drawing my focus there. I opened the email app, seeing the first message in my inbox. In slow motion, I opened the thread to find that I had secured Austin Grainger as a client. Both his entertainment company, and his personal attorney. Wow, this was a major win. Austin, one of the most successful actors in the world, had built an empire with his production company. My thumbs danced across the small keypad as I replied, promising to have a retainer agreement and all necessary informed consent documents to them in the morning.

The exhaustion of the last several days of restless sleep and sad feelings swirled through me like the expensive but terrible scotch I'd drank. Tonight, I was changing my drink, and never planned to allow scotch past my lips again. I poured a double vodka tonic and started for the stairs. Even with all my self-pity, I called it a win that I was able to keep from texting Beau. He needed to be here for me as much as I needed to be here for him.

Beau

Five days later

"Uncle Beau, Uncle Beau, catch it," Dolly, Scott's second daughter, and sevenish year old middle child, said enthusiastically about the pinfish on her fishing line. She sat at the end of the pier beside me, her legs kicking back and forth just above the water in excitement.

"Hang on, honey. Let me get Daisy's bait set," I said, working quickly on Scott's oldest daughter's fishing pole. Daisy Mae was eight—an older acting eight year old, who told me to only use her first name, and sat on my other side.

Kailey and Scott's youngest daughter, Demi, both close in age, were incapable of sitting still for any length of time. All four girls were life-jacketed up and at the end of the dock of the rental property where we stayed in the Keys.

The younger ones celebrated any fish caught with movement and lots of *ewws* and *ahhs*. Unsurprisingly, their antics had run most of the fish away, while Daisy and Dolly appeared to have been trained to stay quiet during fishing.

"Beau, get it! Get it!" Kailey called, jumping up and down behind my back, placing me between her and the fish.

I grabbed the handheld net and scooped Dolly's hand-size fish up and out of the water. "Do you remember what this fish is called?"

"It looks a little different, but is it a pinfish too?" Dolly asked, looking up at me with her mom's pretty smile.

"Yep, that's what I think too," I said. "Wanna touch it before we toss it back?"

Where Daisy was a pro and could handle most of her own catches, Dolly was less tomboy and more girly. She shook her head ardently. Already knowing this answer, I lifted the small fish over my shoulder toward the two youngest girls.

"Do you guys want to touch it?" Just like every other time I'd made the offer, Kailey bounded away screaming. Demi was slower but dashed away too.

"Mommy! Beau's trying to get me to touch the fish." I saw Kailey jump into our mom's lap who sat on the porch in an Adirondack chair beside a sleeping Scott.

Kailey and I were growing closer this trip. Well, as close as a twenty-five-year age gap would allow, but she was simply an adorable handful. She knew I wasn't going to force her to touch the fish, proving my point by running back to me before I tossed it back into the water.

"They're too noisy," Daisy said. I agreed with her wholeheartedly. She got to her feet and handed me her wound fishing pole. "I'm gonna go get a cold drink. My water's warm." As if their leader had spoken, all three girls fell in line with her. She glanced back with a sigh. "You don't have to follow me everywhere."

"I have some watermelon ready," my mom chimed in, standing from her seat, prompting a chorus of cheers as the girls sprinted toward the house. Lauren met them at the back door, taking off their life jackets before they went inside.

While my attempt to teach Kailey how to fish ended in a boisterous affair, I was left with two small fishing poles, a smattering of water bottles, and the warm sun beating down on my body. I searched out Scott, wanting him to help me with all this, but I saw he was truly fast asleep. He hadn't budged as the girls ran past him.

"Hey," Carter said, approaching from behind me. I'd tried my hardest to avoid being alone with him. Carter always wanted to *talk*, but I didn't have anything to say to him. "Want me to take that for you?"

"Are they done for the day?" I asked, already taking measures to end the great fishing experience.

"I believe so. Linda's going to try to get them down for a nap before we go to the fair this evening," he said, gathering the water bottles as he came closer. As I reeled in the poles with my back to Carter, I felt his hand clamp down on my shoulder.

"I spoke with Dash. He mentioned that he's missing you."

I nodded, trying to swallow that lump of bullshit down. He hadn't called and he sure wasn't here with us.

"We truly appreciate the time you spend with us. Both Linda and Kailey really enjoy that you're here. I do too."

I nodded once more. My bobblehead skills were impeccable.

"Beau, have I done something to upset you?"

Dammit, that was too direct. I could tiptoe around the question. I knew Dash had told him that I was protective toward my mom and Kailey after the way my father had treated me. What more needed to be said?

"No," I finally answered, allowing the word to stand on its own merit as I grabbed my fishing gear.

Carter didn't move, trapping me at the end of the dock. I straightened to my full height to face him. Though I wouldn't call it face-to-face since he was around five-foot-ten, I had to look down to capture any part of his face in my visual field.

"It's not that I'm unhappy. I just want my mother safe and for you to continue taking care of Kailey. Outside of that, what I want is irrelevant. It doesn't matter at all." That became clearer to me in every part of my life, but I left that thought inside my head.

Since I rarely allowed myself to ponder anything too deeply, the realization of what I was experiencing mentally bowled me over. I hoped my outward appearance remained calm, because inside this head, it was a shitshow. The main problem with my life, Carter and Dash had in spades. Money made me really uncomfortable and created chaos and greed for those who had it. Men like Carter and Dash never settled for more than enough. Hell, the word *enough* wasn't even in their vocabulary. I was a basic guy who wanted a basic life. What did Dash even look like in my idea of a good life? I couldn't envision him there with me.

"Nothing's wrong. I appreciate what you've done for my mom and Dash. You saved him when he needed it."

There. I'd said it. I was done with this conversation.

"Is that all? You and Dash seem to think you owe me something, but I assure you, you don't. I feel whole for the first time in my life. Your mom completes me. Meeting you, Dash, and Linda has grounded me in the best possible way. I won't ever hurt either of them. I cherish our dynamic."

I nodded but needed time alone to grapple with the vision I had for my life—the one I wasn't currently living. No matter what happened, if I followed my dream, I'd cause pain to people I loved. I blew out a breath I hadn't realized I held.

"Dash wouldn't have his career without your influence," I started, and decided to just say what I thought. "I feel like his father's finally paying attention to his value, which is exactly what he wanted."

Carter smiled instantly. "Based on what I'm hearing, the elder Richmond's quite aware of Dash's accomplishments. Dash told me today that he landed a large client with a sizable portfolio." Carter's expression morphed again as he studied me closer. He furrowed his brow. "You and Dash haven't worked out your differences yet?"

"No, not yet. I'm going inside to lay down for a minute. I'm not feeling my best." The lie rolled off my tongue as I dropped my gaze again then moved past Carter.

"And we need you raring to go. Those girls are absolutely enamored with you." Carter went back to gathering the rest of the snack packages and half empty bottles of water. I glanced out at the ocean, different than I'd ever seen it before. The tranquil beauty of the water lapping gently against the dock, and the sun beating down on my naked chest eased my tension.

So there was another item to add to the list of essentials for my life, I needed sun and water. Dash was exceling in the busy city atmosphere. Maybe we could live separately. It wasn't as if we'd missed talking to each other over the last two weeks. Honestly, we hadn't done much that couples do in a very long time. Dash was evolving into the image of a true Richmond. It was in his blood. Work and success were all that mattered to him anymore. Somewhere along the way the boy I'd fallen for had faded away, and I had no control over his departure.

I rolled my tense shoulder muscles and placed the fishing gear on the deck leading to the kitchen. The ache in my gut told me I'd known the proper answer to our problems for years now. I didn't want to face it, but we'd grown too far apart. Apparently neither one of us wanted to throw in the towel, but ignoring it was making us both miserable.

"Beau. Beau. Beau," Kailey said as I stepped through the sliding glass door. The girls chimed in too, except for Daisy. She was growing up too quickly. The other three were sweet but exhausting.

"He's going into his room," Carter said, dropping the mess he'd collected from the dock onto the kitchen counter. "You girls need to be quiet for him. When are we leaving for the fair?"

"A few hours," my mom answered. "Everyone be quiet. Finish up so you can lay down too. You're going to be up late tonight."

I pointed to the stairs then started that way. Change was coming, I felt it in my bones. All I could do was hope for the best.

Dash

The following day

Although the firm's annual round table discussions didn't allow for phone checks, I slipped my hand into my breast pocket and retrieved the cell the second it vibrated against my chest. Sadly, it wasn't Beau. Though it *was* Beau-adjacent since it was Carter, who was currently vacationing with my guy.

"Excuse me," I said firmly, pushing the chair backward and rising to my feet while sliding my thumb across the screen. I didn't speak until I was away from any prying ears. "Hey."

"You free?"

"Probably not the best time but what's up?" I said, then quickly dropped the professional act because I had to know. "How's Beau?"

"He's fine," Carter said. "Beau doesn't speak to me much, but I can tell he's struggling."

I closed my eyes, *struggling* was such a small word to describe the misery my broken heart faced. "I miss him. So what's going on?"

"I wanted to let you know I'm attending the economic summit this year. Your father will be there."

My eyes popped open wide at that announcement. "When?"

"It begins Sunday evening about the same time Linda drops Beau at the airport. She'll arrive Monday morning, I believe," Carter said, never too good about remembering his packed schedule.

So Beau had moved his itinerary back by a day, probably to add to the point he was trying to make with me. I quickly sifted through my options of whether I should tell Carter to warn Linda about my parents attending the summit, or not. She'd been in the witch's brew before with the spouses and girlfriends of the uber wealthy, but I didn't think she'd ever run into my mom before.

"You've grown quiet, Dash. Do you want to fly out and go to the summit with us? I understand the Richmonds will be there."

I barked out a hard laugh, very unprofessional. "Someday I'll take you up on that. Listen, my sources say my mother and her group of cronies have been biding their time, planning to give Linda shit when they're finally together. So watch out for her."

"I'll make sure she's ready," Carter said.

"Excellent. Keep me posted," I said, lifting a finger when Penny stuck her head out the conference room door to nod me back inside.

"Will do." In Carter's customary way, he disconnected the call without any sort of salutation.

I squared my shoulders and gave a single nod. Time to get back in the game.

20: The What's Happening?
Beau/Dash

Beau

Saturday evening

The chill in the air sent a shiver racing down my spine. There was nothing quite like leaving paradise only to return to Chicago, facing a forty degree temperature drop between the two. I hauled my duffle bag out of the bed of my truck and reached for the case of the new fishing rod I'd purchased in Florida. No matter how I tried, I couldn't shake the longing to still be on vacation. That had less to do with the Sunshine State and more to do with all the tension building in my shoulders since landing at O'Hare. With each mile I drove to the building, my shoulders only grew tighter.

Dash's little race car wasn't in its designated parking spot. I didn't know how to feel about Dash not being home. Our shared calendar had my itinerary. I don't know why I expected him to be here, but I did. Maybe this was an act of retaliation for not speaking to him for so long or maybe he flat wasn't interested in being with me any longer. That probably said everything about our current situation, but I wasn't ready to throw in the towel until he and I had an honest dialogue. I rode the elevator up and walked the hall until I reached the door to our place.

When I entered, a rush of sensation hit me. I felt it to my bones. It was a coldness that had nothing to do with the temperature inside or out. The place was dark, no longer lived in. I wondered if Dash had been home while I was gone. In the living room, I tossed my duffle on a side chair but I was far more careful with my new rod case.

A sigh escaped me unexpectedly. Why couldn't he just be here? That would've sufficed to help ease the argument between us. I rummaged through my bag in search of my phone. He hadn't made contact explaining why he'd be late. His words about not following me echoed in my head. The only message I had was from my mother, checking if I'd arrived safely. I turned an armchair toward the window facing the well-lit entrance and garage, then took a seat to return the text from my mom.

My desire meant something to me. I didn't want to be here, and I'd find a way to go. My heart still wanted Dash on board with the plan. I didn't want to lose him just as much as I didn't want to live the life I currently had. We could fly to one another every weekend. We barely saw each other these days. By spending a weekend with him, I'd actually see him more if he came to me. It wasn't outside of the realm of possibility. We could make it work. An attorney in the firm had a husband in Montana; they traveled on weekends. She said it allowed her all the time in the week to work as much as needed so she could take the time on the weekends instead of being worried about dinners and events during the week.

I steeled my heart and my resolve. Emotional turmoil had no place here, at least for now. From this angle, I'd see him drive into the garage, which would give me time to compose myself, and be prepared to broach the subject. If I failed and we split tonight, where did I plan to go? I didn't know, except somewhere that had an ocean. Not Mobile, and Florida was damned expensive and crowded. I'd have to be able to transfer within FedEx. I had enough money saved to finally buy my own route... I placed my elbow on the arm of the chair, my head rested on my fist. Waiting only strengthened my doggedness to resolve all these lingering issues.

Six hours later, my ass hurt. I'd only gotten up from my chair to use the bathroom. I was in desperate need of a bottle of water and a snack. Yet, I waited, watching intently. I refused to go to bed. That left open a chance of never having this conversation. I practiced my speech, preparing for Dash's counterarguments. He'd have plenty. I would focus on our maturity and the different directions life had taken us. We'd both evolved as individuals. I refused to tolerate any more lonely nights and weekends, hoping for his time.

I no longer intended to change who I was in order to fit into Dash's firm. Having Dash try to change me stung the most. Somewhere close to midnight, a pair of headlights caught my eye. I watched the approach and recognized the sedan as being one from Dash's firm. I rose in my seat and squared my shoulders. That car meant Dash would come in drunk. At least intoxicated enough that he didn't feel comfortable driving. My heart ached. While I was here waiting for his arrival, he'd been out socializing.

The back door of the Lincoln swung open before the driver stepped out to open that door. Dash stumbled out of the backseat, barely managing to catch himself before he took a tumble. Dash had been drinking quite a bit lately, but I didn't remember him coming home like this.

The opposite passenger door opened and Chandler leaped, rounding the trunk in a beelined pursuit of Dash. A wave of heat surged through my body. I clenched my fists at my sides. Any excuses I may have made for Dash were tossed out the window. What the fuck was Chandler doing with Dash?

In an overly familiar manner, Chandler swept Dash into his arms, pulling him close. Dash's arms circled Chandler. When the embrace broke, they exchanged a long glance. Chandler cupped Dash's cheek, caressing there. The entire scene was intimate, beyond friendship.

What struck me was the way Chandler's thumb swept across Dash's lower lip. They looked damned good together. They fit better than Dash and I did. It sure appeared Chandler had taken my place as Dash's newest plus one.

They turned in unison back to the waiting car. Once Chandler had Dash tucked inside, he shut the door then looked up at me. So they knew I was here. To prove the point, he swiped a hand through the air, dismissing me as he went to the other side of the car. They were off in a matter of seconds.

As I watched them drive away, all I saw was red. My chin hit my chest as I breathed heavily, trying to control the need to hit something into submission. Dash wasn't coming home. Chandler had probably told him I was home, standing in the window, and they made the decision to leave together.

As unbridled pain washed over me, my eyelids fluttered shut. My heart shattered into a thousand pieces, falling from my chest. Motherfucking Chandler.

I tried in vain to convince myself that it didn't matter that it was him. Anyone in this situation would be devastating, but deep down, I knew that wasn't true. Chandler hurt worse than anyone else. One thing was certain, I wasn't sticking around for this. Message fucking received. It took all my strength not to tear this motherfucking place apart. I had no time to think irrationally and act on impulse. I was able to land somewhere in the emotional middle.

With heavy footsteps, I marched across the floor then up each step of this ridiculously curving staircase. I'd always found their design to be dumb. After tonight, I wouldn't have to see them ever again. By the time I reached the bedroom, I had a good mix of both anger and hurt roiling around inside me. The sight of the room only intensified my emotions. Framed pictures of us—either alone or together—decorated every available shelf and piece of furniture. Tears sprang to my eyes.

Maybe I'd hung on too long, but dammit, we used to be happy . I overlooked the allure of our better days that had kept me here longer than they ever should. We were only kids when we met. Far too young to make the promises we made. We lived life like an old married couple. Dash had always wanted to appear older to compensate for his youth... I forced my mind to stop as I retrieved my suitcase from a storage closet upstairs. Whatever happened between me and Dash was in my rearview mirror. I only needed to look forward.

I laid the suitcase open on top of the built-in dresser inside the closet. With no discernable organizational system, I threw my clothes inside, many landing on the floor. Fuck it. I wasn't taking any of the shit Dash had purchased for me. I grabbed my uniforms and kicked at the clothes on the floor as I made my way out.

My packed duffle bag, already downstairs, contained everything I needed anyway. With my hands full, I double-timed it down the stairs. As I reached for my bag, the sparkle of my commitment ring caught my eye. Everything in my hands dropped onto the chair. With an emotional pain that seared through my system like a lightning bolt, I yanked the ring off my fat fucking finger. Dammit, my knuckle was bleeding now. Dash's fault too.

I chose not to dwell on the meaning that piece of jewelry held to me. With a deep breath, I grabbed the notepad and pen from the entry table. As the simple words poured from me, I saw red.

"I got it. Sorry it took so long to make this move. I've been in the same headspace as you for a long time. Probably longer than you," I scribbled, feeling petty. I hoped Dash read this as I intended. "Chandler? Of course. Do the right thing and leave me the fuck alone."

I felt adding my name was unnecessary. I left the note by my ring and grabbed my shit from the chair. The finality of my decision liberated my soul as I tried to carry my clothes, fishing pole, and duffle bag to my truck. I shoved it all into my truck's backseat and was driving out of the garage within minutes. I'd get my boat and haul it with me wherever I went. I didn't want Chandler to step a single foot on my beloved fishing boat. "Damn straight." I slammed my fist into the steering wheel to punctuate my words. This was my first step to getting my life back on some sort of track.

If everything worked out for me, I wouldn't ever have to suffer through this city's traffic again.

Dash

Sunday

"Whoa," Penny exclaimed.

Why was Penny at my house? Had I missed a meeting? My head throbbed like a son of a bitch, making it hard to focus on anything other than the drumbeat pulsating against my brain. The light streaming in through the window beat against my closed lids with the effectiveness of the harshest interrogation tactic, designed to torture the toughest criminals. I pressed a hand over my eyes to ward off the worst of it.

"What're you doing here and why does it smell so bad?" she asked.

I lifted my hand and cracked my eyelids open. Huh. I was in my office, which made more sense than Penny being inside my home. When I attempted to speak, I found I had a frog living in my throat with the way I croaked. There wasn't any saliva in my mouth. Fuck, I had to slow down my drinking. Beau needed to get his ass back here and help me tackle my problem before I turned into an alcoholic. I needed to get my shit together and get home to carry out my plans to surprise Beau upon his arrival this evening. We had to find a better way to repair our partnership, and I had to assure my guy that Chandler was never going to be an issue for us again.

I did my utmost to suppress my pain and started to rise to a sitting position.

"Wow, Dash, that's awful." I heard the distinct sound of a dry heave following her words. "I'll contact the janitorial service."

If she had such a reaction, I was certain my stomach couldn't handle whatever she saw. Yet, I cautiously ventured a look in her direction. At least I attempted to use the trash can. That had to count for something.

"Penny," I called.

"Already on it," she said, reading my mind as usual. My bare feet were firmly planted on the ground, with my elbows resting on my knees. "Chandler brought you in before midnight. You were somewhat upright but by the time he settled you on the sofa, you were out cold. He then rifled around in your desk, opening and closing several drawers. Apparently, he didn't know we record everything in this office." That revelation that Chandler had finally shown himself had me pushing through the pain to stand. "The audio in your office picked up Chandler saying you had always been too naïve."

Hmm. Was my current state only due to an alcohol hangover, or did Chandler slip me something more? I never felt this bad before in my life.

"Did he carry anything out?" I asked as I headed for the minibar for a Gatorade, then took several long swigs.

"He shoved something under his overcoat and left you asleep on the sofa. Well, he nudged the trash can closer to you, then left."

I stared at her, and she stared right back.

"I've never seen you looking so disheveled. Is that eyeliner underneath your eyes?"

Dammit. I'd started adding a subtle line beneath my lashes to help make my penetrating stare pop. I used it as a diversionary tactic that seemed to throw people off when looking into my eyes.

"What time is it?" I asked, ignoring her question.

"About noon."

"I need to leave. Beau's expected to be home by early afternoon," I said, rummaging through my pants pockets for my key fob. At the same time, I spotted my suit jacket and headed that way. Maybe my keys were in there.

"I have that he arrived home yesterday," Penny said, confusion evident in her voice.

"Carter mentioned that Beau had rescheduled for today," I said, remembering the small gift box I had bought well over a week ago, which was tucked away in my desk drawer.

"Weird. The system didn't notify me of a change," she said. "I'll redirect the vitamin hydration company to your place. They'll set up an IV, and within ten minutes, you'll begin to feel better. They work like a charm."

"That's fine. I'll be home in roughly twenty minutes. I'd like to take a shower first," I said, dropping the suit coat back on the side chair. Penny would send it off to be dry cleaned.

"Sure, I'll let them know." As I confidently headed toward my office door, I resolved to use willpower to improve my mood. Somewhere in the next few hours I planned to confront Chandler and send him packing, Beau would be invited to go with me.

I was tired of all the game playing in my life. While I had played a part in fostering and manipulating Chandler, it was time for a change. Once I let my guard down, I realized how badly I missed Beau. I was determined to rebuild our relationship. Beau only needed a reminder of how much I cared. We also needed to have regular sex again. I'd been remiss in both departments.

I had a lot to sort through. How had I allowed myself to get so out of control last night? My guy deserved much better than me. We'd find our way, though. We always did.

21: The Chandler
Dash/Beau

Dash

The soothing warmth of the shower worked wonders for my hangover. I positioned myself strategically to allow the water to beat along my upper back and neck, even with the hydration specialist's imminent arrival. Nevertheless, I stayed under the spray until the hot water turned cooler, my muscles loosening up. I'd brought one of Beau's Powerades into the shower with me, taking a decent swig every so often.

My stomach roiled, but the contents stayed down. I called that a win.

Why I had chosen last night to completely overdo was beyond me. I'd been steadily drinking more and more since Beau was gone. I hated the idea of going to bed alone. But apparently last night had been my breaking point. Perhaps it was because he wasn't arriving home for another day. Beau had stayed away longer to teach me a lesson, and boy, had it.

What I desperately wanted to convey to Beau was how often I lay awake at night, watching him sleep. His presence constantly reminded me of my worth and that reinforced my belief that I could achieve the goals I'd set for myself. I was dumbfounded by the reality that my guy didn't seem to realize that he was the glue in every situation of my life. Beau kept my world together.

The problems we had were all on me.

I should've put my pride aside and called him, not have waited for him to call me to make amends.

The doorbell rang, sending my phone chirping like crazy. I quickly left the shower and reached for a dry towel I had placed by my phone. With a quick swipe of my thumb, I responded to the ring. "Hello. Give me a minute. I'll buzz you in. You can set up in the room to the left of the door."

"Yes, sir," he replied, which always made me feel wiser than my actual age. I pushed the option to open the door and continued rubbing the towel over my body. I took my hairbrush, quickly raking my damp hair off my face. I usually preferred to dry it properly, but I had a lot to do before Beau arrived home. My appearance was the last thing on my mind.

I grabbed my robe hanging by the bathroom door and put it on as I went through the bedroom. I loved this gorgeous home. I loved that my almost mother-in-law married a generous, loving man who'd offer this place to Beau and me for such an extraordinarily low price.

As I trotted down the staircase, the technician was already set up. He was gloved up with an IV bag ready to go. "Mr. Richmond?" the guy asked.

"Call me Dash. Mr. Richmond is my father. Should I sit here?" I asked about the comfortable side chair he had pulled into the center of the room.

"Yes, sir," he replied. The entire process lasted no longer than twenty minutes. I had undergone similar procedures before. I found the whole experience relaxing. Something about my body receiving the nutrients and hydration it craved made everything right as rain. A yawn slipped free, and my eyelids drooped. Perhaps I should reconsider my options. Maybe I should rest until Beau arrived home then wake and plead for forgiveness.

With a series of long yawns, I let the attendant out and started for our bedroom when I spotted Beau's commitment ring on the entry table. Even in my exhausted state, warning bells rattled in my head. Then I saw the note, written in Beau's unique penmanship. Time slowed as I held both, reading Beau's words.

My heart sank as I read the note. What had Chandler done? The ink looked bolder on Chandler's name, as if he'd pressed harder, penning it with malice and jealousy. No. *No.* What had Beau seen?

Beau had already come home?

How? With both the ring and note gripped tightly in my hand, I took off in search of my cell phone. Was there any chance I'd missed him this morning? Panic and anxiety gripped me. Every muscle in my body tensed. All my arrogance of the last two weeks, my convictions of not being the first to reach out, mocked me as I slipped easily back into my old self—a person I hadn't been in so long.

Before I tanked, I found my phone on our bed and quickly dialed Beau's number. It started ringing before I ever had the receiver to my ear. My gaze flitted around the bedroom, landing on the open closet door. With a singular focus, I moved toward the closet as Beau's voicemail activated.

"Babe, what's happened? I got your note and have your ring. It needs to be back on your finger. Please call me." I didn't hang up as my foot knocked against the door, very afraid of what I might find as the overhead light automatically lit the small space. Beau's clothes were scattered everywhere. An open suitcase lay cockeyed on the floor. He'd never intentionally leave such a mess. I pressed the call button again, but it went to voicemail. Beau was ignoring my calls.

I squeezed my eyes shut. Dread coiled in my gut. Every choice I'd made since our happier days felt like a misstep. All leading us to this heartbreaking moment. My heart ached. My thoughts turned desperate. If only I could find where he'd gone, I'd rush there and bring him back home. *Penny.* I'll called her. She regularly worked miracles. If anyone could find him, it was her. I took a deep centering breath and dialed her before my panic turned into hysteria.

Beau

Indecision had finally taken hold of me. My heart fucking hurt. The pain made me frantic. The grounded man I always aimed to be was becoming erratic. Exhausted, I'd pulled into a motel in Oklahoma City. That was three hours ago, and I hadn't slept a wink since I'd arrived. Instead, I passed time by staring at the ceiling, wishing for anything to take this pain away. Raw emotions simmered just beneath the surface, with an enormous pain and just that same amount of fear.

Why had I chosen to leave? At the time, I'd thought making the first move meant I was in control, but I wasn't at all. A clear voice inside me insisted that Dash hadn't betrayed me. That I hadn't witnessed what I thought I had. Yet, I countered that thought with the idea that the eyes never deceived.

Chandler was aware of his actions and had easily led Dash away from me. Their embrace wreaked havoc on my soul. Chandler spent all day and probably most nights with Dash. They fit together in a way we did not. From my position on the bed, my legs hung over the mattress. I kicked my feet to help lift myself to sit on the side of the bed. I might have accepted Dash randomly fooling around with anyone but Chandler. Dash had to know that I'd never go for Chandler being the other guy.

I hadn't been the one to break us up, Dash had orchestrated our split. He was fully aware of my return date. It appeared on our shared calendar.

I rolled back on the mattress again, bringing my palm to my chest and gently rubbing the dull ache that lingered there. My hand felt naked without my ring. The rattle of my cell phone connected to the charger by my nightstand caught my attention. It could only be one of two people, either Scott or Dash, my mom was occupied with Carter. With more strength than I realized I possessed, I let the call go to voicemail.

The phone rang again. I was more content when the damn thing had died about halfway between Chicago and Oklahoma City. I suspected Dash was relieved that I'd gone. He might want reassurance that I wouldn't try to have Carter find a new attorney. Maybe I should consider asking for a cut in the revenue obtained from Carter. A devious smile pulled at the corners of my lips.

I understood I wasn't particularly likable. That was an undeniable fact. But, Dash had liked me once. Where had it all gone wrong? I knew the answer, deep down, I was a country boy through and through. A guy who was caught in the middle of two worlds. I struggled to navigate the world of sophistication and wealth, and rednecks wouldn't like me for being gay. I was basic, and Dash was all the things I wasn't. We were as opposite as two people could possibly be.

My phone rang again. I ignored it...again. Instead, I focused on the memories of the great sex he and I had shared. Dash took it as rough as I could give it. I was sure going to miss driving into my guy's ass. Hell, I already missed it. It'd been so long since we were together in the same headspace. Years, in fact. I heard my phone rattling again, but I'd been awake well over twenty-four hours.

My thoughts turned blissfully numb as my eyelids grew heavy. A giant yawn escaped. I reached for a pillow and bent my legs. In the recesses of my mind, I heard my cell ring again, but I was finally slipping into sleep. I'd deal with it later.

Dash

From the elevator, I reached my assistant's desk in five long strides, even though it usually took seven. I started speaking as soon as the elevator doors opened to our floor. "What do you have on Beau?" I asked.

Her fingers flew over the keyboard at a rapid speed, and her back faced me.

"I have access to his credit cards. The login's auto filled. If you haven't found anything, search those."

"Got it," she said, not sparing me a glance. I maintained my urgent pace, heading into my office to figure out what Chandler had searched for.

"Chandler's not responding. It seems his phone is turned off," she called.

My suspicions about Chandler were confirmed when I rounded my desk to the private drawer I kept locked at all times, but he'd had access to my keys last night. The drawer opened without having the key to release the locks. Immediately, I saw Carter's file was missing.

A smile split my lips, he'd fallen for it. I had duplicated the files, inflating the estimates on all of Carter's bids for the next year. Whoever Chandler gave that file to—and I was pretty sure that was my father—wouldn't win a project for however long it took them to realize they'd been played. I gave a mental fist pump at the win.

Beau's handsome face came to my thoughts. He'd be happy. We'd celebrate the success. I picked up my landline and dialed Beau again. The worry that lay just below the surface had me ducking my head and closing my eyes. Four rings then voicemail. "Beau, call me when you get this." I couldn't keep the begging quality from my voice. "Please, baby, call me."

The phone was barely in the cradle when Penny came into the room. Normally, she knocked, but we were too far into this shitty day to abide by such manners. "I discovered a charge for a motel in Oklahoma City. Various gas station fill-ups lead me to suspect the charge is valid. I printed the statement and pinpointed the locations." As she spoke, she laid each piece of evidence in front of me.

"He's already made it to Oklahoma City? How is that possible?" I wondered aloud, picking up the sheet with the map on it. Was he on his way to Dallas? Without too much real thought, I lifted the phone again, dialing Amelia.

"Dash? Are you okay?" Amelia answered in the same caring way she always had. This time, I forewent my normal playful tease about her being overprotective.

"I believe Beau's heading to Dallas. If he shows up there, will you call me?" I asked.

"Why don't you know?" she asked, her tone edging toward worried.

"I can't get into it right now. If he does arrive, I need you to talk up what a good guy I am. I'll fly home on the first flight out."

"Dasham, what did you do?" she asked sternly. "Beau's a good man."

"I know, but now's not a good time to explain. Call me if he arrives," I said, letting that be enough for now, and hung up the phone.

Absently, I thumbed through the files of other construction companies I represented. Those files were filled with blank copy paper. Although my only real worry was Beau, I had to confront Chandler. Make a big deal about the theft and inflate the importance of the files containing sensitive information not meant to be seen by anyone else. If one man represented the epitome of a bottom dweller, it had to be Chandler.

"Can you continue to follow Beau's card?" I asked. "At least that'll give me a direction."

"Dash, I love Beau. I do," Penny started. "But are you certain you should go after him?"

My head jerked up as I rose from my seat. "What's that mean?" What a ridiculous thought.

She lifted her hands in some sort of gesture of peace. "You both have changed. You're devoted to your work, spending well over a hundred hours a week here. I've been in this for too long. People like you have a hard time maintaining any sort of relationship. You're married to your job."

I gazed at her in disbelief. Why was this the first time I let that philosophy sink into my thick skull? Because I'd discounted it. My arrogance pushed me to believe I could handle my personal and career growth. How dumb was I?

I didn't show Penny my cards. I rarely did until I had time to consider it all. "I understand your perspective." That reply would have to suffice. As I rounded the desk to leave the office, I added, "I'm going to find Chandler."

"You know, this is the first time I've seen you like this. I like the hair falling down on your forehead. It makes you look younger," she said, propping her shoulder against the doorframe. I almost rolled my eyes. She'd nailed the exact reason I kept it swept up all of the time.

I lifted my hand to my head, realizing I hadn't even dried my hair today. I never left the house with my hair in disarray.

"I don't think you heard me," she called.

"I heard you." As the elevator door slid open, I stepped inside in full find-Beau-beast-mode. He'd gotten my attention. Decision made, I couldn't live a proper life without him. Maybe I hadn't done right by him, but I always knew he was my anchor. Fuck this job.

22: The Ocean
Dash/Beau

Dash

The firm had placed Chandler in one of the small condos designed for traveling lawyers who came to Chicago for various reasons. I parked in front of the ground floor unit and noticed the partially open door. That couldn't be good. I approached the front door then nudged it farther open with my toe.

"Chandler," I called out, but received no reply. "You here, buddy?"

Again, only silence greeted me. I stepped fully inside, and my eyes widened. What a mess. What had Chandler gone through that led him to live in such filth?

"Chandler, are you here?"

What did it say about me that I'd rather have a vagrant living here than believe Chandler, a guy I'd known forever, had turned out to be such a trashy person—literally? I had to gather my courage and steel my spine to continue inside the house. All the lights were off. I flipped the switch on in the bathroom. It looked like it hadn't been cleaned in months. The bedroom was in the same condition. All of Chandler's clothes were gone, empty hangers lining the closet.

The hand I hadn't used to touch anything, covered my eyes as the sheer magnitude of what Chandler had done settled heavily on my shoulders. Worry fueled my thoughts. Chandler was acting with my father's blessing, ensuring I lost everything. Why hadn't I shielded Beau better? I patted my front pockets then the back pockets, searching for my cell phone, only to realize I'd left it in the car. I left the apartment, locking the door behind me. Once I was tucked inside my car, I worked the display screen to call Beau's number. It rang four times before going to voicemail. Why wasn't he answering?

"Beau, whatever Chandler did was with malicious intent. I have no idea what caused you to leave, but Chandler's actions were premeditated. It all came to a head last night. Please call me. I love you. Carter told me you changed your plans to come home on Sunday. We can leave Chicago together. I see what I've become, and you deserve better from me. Please call me."

I pressed the end button and stared through the front windshield, feeling more isolated than ever before. My palms grew sweaty, prompting me to clench my fists. A large part of me wanted to drive to Oklahoma City right then. That same part of me wondered if Beau was feeling as lost as I was right now.

Penny's name came across my screen before the ring chimed.

"Yeah?" I answered.

"Beau just filled his tank at a gas station in South Oklahoma City."

"Thanks, Penny. You've been great today. I'll monitor his charges tonight," I said, not thoroughly convinced I shouldn't go after him.

"I don't mind. If I see something first, I'll call you," she said.

"You're going above and beyond your role," I said truthfully.

"Keep that in mind for my upcoming employee evaluation. Ciao," she said before the call ended. With a deep breath in, I realized I was going home alone, left to wallow in my own sorrow. That thought frightened me. I was all too aware of how deeply I could sink because of Beau. He had to let me back in. I couldn't endure a life without him.

After several hours of repeatedly calling Beau's phone, I finally decided to check with the motel. I should've done it from the second I heard about the motel charge. Why hadn't I? I couldn't say, but I was still dealing with a mammoth hangover and seriously troubled by Chandler's actions. Fucking Chandler. Even though I'd sensed my relationship with Beau was diminishing, I'd allowed Chandler to sneak in and hurt Beau again. What an arrogant fool I'd become. A joke of a human being.

I grabbed a bottle of rum from the bar on my way to our chairs that offered the perfect view over Lake Michigan. I took a healthy swig directly from the bottle. This liquor went down much smoother than scotch ever could.

With a sigh, I slumped back into the chair. It was time to digest that my tenure with the firm was coming to an end. Tomorrow, I'd begin cleaning up my cases, preparing for a transition. The few clients that had relied solely on me, a contingency in their contracts that only I handled their accounts, hopefully went with me wherever I landed. Luckily, untangling myself as a junior partner would be infinitely easier than if I'd been made senior partner already. I didn't yet have an equity position in the firm.

I dialed Beau one last time, desperately hoping he'd answer. If he did, that had to mean he wanted me back. My stomach knotted as the fourth ring started and seemed to drop to my toes when the voicemail answered again. My head swam, and I took another swallow of the rum then dialed the motel.

"Motel 6," a man whose voice might have seen better days barked.

"I'm looking for Beau Brooks, a guest of yours," I said, my chin hitting my chest, my fingers crossed.

"He checked out about four hours ago." The call ended abruptly. So much for customer service. *Dammit.* My poor choices were glaringly evident, deepening my understanding of why my wonderful mister had walked away. Why had I ever agreed to keep Beau at a distance? Especially when he sat at my office for hours watching me do all the mundane and grunt work tasks a first, and second year attorney was assigned. I loved those memories. Dinner by lamplight in the file room we affectionately referred to as the dungeon.

I wasn't always the man I became. The idea that I thrived by carrying my father's attitude toward life made me physically ill. Manipulation wasn't my way, but I'd done that so many times I'd lost count. Even with Chandler, I'd manipulated that situation to see what he was up to. I didn't feel bad about that. But Beau? That one I didn't feel good with at all. I closed my eyes, listening to the silence of the house. Despite what anyone thought, I'd never lost my desire for my husband. Or for the dream that we'd have children someday. I yearned for a handful of little ones to love and explore the beauty of the world with.

Why had I allowed Beau to live such a lonely life? The first time he'd left me, that had been my father's fault, even though neither of us knew it at the time. This time, it was my father's destructive DNA manifesting inside me. And I'd let it happen. Beau would be far better off without a Richmond in his life. Unfortunately, I wasn't the kind of person who'd grant him clemency from his life sentence with me. I didn't want to give him an opportunity to see if he could be happier without me. I would be the one to make him smile again.

I went to the medicine cabinet in the kitchen. Beau was good about leaving my sleeping pills out for me. I'd taken that simple gesture for granted. I'd taken everything about us for granted, but Beau had sure gotten my attention. Please let him be heading to Dallas. Please. It meant I still had a chance.

Beau

Driving into Dallas along Interstate 35 East felt completely different tonight than any other time before. After getting some sleep, I was in a better position to make decisions on where to go. I just had no idea where I belonged. The last time I'd experienced happiness was in Sea Springs, where my grandparents always made my visits memorable. It was where my mom's heritage could be found.

If I stayed on the outskirts of town, I could avoid Richmond Resorts and the family land that had been ours for generations. It seemed the direction I was supposed to go or at least the direction the truck was taking me in. I had several hours to go to make it to Sea Springs. Maybe if my grandparents' land ever became available, I could buy it to keep it in the family. I understood why my mom's family had cherished that place. The proximity to the ocean nourished my soul.

The reason I'd ignored all the relationship warning signs—right up until Chandler arrived, that is—was to avoid the pain currently ravishing my heart, cutting deeper than any other time in my life. And I didn't need to allow my thoughts to go willy-nilly right now, I had to drive safely to get there in one piece.

Time was the only remedy to heal life's traumas. I wasn't convinced that what Dash and I lost was something I could heal from, but I'd give it a try. Perhaps one day I might find someone who resonated with me. Pain slashed over my heart again at even the suggestion.

I pushed those thoughts aside and turned up the country music station, humming along with the melody. Carter had told me years ago that the mind couldn't think of two things at once. He wasn't wrong. I made a conscious effort to think of anything other than Dash. And there he was again.

I fucking hated Chandler.

Dash

Monday

The grit in my eyes, along with the red rims surrounding them, prompted Lon, who planned to be in court today merely as an observer, to decide to argue the case instead of me. I was put out by the call. Despite having sleep deprivation, I was exceptionally skilled at my job. I could win this case with my eyes closed. Which they really wanted to do.

I glanced down at the cell phone that had remained in my grasp without interruption. Beau hadn't called me back.

His debit card was now sending me alerts with every new transaction. He had stopped for gas in Waxahachie, Texas, and then again in Houston. Where was he headed? Surely not to Sea Springs where our world had fallen apart the first time. What were his intentions?

"Dash, you ready?" Lon called from the end of the bench I'd sat in behind him. I looked around, astonished to see a nearly empty courtroom.

"It's over?" I asked.

"Yeah, and I said your name a few times." The scowl on his face wasn't one usually directed at me and his tone had a tinge of anger lacing through it.

"Was the case dismissed?" I asked, standing and working my way out.

"Yes," Lon said, more irritated than seconds ago, but I didn't give a shit. He'd be truly pissed once he learned my intentions of leaving the firm. But I wasn't ready to divulge that information yet. And I'd stopped caring about his feelings a long time ago.

I nodded, glad to see the case ended in our client's favor. Once we were alone inside the elevator, he locked stares with me.

"Penny shared what occurred. Which one's bothering you? Beau or Chandler? Fair warning, it better be Chandler. You risked our company by bringing him in. We have no idea what he might have had access to."

I raised my hand, hoping to stop the reprimand Lon was intent on giving.

"Don't belittle my intelligence. Everything he was involved in was staged. He left with paper files that held no significance. But I assure you, he'll face consequences for whatever he did to Beau." I didn't look away from his stare as I spoke with sincerity and zero hesitation. Chandler was far from finished with me.

Lon gave an exasperated sigh. "You still don't get it. Men like us don't have relationships. We can't give what a relationship needs in order to thrive. Our love is law." He waved his arms wide. I imagined he wasn't referring to the elevator, but rather the courthouse as a whole. "It's simply the reality, Richmond. Accept it and move on. You've made your choice. Honestly, he lasted longer than I expected."

Whether Lon believed it or not, I did pay attention to him. Though, what I did with his wisdom might be different than he'd intended. "Why longer than you thought?" I asked as the elevator opened on the first floor. Lon nudged me out, and I complied though I'd rather stay on and finish the conversation.

"I don't know too many people who'd stick once they learned they were too country to take part in firm events," Lon said, shoving open the outside doors for me. "Especially after they tried so hard to fit."

Beau had appeared to be relieved that he no longer had to be my plus-one at client dinners. I had taken Beau at his word, but what if that actually hurt or embarrassed him? The concept was too upsetting to consider. I never wanted him to think I was ashamed of him.

"Don't strain yourself overthinking," Lon chastised, guiding me toward the outside parking lot. "You could discover what transpired the night he left by accessing the security cams from your building."

I halted so abruptly it felt as if the soles of my shoes stuck to the pavement. What was happening to my brain? How had it not occurred to me? Even after we'd used the cams in my office to ferret out Chandler's misdeed, I still hadn't thought to access our home security data. Instead, I was just continuously dialing his cell that was now permanently turned off.

"Take the next few days off because no one needs to see this." He waved his finger up and down the length of my body. I followed his gaze, uncertain about what was wrong. He had a point. My dress shirt was nearly fully untucked, and I was wearing mismatched shoes. "Get your head right and come back ready to tackle the world. We need you on your A game."

My mind resisted his instruction, not due to my dedication to the job, but from the dread of being left alone inside my own head. I feared I wouldn't survive the company I'd be forced to keep.

"It's not open for discussion. Let's make it a solid week. You haven't taken time off since you started. Take a vacation. Go to one of those all-inclusive resorts or go see family. I won't allow this to detract from your senior partner vote next month."

Wow. The vote hadn't crossed my mind. The pressure of becoming a junior partner had me wringing my hands for months. Now, faced with something as significant as a senior partner—a full equity partner—I didn't appear to give a single shit.

My answers were taking shape whether I wanted to accept them or not. Beau had yet again clarified my priorities. He was number one on the list—my list, any fucking list. I kept that news to myself and nodded. I'd take the week with the hope of resigning by the time I returned.

"You stopped paying attention again." Lon shoved me in the direction of my car. "Go home. Keep your phone on for any questions."

With a glance at said phone, I saw a new notification run across my screen. Without a concrete plan in mind, I decided to pack lightly then head to the Houston airport. Beau had booked a room at an inn located on the far side of Sea Springs. If he wouldn't talk to me by phone, then he was going to deal with me in person.

23: The Bath
Beau/Dash

Beau

Two days later
Sea Springs, Texas

I scratched my itchy facial growth, realizing that my reluctance to shave might not have been my best decision. When the itch crept up to my scalp, I had to remember the last time I'd taken a shower. It must have been the night before I returned home... Wait. Chicago was never truly my home, and I refused to accept it as such. The last place I lived that felt like I belonged was my grandparents' house. They always told me that their place would be mine someday.

My eyes narrowed. Man, I was going emotionally lower than low. I also needed to bathe. As I lifted my arm to check the smell of my pit, I was relieved to find it wasn't that bad. So much like I'd done since arriving, I aimed the remote at the television and flipped through the channels to find something to watch.

I'd spent the better part of my hotel stay in this bed, either snuggled under the covers or lying on top like I was doing right now. My Dash-induced depression weighed heavy on me.

When I first arrived, I decided to give myself a solid week before I pulled my life back together. I needed a job—FedEx canned me for leaving without notice—and a new place to live. I also had to find somewhere to keep my boat.

A knock interrupted my pity party, causing me to glare at the door. Since I'd declined housekeeping, and had the snoozing door hanger on the door, no one should be bothering me. So I'd ignore them until another knock, much louder and longer this time, had me sitting up. Anger licked up my spine.

I flung the remote on the mattress as I headed for the door. Another knock sounded at the same time as I peered through the peephole. I only saw darkness, which was weird. Fuck that, I jerked open the door, swinging it wide. There stood Dash, looking as dashing as ever, wealthy and runway ready. My senses were assaulted, but somehow my brain stayed clear. I clasped the side of the door and sent it slamming shut.

Naturally, Dash denied me the satisfaction that came from hearing a slam. His foot stopped the door from closing, allowing him to enter my room uninvited. "How the fuck did you find me so fast?"

Dash didn't immediately answer. He looked me up and down then up again. I zoned into the red rim around his pretty blue eyes, I'd missed that on the first glance. Otherwise, he was on point, his slacks and fitted button-up shirt framed him perfectly. When his gaze shifted around my room, I followed to see what he was seeing. Only then did I see the pigsty I'd created. It didn't matter. Pinning aside the depression and hurt from moments ago, I focused on his superior attitude, my back went ramrod straight.

"Why are you here? I was pretty damn clear with my note."

Dash refocused on me. "I apologize for losing my way. Come home and let's work out a home balance that suits us both." His tone was an octave higher than angry which meant it was still not that of a man begging for forgiveness.

"No. Now leave," I said, my frustration directed at him and myself for drinking him into my thirsty soul. It would be so easy to do as he suggested, but dammit, he hadn't asked. He'd commanded. He hadn't addressed the Chandler issue or why he hadn't come home the night I arrived back in Chicago. Instead, he came with that lawyerly air of superiority. As if his simple statement was all it was going to take for me to drop to my knees, suck him off in appreciation of his kindness.

"I won't leave without you. I reviewed the security feed from that night and saw what you obviously did. I regret putting myself in such a compromising situation. Nothing happened between Chandler and me. I woke up the following day in my office. Chandler had taken my files and disappeared. It's a convoluted situation, but I take responsibility, and I apologize once more." I didn't retreat as that felt like surrendering control. Instead, I towered over him, explaining my new truth.

"I'll never return to Chicago. My life isn't tied to that city anymore. You no longer hold that place in my heart. We've drifted apart. When you chose to exclude me in your dinners or cocktail hour..." I shook my head. I had to be succinct or tears might build. "I embarrassed you and your company. I should've taken off when you took their side."

"You've never embarrassed me," he said firmly, and I cut him right off.

"I know what I heard. You thrive in that world. The wealth, the prestige. Everything you've created serves as proof of what you lost when your family kicked you out. You deserve all the success. I want a simple life. We were always back to this unresolved conflict. We're too different," I explained to his shaking head.

"What I've accomplished was for the benefit of you. The money I've earned and the life I've provided was all with you in mind. Rock climbing isn't cheap. The gear and trips come with a cost. Yet, I've rarely been invited to go with you."

I laughed right in his face. "You were invited, but I got tired of the constant rejections. And my hobbies are far cheaper than the cars you keep buying," I shot out, my willingness to compromise was fading fast. Fuck him for bringing up the activities that kept me sane through all the hours I spent alone. Fishing and climbing were literally all I had anymore.

"Beau." Dash sighed, clearly frustrated with me. I sensed the way he insinuated that I was being foolish. Fuck him for making me feel inferior yet again. "We've made commitments to one another. We are meant to be together."

I shook my head, remembering who he and I were right now, not the past. "We were kids who settled into life like middle-aged men. We've never dated anyone else. We've drifted apart because we are opposites in every way. I need time to sort out my life, manage my bills, and live within my means. I want to know what it feels like to be independent." I was seconds away from saying that I couldn't live with the complications and manipulations of a lawyer when tears developed in Dash's eyes.

"While all that may be true, I can't bear the thought of losing you," he said. I didn't disagree. I've mourned him these last couple of days. "Please, give me something to hold on to. Some glimmer of hope."

I watched the tears gather enough momentum to roll down his cheeks. Oh, that was too much to see. My head hung low, and my eyelids shut. I caused his pain, just like I caused my own. It didn't change the fact that he and I had grown apart, and I placed the blame squarely on him. I had remained basically the same person I'd always been.

Dash inched closer to me and leaned in, his fingers intertwining with mine. The tender grasp felt both familiar and secure. And those feelings turned out to be a façade. Dash hurt because he'd lost. After all the years of fighting for his clients, he'd become a man who'd lost sight of what life looked like. He wanted me to go back to Chicago, and sit in that house alone, waiting for him to eventually return. I refused to be a possession again.

"We need some time apart. Emotion can't dictate this decision. You need to really consider what's important to you. I do too. It's unfair of me to ask you to live the life I want to live."

"Please," Dash whispered. I simply shook my head, proud of myself for standing up for myself no matter how much I wished life hadn't turned out the way it had. "Then how long, Beau? How much time do you need?"

"I'm not sure." When I noticed the pain break his strict control over his face, I relented. Certainly with time he'd fall back into his life without me in it. "Give it a year. We can reevaluate our lives one year from now."

Dash let go of a sigh and wiped away his tears, squeezing my hand tighter than before. "And this is where you want to live?"

"It's the first place where I truly felt happy being myself. I need to get back there...the understanding who I am part. I won't go on the side of town where the resort is, but I'd like to maybe buy or rent a place close to the bay. I'm not sure. You have to give me time to find out who I am," I said.

He remained quiet, I saw the urge to argue bubbling just beneath the surface, but he held it in, only giving a single nod. "I've only ever wanted your happiness. I want to be able to communicate with you."

"I'm not sure that's a good idea. You've been at my back, taking care of everything, since the first time I saw you. I feel like we need a clean break."

Dash wiped his cheek while releasing my hand. Not a single word was said. It was weird for him to give so easily. He left my room, shutting the door snugly. Wow. I collapsed onto the edge of the bed. That conversation may have been the hardest one of my life. Did I truly mean what I'd said? Yeah, I did. My convictions were firming up.

Did that mean Dash was permanently out of my life? Maybe. Probably. It crushed my heart to think such a thing. At least I developed a plan for my future. My sole focus was on progressing, definitely not the striking blue eyes of the man I loved. First thing on the list was a shower, then I needed to find a job. After that, who knew? Maybe finding a house to live in. On my short walk to the en suite bathroom, I considered getting a dog. I'd always wanted one.

Dash

One week later

I was utterly uninspired. My vibrance had vanished. Of course, I was aware of it, but it seemed everyone in the office noticed too. It didn't matter though. Beau brought happiness and normalcy to my life. Two qualities I cherished, now gone, maybe forever. Perhaps I needed a counselor. Eventually, I'd seek one out. Maybe.

In front of my desktop, I stared at the screen, my fingers poised to type, but my thoughts were solely on Beau. What was Beau doing right now? Had his job allowed him to transfer? He certainly had enough money to pursue his dreams. Once I sold our assets, I'd ensure his share went to him. Maybe I'd talk him into a high-yield savings account.

I loved Beau deeply. He was my breath, my wings, my reason for living. How was I ever going to live without him? Well, I refused to find out.

"Is this serious?" Angela, the firm's managing partner, asked from my open office door.

I needed more context than the piece of paper she held in her hand. "About what?"

"You know exactly what I mean." She stepped further into my office, prompting me to abandon what I was doing on the computer.

"My resignation?" I asked. "Then yes. It's serious."

Her penetrating gaze, a trait common among lawyers, seemed to bore right through me. Since it didn't affect me, I waited as she crossed her arms over her chest. "I'm disappointed in you."

I barked out a harsh laugh. "You'll have to get in line. The number of people disappointed in me is growing."

She found no humor in the situation whatsoever. I took a centering inhale then exhaled slowly, hoping to manage the sudden bout of anxiety. "I'll stay on until we get my clients reallocated. The contracts that have me listed as a requirement, I'll talk to them." Which was a lie, I wanted them to go with me as I started my own practice.

"Dash, you're an exceptional talent, one of our very best hires. What does it take to get you to stay?" Angela leaned against my desk, her knuckles resting on the top as she stared down at me.

"I genuinely love my job, but I can't live without Beau. My life's with him by my side. I'm sorry," I said with finality.

"I'll talk to him," she offered.

"Please don't. I'll be available to answer questions or to consult with anyone," I said, ready for this conversation to be over. My fingers went to the keyboard again, poised to type. She didn't leave.

"Who do you recommend take your clients?" she asked.

"Donna Abrams. We're very similar people," I said. "She hustles and deserves the leg up."

"Let me talk with the partners. Does Lon know?"

"I suspect so." I said before I took the week off.

"Richmond," Lon barked from his office three doors down from me. I saw Penny flinch at the outburst. Her concerned gaze sought mine.

"I see he's learned," Angela remarked with a smirk. With reluctance, I got to my feet and started out of my office, Angela on my tail.

"Don't forget to bring up Donna," she said with an air of humor and elitism. I glanced over my shoulder at that remark, trying to read between whatever lines she had going. What was wrong with Donna? The answer was inconsequential. My plans were already in motion. I was relocating to Sea Springs. My year of solitude didn't imply that I wouldn't be around him. Maybe, after a couple of months apart he'd want me back. It could happen. Maybe?

24: The Dixie Duke
Dash/Beau

Dash

For the first time in more years than I could remember, I returned to my dark, lonely home before six o'clock in the evening. If I'd made this more of a habit, my love would be here to greet me. As I entered, I switched on the overhead lights and headed straight for the bar to pour myself a vodka tonic with a healthy dose of lime. In the long to-do list I'd made for myself, I needed to work on my alcohol consumption, but that was further down the list. I needed the liquid courage to help get me through the next few weeks.

Glass in hand, I went for the wall intercom system and pushed the button to begin playing the music I craved all over the house, picking up where I left off last night. I was working my way through the Aretha Franklin era. The depth of the lyrics along with the scale of the music had so much more feeling that engaged the senses. Especially from where I found myself today.

I took a hearty gulp of the drink and sat in the seat I'd moved closer to the framed pictures of Beau. The task list I made last night sat on the nearby end table where I left it, pen on top. I picked it up and quickly marked through the first goal of putting in my resignation at the firm. I took a larger drink this time, reliving the afternoon chewing-my-ass-out session that Lon had been intent on giving me. The next few items on the list were going to be challenging but none more difficult than quitting my dream job.

Item number two was to call Carter and catch him up on my changes. He'd sold Beau and I this penthouse. Although Beau had always been reluctant about this place, I'd never been short-sighted. The property was deeded in my name with Beau entitled to half. With the housing market on fire, I could likely sell the place quickly. My half would fund a start-up law firm in Sea Springs as soon as I could get there.

I stuck my finger in the knot of my tie and reached for my phone in the breast pocket of my suit jacket. Carter's contact information was drilled into my brain, so I dialed the number I knew by heart. Carter had become a father figure to me. We had developed a close bond, and I found I craved his support more than ever.

"Carter," he said, the king of the fourth-ring answer. Kailey's giggle had me grinning. She had such an infectious laugh. Linda had to be nearby. They made a dynamic duo, having used their differences to create an even healthier twosome.

"Do you have a minute?" I asked.

"Only a minute. It's family time. What's up?" he asked.

I weighed the decision of talking to him with Linda in earshot, but the silence and loneliness of my house were getting the best of me. "I'm planning to sell the penthouse. I've contacted a couple of realtors but wanted to talk to you and get your approval first."

"Why're you selling?" he asked. I heard movement and Kailey's voice fading.

"Have you heard from Beau?" I asked. Beau and Linda were quite close.

"Not since his visit," Carter said, his tone edging toward concerned. "What's going on?" Well hell, what did I say now? When I took too long to answer, Carter pushed. "What's going on, Dash?"

Backed into the corner I'd put myself in, I let go of a pent-up sigh and stared at the picture of Beau's rugged body scaling the side of the mountain. "Beau and I are on a break." The confession tasted like acid on my tongue. "We've broken up."

"I sensed something was really off between you two, but I couldn't get Beau to talk to me." Wherever Carter had gone, he returned to Linda and Kailey, because he asked someone other than me, "Have you talked to Beau?"

"No," Linda answered, concerned. "Why?"

"He and Dash are on a break."

"What?" she asked, moving closer to the phone. "What happened?" I heard the panicked pitch in her voice, knowing I'd put it there. Damn.

"I'm putting you on speaker, Dash," Carter said. "Tell us what's happened."

What did I actually say? How much did I expose? "I'm not a hundred percent certain what happened. No, that's not right. It was all on me. But Beau arrived home from his vacation earlier than I realized. I'd been drinking all day. It gets fuzzy after that, but I came home to a note that he'd chosen to leave me. I tracked him to Sea Springs—"

Linda cut me off. "Sea Springs?" she asked, confusion in her tone. "Why?"

"I was just as surprised as you. I went to bring him back home, but he refused. He's on the other side of town from the resort and your parents' old place. But, I don't understand why he chose Sea Springs either." I took a longer drink of the vodka, needing something strong to finish this conversation. Rehashing the bad decisions that caused me such severe pain was hard to do.

"You went to bring him home and he didn't go with you?" she asked.

"Yes." The heavy weight of my heartache was stated in a single word.

"I'm going to call him," she said.

"She's gone. What's your plan?" Carter asked.

"That's why I'm reaching out. I resigned today and plan to put both my homes on the market unless you want this property back. Beau has sound reasons for leaving. He's not wrong. Ultimately, he's unhappy living in Chicago and even less happy with who I've become. Both are fair points. He needs a year on his own. So I'll take this time to relocate and do my best to win him back."

"Huh," he said. "That's unfortunate, Dash. I'm sorry."

"Me too. What do you want to happen with this place?"

"It's yours now. I handed it over to you two," Carter said.

Good. Finally something was going my way.

"Beau's unhappy here. I'd like to put it up for sale so he knows how serious I am about winning him back. The money will be split down the middle," I explained.

"We have time to sort out the specifics, but do what you think's best. Will my account with the firm go with you? We added that requirement to the contract, correct?" he asked.

"Yes." More relief assailed me. While our contract did stipulate his account would go with me, actually knowing Carter would stay in my corner made life suddenly more bearable. "Please don't hesitate to say that you'd like to stay with the firm. I can take it." Except I lied. I couldn't take it, not at all.

"No," Carter said with a small chuckle. "I've only signed with your firm for you."

"Good. I'll work hard for you. One last thing. I planted some erroneous information on the properties you've bid on. Richmond's responsible for the breech of the data," I explained. That looked like the only right decision I'd made in a long time.

"We encountered your father at the conference. Linda talked you and Beau up to everyone. She has such a talent at getting under their skin. It was a great moment for us both." The smallest of smiles curled at the corner of my lips while I tried to visualize my father's anger at hearing good things about me. I was surprised he hadn't had a heart attack right on the spot. "I then clutched his shoulder and told him that you were like a son to me."

All right, that was funny. "How did he respond?"

"Well, the best way to describe the interaction would be to say that he'll be avoiding me in the future, I'm sure," Carter said, clearly proud of himself. "A flush crept up his neck. He doesn't appear to be a healthy guy."

"Very good. Thank you for sharing. I wish Beau was here. He'd love to hear all the details," I said. Sadness crashed over me again, back in full force. "Listen, I'm going to go. I'll keep you updated. If you remember any other details about my father, call me. When I transition your account out of the firm, I'll make contact."

"Dash, take care of yourself. You and Beau showed me what love looks like. You're the reason I have a family today," Carter said, his tone reassuring.

"Thanks, Carter. I'll reach out soon." I disconnected the call to place another to Beau. He still wasn't answering, but that didn't seem to matter to me. I had a routine of calling my love every morning and then again in the evening. I texted him throughout the day. Of course, he didn't respond, but I just couldn't let it go. Yes, we were different people, we always had been, but that was our strength. Beau just needed to remember.

Beau

The sorrow reflected in all the dogs' eyes tore me up. If I had my way, I'd take them all out of this no-kill shelter and find new homes for them to live out their days happily. I walked the aisle lined with cages, keeping my focus on a German shepherd mix.

"Here they are," an attendant said, entering the room a few moments after me. I noticed a top cage behind the door that I'd missed when I'd walked in. Four pint-size puppies were inside.

"What happened to bring them here?" I asked. The best I could tell, they looked very much like purebred shepherds.

"Their mom had to move across country with her owners," she explained. "They're new here. Six weeks old and have had their shots."

I stood in front of the cage, peering inside. Two of the little ones caught my attention. They roughhoused together, jumping and rolling around each other. They were cute. I hadn't considered adopting two, but they seemed to fit really well together.

"These two," I said, pointing to the playful duo. "What's it like to raise two German shepherds?"

"They're generally intelligent dogs. They're playful, loyal, and full of energy. With proper training, they can be great companions. I think taking two will help with separation anxiety. The number one downfall of German shepherds is the shedding. It's a daily battle to keep up with the hair."

Hmm. Given the smallish townhouse I'd just rented across the street from the ocean, I didn't imagine it'd be too much trouble to sweep up the hair.

A wave of melancholy rolled over my heart. If Dash were here, he'd have researched all the facts about all dogs, knowing the advantages and disadvantages of each breed. But I needed something to occupy my mind and fill my time. Without giving it much more thought, I pointed again to the two puppies that had caught my attention. "How about those two?"

"They're cute. Always rambunctious," she said, not too concerned to open the cage to reach in for their collars, then verified the information on the clipboard in hand. "One's a male, the other's a female. They've been given the name Dixie and Duke, but you can change them if you want. Of course, you can, they'd be your animals."

Her questioning gaze lifted to mine.

"Is it a problem to have a boy and a girl?" I asked.

"No, it's actually better for the family dynamic."

Okay. My head swiveled back to the pups. I got momentarily lost in the coincidence of all the D names in my life. Suddenly, the one on top, lifted its head and stared at me intently. My heart connected in a big way. The other, the one pinned down, followed the look from its upside down position. The three of us bonded in that moment. So I was doing this, and they'd keep their names.

"Can you help with training? I need to get them potty trained, then trained trained. If that makes sense."

"Absolutely. We'll provide you with several resources to look into. We have a potty-training pamphlet. It's not difficult to train. Consistency's the key," she said, nodding in encouragement. I nodded too. Why? I didn't know.

By the time we talked it all out and I paid the fees, and signed the paperwork, the puppies were brought to me. They were so stinking cute in their shared carrying case. Except, for the first time since entering this kennel, I became intimidated.

What did I know about taking care of anything? I didn't even have a job yet, but I did have a fat bank account from ten years of working while barely spending a dime. I was still anxious as hell as I took the handle of the case and lifted it to stare at the two beings inside. Man, I was an emotional mess. Forget the intimidation. A burst of joy ran over me, and it was a beautiful feeling I hadn't experienced in years.

"We'll help you carry everything out," she said, not waiting for my reply. She scooped up a small box she prepared, filling it with food and other essentials they said I'd need.

"Nah, I hadn't gotten that far. I wasn't completely sure I was adopting today," I said, putting the puppies' crate in the back seat, placing the box in beside them.

"All right, enjoy your pups. I packed instructions for neutering and spaying so you can educate yourself. They'll need special care post-op," she said as I got into the cab and started the engine. My phone connected to the truck and then simultaneously rang. I barely glanced at the caller's name, feeling like it was one of Dash's many calls a day, but this time, my mom's name appeared on the screen.

"I have to take this," I said, reaching for the armrest to shut the truck's door. "We'll see you next week."

"Thank you," she said, stepping away from the truck, lifting a hand to wave. I answered the call while shutting the door.

"What's going on?" I asked. She rarely made contact outside of our regularly scheduled Sunday evening calls, choosing to text me throughout the week.

"Where are you? What happened, son?" Her voice mirrored the sadness I've been dealing with for weeks.

"So you know?" I asked and left the truck running in the parking lot of the kennel.

"Carter's speaking to Dash right now," she said. "I heard that you two are on a break. What's going on, Beau? Where are you?"

"The what happened answer is that he and I grew apart. I've been battling with it for a while. The evening I got home from being with you guys, Dash wasn't there, which was normal, but when he arrived, he was so drunk. Another guy jumped out of the car and took him back inside. I watched it all. Arms around each other, holding each other close. I took off that night, and that's the whole story. He showed up here. If he wasn't so damned cocky, I probably would've gone back with him, but I didn't. We're done."

"Oh, Beau, I'm sorry. I knew things were off, but I didn't understand how far it had gone," she said. "Come here. We have plenty of room for you. It'll give you time to build a plan."

"I'm in Sea Springs. I rented a place close to the beach. It's small but enough for me. I never felt comfortable living in those big homes. There's a lot of space in them to feel lonely." My new puppies gave a baby bark, drawing my attention to the rearview mirror. Both dogs were side by side, staring out the front of the cage. I lifted a finger to my lips, glancing back at them. "Shh."

"What was that?" she asked.

"I adopted two puppies today. They're in the back seat." My mom fell silent for so long that I had to check if she was still on the call.

"You there?" I asked.

"Beau, sweetheart, you went to Sea Springs and adopted two dogs? Are you okay? Should you be making so many life-changing decisions right now?"

Her worry caused me to chuckle. "I'm on the opposite side of the city from where everything went down. I always liked coming here to see nana and paw. Sea Spring's feels like my home. As for the dogs... I planned to adopt one, but his cellmate was funny and cute. They felt like a package deal. I don't know how to care for a pet, but I'm gonna try."

"What can I do to help you?" she asked.

"Nothing. I'm taking things day by day. I miss Dash, but I miss the old Dash, not the person he's become."

"I can't believe he was with another guy. He never struck me as that type of person," she said.

"I'm okay, Mom. Better now that I'm out of Chicago. I gotta get us back to the motel and read all the stuff the kennel sent home with me. Tomorrow I'm taking possession of the townhouse I rented. I gotta get furniture and stuff." As I spoke, Dash's name popped up on the screen. The man never gave me a break. Of course I let it go to voicemail.

"I'm sorry for what's happened. I want the best for you," she said.

"Tell Carter I have no issue with him working with Dash. I know they're close. I don't know if he'd even consider not working with him, but I don't want to know about it," I said.

"I'll tell him. Beau, I love you. I'm so proud of the person you've become. Don't discount Dash just yet. See if he makes the changes that put you two together again. Remember when times were good..." Her sad voice bothered me, but I wasn't in a place to relieve her just yet.

"I'm okay, Mom. Trying to keep busy to distract myself. I'll call you once I settle into my new place," I said. "But I'm hanging up now. I gotta get on the road."

"Bye, sweetheart. I'll call you Sunday night."

"Bye, Mom." I hung up, pushing her worry away. It was tough to end any relationship, but mine and Dash's love story was unique and genuine, taking us from childhood into adulthood. When the bond started to break, I should have left. I gave a quick glance over my shoulder, realizing that my energy was now focused on these two dogs. We were going to be just fine.

25: The Practice Dash

Spring, 2015
Dallas, Texas

"Dasham, they're leaving now!" Amelia shouted from the front porch. Meanwhile, I was taking a final walk through my Dallas home before handing it over to the new owners. As I moved from room to room, I reminisced about the special moments I'd shared within these walls. Whether with Beau or during those times when I waited for him to arrive, I sought refuge here. I had a deep love for this place. It held an irreplaceable spot in my heart.

Leaving my life in Chicago was far easier than moving from the home that Beau and I envisioned for our future together. "We'll arrive in Sea Springs before the movers do, don't worry," I called, slowly making it back into the living room. I gazed out the floor-to-ceiling windows, looking over the backyard when my cell phone rang. I had long since given up the hope that Beau might be calling. I pulled my phone from my pocket to see Joy's name on the screen. Luckily, she drew my attention before I crashed emotionally under the weight of these memories.

"Hey," I said when I answered, then changed course toward the front door. My life was no longer tied to the past, but in the future. I had a long way to go to finish this transformation to bring Beau back to me.

"Hey, guy. What's going on?" Joy asked. I stopped long enough to lock the door then stepped back to take in the view of the porch and yard. If I ever had the opportunity to recreate this vision, I certainly would.

"I'm saying goodbye to my Dallas home. The new owners take possession in a few hours. Perhaps sooner. Either way, Amelia and I are leaving," I said, glancing toward the woman I considered my backbone as she stood waiting by the car. No joke, she was tapping her foot in double time rhythm, picking up my slack in just about everything.

"Ah. I didn't realize the move was today." Her tone changed, becoming compassionate, which was strange from her. Sarcasm was her usual way. She whispered in conspiracy. "I got news to share."

"I'm ready," I said, starting for my sports car in the driveway. My finger twirled at Amelia, urging her to get inside the car and leave the evil eye here at the house.

"Chandler's taking over Granddad's legal department. He's secretly been transitioning into the position for months. I just found out."

I let out a loud, spontaneous laugh. The perfect comic relief to lift my spirits.

I dropped down into the driver's seat and waited for Amelia to take her seat. "Chandler's the new head of my father's law department." Since Beau and I were knee-deep in this break, my current relationships were with Beau's voicemail and with Amelia who was joining me in Sea Springs. She'd be my new receptionist at a law office I hadn't opened. What I hadn't said aloud was that while she'd managed my life for years, I wasn't overly confident in her actual office skills. I'd likely need to hire a paralegal soon.

"No," she exclaimed, her sudden cackle had my grin spreading wider.

"Have you heard anything regarding the property bids he has out?" I asked.

"Yes, that's how I learned about Chandler. He's not being blamed. Instead, they're putting it on you. Something about a bid on some property or something like that. But it's your fault that Grandad's lost some business. Chandler's become a legend in Granddad's company." With her use of the term *legend*, I bowled over in laughter. My father deserved what was coming at him by placing Chandler as the head of anything.

"I'll call you back once we get on the road," I said, juggling the phone to shut my door and start the engine.

"Let me text you later. Jordan's getting married, and we're starting a weekend full of activities," she explained.

"Who'd marry Jordan," I asked, honestly shocked. The call transferred to the car. Amelia's face scrunched up at the mention of Joy's brother.

"It's not a good situation, I assure you," Joy said. "I have to go. I'll call you soon. Ciao."

I appreciated Amelia more than I could say. She and I were aligned where my awful family was concerned. I clasped her hand. "Thank you for coming with me."

"Your nice words aren't going to distract me. You're to drive the speed limit with me in the car. Otherwise, I'll have a heart attack before we leave Dallas." Of course. She'd moved on to other important things to fret about.

"If I follow your wishes, I'll drive like a turtle and we won't arrive until sometime next year," I teased, gripping the gearshift then shifting into reverse. I cautiously backed out of the driveway.

"I sure liked living here," I murmured as my gaze locked onto the house momentarily.

"I know you did," she said, reaching for my hand. "But you lost your way, Dasham. We have to keep that from happening again. You deserve a good life. You're a good man."

That had become the primary objective for my life. In an effort of self-preservation, I'd finally stopped beating myself up for what I'd become and promised to only look forward. I pushed into first gear and drove away without looking back.

Two weeks later
Sea Springs, Texas

"The outside sign has arrived," Amelia called from the reception area of my newly leased office space.

The property had two floors. Downstairs consisted of three rooms. The front space was big enough for Amelia's desk and another desk for a paralegal once I was able to hire one. My office was located in the back, which was a decent size and offered privacy for client meetings. The last room on this floor was a bathroom. Along the side of the front room was a staircase leading to the top floor which currently housed my extensive wardrobe. If it worked out, and my little firm grew, the second floor could provide additional office space for any associates I hired.

Amelia and I had been working hard, painting the walls in contemporary colors and modernizing the space before my new desk and office furniture arrived tomorrow afternoon. I wished I could say I'd been financially frugal with my purchases, wanting my start-up to pay its way, but that wasn't the case. After I'd learned Beau was the local UPS delivery driver, I'd had no choice but to work with companies who used UPS for their deliveries.

After tomorrow's delivery, I'd arranged to have something arrive every day for the next month. For much of the last fourteen days, I'd searched for Beau in the local area. I did my best detective work, but unfortunately, I couldn't uncover much about him. Nothing at all, actually. Except my neighbor with the office to the right of me said he was our UPS driver. Hopefully, Beau sees my antics as devotion, not stalking. Worst case scenario, he'd move again, forcing me and Amelia to follow. Eventually, I'd wear him down.

"It looks fantastic. The logo pops," Amelia said. As many times as I'd crawled up and down this ladder, I was reluctant to do anything more than finish painting the back wall corner, but she wasn't wrong, from this angle, the sign looked great.

Dammit, I had to see. I crawled down, carefully walking over the drop cloth that we'd used to protect the newish flooring.

From this angle, I was proud of our progress and even happier to hang my sign underneath the awning outside. I liked color even though I rarely had it in my life. Well, until now.

"It turned out quite nicely. Let me wrap up the corner. I'm nearly finished then I'll hang the sign." I turned back to my painting task but stopped first to look through the brackets and hooks that accompanied the sign. "Can you call the guy who's going to etch the front window? I sent an email last night with the logo. I don't believe I've heard from him."

"Sure, I'll call him." Amelia was truly putting in her best effort to assist, and she was making an impact. She managed her chores with precision. I didn't think she ever tires.

As much as I wanted to hang the sign, I left her to her work and went back to finish the painting. Just as I suspected, the remaining wall took only a short time. Much like I'd done every time I painted, I glanced down the length of my body, searching for any splatter. Dressed in jeans and a University of Chicago sweatshirt, I opted for a classic Beau choice with a baseball cap worn backward on my head. No drops violated my ensemble. Huh, who knew I had a backup plan if law didn't work out. I could be a professional painter by trade.

I folded the ladder, lugging it outside to hang the sign, then went back for the sign itself. The task seemed pretty straightforward. Hooks and chains hung from the awning. The sign was designed with holes at the top to hang it securely in place.

"Need my help?" Amelia asked, walking out of the office with me.

"I feel like I've got it," I said with more confidence than I actually had. I climbed the ladder, cradling the sign against my chest with special care. The last thing I wanted was to lose my balance and have both the sign and ladder crashing down on me.

I steadily made my way up the rungs, as if dealing with the finest china. I hooked one side then balanced to do the other side.

"It's perfect, Dash," Amelia said. Great, the office was coming together nicely. On the last rung, before my foot hit the front stoop, a sudden honk drew my and Amelia's attention to the street. A brown box truck was stopped directly in front of my office. Beau was staring at me.

The love of my life, the most important person in my world, appeared dumbfounded. I lifted a hand to him, grinning the smile I knew he loved. I hadn't seen him face-to-face in months. My body tingled at how handsome I found him. He was fit and tan, his hair cut into a style I couldn't see with his backward baseball cap in place.

Oh man, nothing about my love for this man had changed. If anything it had only grown while we'd been apart.

Amelia was hovering near the door. "Is that Beau?"

His stare switched to Amelia who waved toward the UPS truck. After another unnecessarily loud honk, Beau repositioned in the seat to drive away. The impatient vehicle behind Beau drove past us, shooting me the finger as if I had stopped in the street.

"Now, he knows we're here," Amelia said happily. I completely agreed with the sentiment. My heart smiled for the first time in a long time. "The sign looks great. The most prominent one on the street."

I turned to look down at the other shop signs. Mine did stand out. What a difference a cool font made. The smile I'd given Beau stayed on my face. I'd never doubted my decisions to liquidate everything and move to Sea Springs, but it was nice to have the reassurance. For sure, Beau loved me, and I was here to stay.

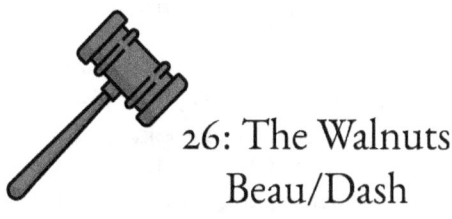

26: The Walnuts
Beau/Dash

Beau

Sea Springs, Texas

"Mr. Beau," Amelia said, lively. "Hello. I missed you." True to form, she moved around her desk to envelop me in a warm hug. I embraced her just as tightly, balancing the small package and scanner with one hand. "I have something for you. Don't leave."

Naturally, she didn't make it easy on me to slide in and out with only a quick greeting. In her enthusiasm, her hands waved in the air as she rushed back around her desk. That was when I noticed Dash leaning against the doorframe to what must have been an office, arms crossed over his chest, appearing as if he had all the confidence in the world, which technically suited him perfectly. Man, he looked incredibly good. So good. His stare was locked on me, but he didn't say a single word.

"Dash and I baked these for you last night. They're chocolate chip cookies," she said proudly, bringing up a festively decorated tin from a drawer at her desk. Her gaze shot back to Dash, as if to include him in the conversation.

"With walnuts," Dash added. My mouth watered. I missed lunch today to make time this afternoon for Dixie's veterinary appointment.

"With walnuts," Amelia repeated, completely aware of how much I enjoyed her cookies. I hadn't had them since her last visit to Chicago a few years ago. She handed over the container as if presenting me with a special prize. I scanned the barcode on the package and traded it for the cookie tin. The delivery required a signature, so I passed over the handheld scanner for Amelia to sign. She was much better at juggling the load than I had been.

"Thank you. It's hard to believe Dash was in on this," I said, my attention divided as I clicked through the screens to submit the delivery details.

"No, he really did. The Airbnb he rented has a beautiful kitchen. So big." She beamed broadly at Dash. "He's such a good man. It was all his idea."

That was even harder to believe. Dash hadn't spent time in the kitchen since he graduated law school. The sudden silence quickly became uncomfortable. Rather than brush aside the tension, I focused on Dash, getting serious, draining all the joy from the room. "What're you doing?"

"Keeping an eye on you," Dash said, smugly, lifting one shoulder as if the answer were obvious. His nonchalance was a too familiar reminder of the person Dash had become. He added a smirk to complete the picture.

My focus shifted to Amelia. "I appreciate the cookies. I'll definitely eat them all."

"Dasham, share what you want him to know," Amelia scolded.

"I'll answer when he asks questions he doesn't already know the answers to," Dash said, his intense gaze fixed firmly on me.

I let out a sharp bark of laughter, turning away from him. Let the games begin. As I started toward the door, I heard Dash's sure stride and the soft click of his loafers behind me. When I glanced back, Amelia was nowhere to be seen, and Dash was closing in on me.

"Ask the question you truly want an answer to."

Dash halted inches away from me, making it impossible to open the door. I cast a sneer over my shoulder. He came in so close that his unique scent of cologne wreaked havoc on my senses, frustrating me.

"Back off me," I said and flipped around, ready for the confrontation. Dash stayed right there, holding his ground, way too close for comfort.

"That's not the question," he said. His sultry voice had the same medicinal balm as the gentle breeze coming off the ocean. And I had to get the fuck out of here before my defenses lowered more than they were.

"Why're you here?" I asked.

"You know that answer too," Dash said, shaking his head. Irritation had a single brow lowering. "I'll share the answer anyway. I resigned from the firm a week after you didn't come home with me. I've sold the penthouse and our Dallas home..."

"Dallas is your home," I murmured, definitely, knowing that he had always referred to the house as ours.

"It was our home. It was built to be the place you and I resided," he insisted, stepping in slightly closer. I stayed rooted to my spot, not due to any manly pride, but everything about him overwhelmed me. He always fucking did this to me, made me unsettled. I didn't like it. "Chandler was there to gather information to report back to my father. He thought he was setting me up, but I knew from the beginning. When you left, he took the opportunity to attempt to ruin me both professionally and personally. The latter worked flawlessly."

"Our problems began years ago," I stated, and started to edge past him. It was time for me to leave. When I moved away enough to open the door, Dash's firm hand slapped down on the wood, keeping it closed.

"I take full responsibility for what happened. I sought revenge against my father, and I lost sight of the fact that I had become him. I apologize for my behavior. After I left the firm, I saw what I'd become. Have dinner with us. Amelia's making her tamales that you like. We can discuss what our future looks like together."

Still facing the door, I closed my eyelids and remained silent for several long seconds before straightening my spine. For the first time in months, the boundaries I'd placed on our relationship began to blur. I found it unsettling, as I was just getting past the end of our relationship, now learning who I was as a man. I didn't know what our future—mine and Dash's—looked like, but I wasn't ready to go back to the life we'd shared. With the way Dash dominated me, he wasn't as changed a man as he pretended to be.

With him surrounding me, my body tightened, and I had to get out of there before my resolve cracked.

"Beau, I love you. I miss you. Nothing's changed for me. Please talk to me so I can resolve your concerns and we can become a couple again. "

I had to leave. With a force that was fueled by urgency, I flung the door open and started jogging toward my truck before anything more could be said. My quest to find my true self had nothing to do with love, unless it was about loving myself.

Of course I loved Dash, that was never in question. I hadn't left him because I fell out of love with him. I'd left because I'd lost myself, if I ever knew me at all. I just refused to allow the bond we'd always had to control me ever again. Once I figured myself out, I'd decide what I wanted in a relationship. He'd have to wait or move on. That was just how it would go this time. I finally had control of my own life, and I wasn't going to relinquish it based on a few words of devotion.

Dash

Weeks later

For as long as I had searched for the area Beau lived, I never expected to stumble on him randomly, on a Saturday evening, while driving on Oceanside Drive, the scenic route of the Gulf of Mexico. Another surprise was that he had two spirited German shepherds on leashes. I didn't stop or pullover, but I drove slowly as he jogged across the street, looking hot as hell in the tight -fitting athletic wear, and gave some sort of command to the dogs.

Still on the leash, they came back to his side taking a seat. Pretty damn impressive. He unleashed them both and threw out a hand. The three of them jogged on the beach together. After a few seconds, the two dogs bolted, running freely. Beau called out something, I didn't know what, but they ran into the surf, happily traipsing through the water.

Beau continued to follow, jogging behind them. He had earbuds in his ears. Music was new to his workout. Maybe. I hadn't seen him exercise in years. The time I'd wasted that I'd never get back haunted me. A long, irritated honk from behind snapped me back into reality, but my focus remained on Beau. I pulled over, so taken with the way Beau handled himself and the dogs that I couldn't continue my drive.

When they were too far away to be seen, I glanced on the other side of the road at the townhomes lining the opposite side of the street. A dark blue jeep was parked beside the townhome on the corner, and the tiny voice of intuition whispered that it belonged to Beau. I couldn't contain my smile. Beau had made a good life for himself. Seeing Beau happy filled me with immense satisfaction. It was what I'd always wanted for him.

I drove slowly along the side of the road and turned into the parking lot ahead. I circled around, until I was back on the street, heading in the opposite direction I'd been traveling but in the same direction that Beau had jogged. I'd give up everything to be jogging with Beau right now, involved in his dogs' lives. It had been this town, this beach that had set my life on the trajectory of Beau Brooks. I was never going to get that man out of my head. I didn't even want to. I stayed in the far right lane, slowly driving until I saw they'd made it to a private beach. There was a dog park there, the German shepherds were popular among their peers. Before Beau could reach the park, the other animal owners were already welcoming them.

That same attention that was once directed toward me now felt distant, almost an unachievable memory. What a fool I'd been. With roughly four months left on my one year sentence, my determination strengthened to bring us together on that day.

When my heart gave an ache that wouldn't release, I marked the location where I'd seen Beau and started in the direction of the Airbnb. As always, disappointment in myself made it impossible to think clearly.

What happened that urged Beau to decide on two dogs? Were they male or female? Beau had gotten dogs and I wasn't involved in the decision. Switching gears, I thought about how hot my guy was while jogging in his tight running shorts and fitted tank top. He was beautiful. Still solidly muscular. It seemed his body was just made that way.

Desire raced across me. Visions of Beau moving over me replaced everything else. I needed Beau inside me. My own fist on my cock tonight just wasn't going to do justice to sex with Beau.

I wondered if he'd discovered another rock-climbing club. What happened to the dogs when he took his trips? Did they join him on his adventures? They appeared to be very well trained. Had they come to Beau that way or had he taught them? I could only speculate on any answers. I had no idea. Sadness stamped out my desire.

If I ever had an opportunity to bury Chandler, I'd take it without looking back. His payback was coming.

Beau

One month later

I burst into Dash's office building, startling the shit out of Amelia in the process. The front door rattled under the force I used. When the damn thing bounced off the wall, coming back at me, I had to resist the urge to beat the hell out of it.

I didn't say a single word as I stomped my way to Dash's office, forcefully pushing open the closed door. Dash was in a meeting with someone, but I paid no attention to the other person, and didn't give a fuck about professionalism.

"What the hell's all that money in my account for?" Although I asked the question, I didn't wait for an answer. "However you got it into my bank account, take it back. I don't want it."

Dash glanced at his client sitting across the desk from him and nodded her out of the office. "I'm sorry, but I need to handle this matter. Feel free to call me anytime tonight with concerns. Otherwise, meet me at the courthouse at eight thirty tomorrow morning. We'll talk more then."

The woman shot a worried glance my way, but she still nodded at Dash, snatched her purse from where it sat by her feet, and zipped out of the office like she was late for a race. As soon as she was gone, I again zeroed in on Dash. "I have four million dollars that needs a place to go. I don't want the money. Take it back. Put it wherever you want."

"No," Dash said, waving a hand dismissively. "I need to prepare for a full day in court tomorrow. Would you like to continue this conversation over dinner tonight?"

Oh fuck you, I wanted to say. I hoped the insult stayed on the inside of my head, but I wasn't sure. "You're a smug bastard. If you don't take the money back, I'll donate it all to charity," I countered.

"I figured you would, but it's yours to do with what you want."

Dammit. My head was about to explode. I didn't want the money. Why was everyone always trying to give me money? It didn't take a rocket scientist to figure out I wanted to live off what I made. Even more upsetting than the money was the way Dash ignored me. For months, he stalked me, putting himself in front of me all the time, and now, he chooses not to care? Dash sat in his chair and sifted through the paperwork on his desk.

"For now, I have court tomorrow. I need time to prepare. Will you send Amelia in on your way out?"

"You're always prepared. Stop the act."

Dash paused the fake rifling through papers on his desk and leaned back in his seat. "You've got me there. Have dinner with me tonight."

At that moment, my brain nearly short-circuited. Heat rushed to my cheeks as fire burned my senses from the inside out.

"You're breathtaking while angry."

My hands flew up in frustration as my thoughts tangled, fueled by my anger. Four million dollars was an enormous sum of money. I.. What.. Ohmigod... Why did what I want never matter to anyone?

"That money is from the sale of the penthouse. The Dallas property income will be available in the next few days. Your half will be..."

I couldn't bear to hear another word. No matter how hard I tried, this man kept throwing me off. Yes, I was angry, but I loved him more than I could say. Now those emotions were mixed into everything else. Left with nothing more to say, I pivoted out of his office and stalked toward the exit.

"I warned you he wasn't going to like it," I heard Amelia say. I left the office, before Dash responded. If Amelia grasped my wishes, why couldn't Dash? Man, I needed to take time to compose myself before getting behind the wheel of my truck, but I didn't.

What did I do with the money? How did I even handle such money? Did I let it hangout in my checking account? That seemed wrong.

Another louder voice inside my head screamed something obvious that I had completely missed. It pointed out that Dash seemed to view our relationship as if we were broken up, dividing our assets as if we were dismantling every aspect of our lives.

I didn't like that one single bit.

27: The Fresh Treats
Beau

One month later

Having no real idea what I was doing, I sat across the booth from the town's top realtor/financial advisor, Ford Johnson, a guy I'd met while delivering packages. Between us were several sheets of paper scattered across the table, two cocktails were pushed to the side, making sure any condensation from the glasses didn't alter the contracts I was about to sign.

I stared down at the sheets of paper, having no idea what I was doing. Dash always handled our finances. Funny how after all this time, I still thought about Dash and me as a couple. Another realization was that I'd taken much of what Dash offered me for granted.

It didn't help that my thoughts were consumed with the emotional side of what I intended to do with my grandparents' old property.

A whirlwind of questions lapped around my mind. Did I possess the skills necessary to rebuild their home? One of the spec pages was a rough illustration of their old home drawn by a local architectural firm. If I signed off on these contracts, they'd draw up blueprints to rebuild the house.

Although I didn't understand how to read a blueprint, I hoped to learn sooner rather than later. Ford planned to hook me up with a company to help guide me on city permits, and how to find the various trades that I was unfamiliar with, such as electrical, plumbing, and the newest safety equipment and features that the city now required. I planned to put together the framing of the home by myself.

My goal was to craft an exact replica of the previous home, all three stories, to pass down to future generations. Pass down to whom? Well, I guess that would be my little sister, Kailey. If she has children...

"Have I overwhelmed you?" Ford asked, gathering the pages in front of me and placing them in a neat stack.

I smiled, embracing the reality of the situation. "Completely overwhelmed, but in a good way."

As I stared at him, my mind lingered on my life here in Sea Springs. How would Dash feel about what I planned to do with my money? I guessed I was making Sea Springs my permanent home.

"Remember, the property's been rezoned. It's only residential. You can no longer run a B&B or list as a short-term rental property. The patch of land on the other side of the road, can be used as a commercial property, just not the area where the home is placed."

I nodded, secretly thankful that the house would be a home and nothing more. The only other person who mattered in the design was likely Dash. I wanted him comfortable there, even if it wasn't his permanent residence. I didn't understand the changes inside me. For ten or so months, my thoughts on Dash were of us being separated. Now, in the final stretch of my imposed hiatus to find myself, I was beginning to see us as a couple. At the year mark, I was more than willing to date him again.

My guy brought a smile to my lips. He was beating me down like a sledgehammer through the carefully erected walls I had put in place. For some reason, I believed his constant apologies and his explanation. I always had. He wasn't a cheater. Arrogant, absolutely. Most times when he trapped me in one way or another, I experienced solid rock-hard arousals.

Maybe what changed my mind in the last ten or so months was that I'd never considered dating another guy. I hadn't even swiped right on an app. I only wanted Dash. The way I plumped in my blue jeans at just the mere suggestion said it all.

"I lost you again."

This time I laughed at myself. "I'm lost to it all. So what's the offer we're making?"

"Between you and me, the company that owns the land has been liquidating assets. Something happened there. I think we go ten percent below asking price and see what happens."

Hmm. Did Dash know that his father's company was selling properties off? "What about the property next to it with all the trees?"

"I haven't heard back from the owners. I'll reach out again," he said, nodding.

Wow. Expanding on what my grandparents owned had to make them proud, my mom too. "Okay. We're doing this. And you remember they aren't to know it's me buying the property. Right? A hundred percent they won't sell..." Out of the corner of my eye, I saw Dash outside, staring into the café, smiling and lifting a hand in a wave. Talk about wearing me down, how did he always know where to find me? Instead of ignoring him like I normally did, I lifted a hand in return. His face lit up in a bright grin as his gaze moved to Ford. His expression morphed into a deep frown. His brows dropped into a hard V as his accusing stare landed back on me. A mix of anger and disbelief had him backtracking for the café's door that he had already passed by.

I had no understanding of what triggered his disapproval, but suddenly, the front doors banged open, the bells on the knob rattling like crazy. Every diner turned Dash's way, but his gaze fixed solely on my table. Not on me, only Ford.

"I've also arranged high-yield annuities for the four girls. The paperwork is here." Ford lifted additional paperwork to put in front of me. "Also, I've arranged for Scott Lee..."

"Who the fuck is this?" Dash asked, sliding into the bench seat next to me. I'd never seen him like this. He was hot and bothered and hip-bumped me to scoot my ass over to give him more room. When his left hand landed firmly on the table, I couldn't help but notice that he still wore his commitment ring. Realization dawned as he wiggled his fingers to make sure it was seen. My guy was jealous.

"Dash, what're you doing?" I asked.

He hardly cast a glance at me. His eyes shot daggers at Ford.

"Who's this?" Dash asked, tossing out his right hand. "You know he's my husband, right? You're spending time with a married man."

Gauging Ford's response, I wasn't quite sure where he stood. I picked up an emotional range somewhere between alarm and humor.

"Dash, this is Ford Johnson. He's my financial advisor and realtor."

Dash kept a close watch on the guy, clearly skeptical. "Jack of all trades, huh? How does one become an expert in two different fields?"

"Dash, hold on. He's helping me with purchasing some land..."

"I'll give you two some space to chat," Ford said, sliding a decent size stack of paperwork to my side of the table. "Take a look through the contracts, decide what you want, and stop by the office. I have a notary on staff." As he spoke, he slipped across the seat, dragging his briefcase with him. He stood ready to bolt at first chance. "I've heard about you, Dash. You have a strong track record in court. I wanted to stop by to discuss the possibility of collaborating with you."

"You're out with my husband..." he started, his tone turning nasty.

"Dash, stop," I said firmly. "Ford, I'll show him what we're working on. He'll understand soon enough. Thank you for meeting with me." Ford never looked back.

"Why do you need a financial advisor?" All of Dash's attitude pinned me in my spot. "I'm right here. I'll handle whatever you need."

"You embarrassed me," I said, though deep down, that wasn't entirely honest no matter how much I wished it were. I enjoyed having him here next to me in the booth, something we'd always done when we'd gotten back together the first time. A shared dessert would arrive at the table with one spoon. He'd choo-choo train the bites into my mouth, and we'd laugh. The memory was so vivid and special I wished it were happening right now.

"No, I didn't. You weren't embarrassed at all. Why were you here with him?" Dash asked. "Was this some kind of scheme to show me what you went through? Because I don't like it at all."

"If you believe I'm trying to get you back for Chandler—" I ignored the snap of Dash's finger and how he pointed at me as I continued to speak. "Then you're admitting that there was something going on with Chandler."

"I had no involvement with Chandler. How often do I need to say it?"

I held my gaze steady on him for what felt like an eternity, hoping he would grasp the meaning. It took him more time than I anticipated based on the indignation written all over his expression.

"Ford's a UPS client. He's married to a woman, has a few kids, and is trying to start a business for himself. He took care of a few things for me." I patted the stack of paper in front of me.

"What're you trying to do?" Dash asked and rolled his shoulders and neck. At least he tried to be reasonable as he reached for the stack. I placed my hand over his to prevent him from taking them away from me. Dash was such an intriguing guy. Stealthily, he flipped his hand around underneath mine, threading our fingers together. I didn't withdraw from his touch. The weight and feel of his hand in mine caused my fingers to close over his. "Please stop pushing away from our bond. I'm ready for us to be a couple. I'll always put you first, just as I know you do for me. This time apart was essential for me to gain clarity, but I'm back on track now. I promise."

Dash apologized so often that I did believe his sincerity, making my next words painful to say. "We decided on a year apart. I've undergone some significant changes to my life. You may not appreciate the new version of me," I confessed.

"That's impossible." He shook his head sweetly as if I was absurd. "Show everyone that you're taken," he pleaded, placing the ring on the table. "Please. You're too handsome. I can't take another moment like the one I just stumbled upon."

He carried my ring around with him. His love for me remained unchanged. My heart connected then ached at the worry on Dash's face, and I tightened my grip on his hand. With my other hand, I instinctively reached for the ring. It felt as right in my palm as the handhold did.

"Hold on to it. For some reason, sticking to our time apart matters to me. This way, there won't be any doubts about us rushing back into each other's lives. It wasn't only you that grew apart, I did too."

Tears welled in his eyes. Not quite enough to spill over, but they were there, nonetheless. "I love you, Beau. I miss you. Nothing's changed. What if you meet someone and want to replace me? I don't like it."

What did I say? Dash's special scent and striking face tugged at my heart strings. I didn't want to lie to him, yet wasn't ready to speak my truth. It almost killed me to lose him. The only way I survived was to stick with the calendar and move myself forward systematically through life. Dash began to nod at me, swallowing a lump in his throat. His attention went to the papers below our hands. "I know you want us together as much as I do. I'll wait the six weeks."

The handhold continued, now on the table, as he read the first few pages. His ability to speed read and retain information always impressed me.

"You're buying your grandparents' land?" Dash asked. Bewilderment crossed his expression. "That brings you closer to the resort."

"My goal's to create a replica of their house that feels less like a B & B and more like the home it was intended to be. The purchase includes a swath of land in front of the house, my grandparents owned that too. It's sort of in front of the house, you cross the parkway to get there. The city bought the land for the road. The part on the other side is zoned for commercial use and leads directly into the bay with easy access to the ocean. If it works out, I can build a dock and start my charter service." I explained a plan that I hadn't said aloud to another person. Insecurity messed with me. What if I couldn't handle the project?

"Allow me to make a few changes to the contract. I want to guarantee your privacy. I doubt my father's company will sell to you if he has any idea it's you."

"I agree," I said, nodding. "They're selling a lot of land around here. Ford said they were liquidating assets."

Oh, there it was, Dash's satisfied grin. Whatever he had in motion, must be working.

"I heard the same thing," Dash said, flipping through the pages. His stare jerked to mine. "You're giving Scott five hundred thousand dollars?" Dash asked, surprised. "Are you sure?"

"Yeah. Each of the four girls will have two hundred thousand dollars in an annuity. Scott's will be an annuity too, I guess. The bank told me they could live off the interest," I explained, reciting some of what the bank manager outlined, or what I remember he said. "Maybe it wasn't an annuity? A high yield...something or other?"

Dash chuckled at my confusion. "Some things don't change," he teased.

"All right, now. I want the girls' funds secured until they reach twenty-five, but I want Scott to have access to all the money. I guess. He's been a good friend. Like a brother to me."

"Is he aware of this?"

I only shook my head. Dash's expression turned doe-eyed. "You're a good man."

"I'm not," I replied. "I don't want the money, and you won't reclaim it. Scott carries a heavy burden, and he protected me when I couldn't protect myself," I explained my reasoning. "And he had my back when I came out. I might not have gone to find you without his interference."

"I've never seen anyone more selfless in my entire life," Dash said. "I've often felt the same way about Scott. I owe him."

I kept my thoughts to myself, particularly regarding Dash's selflessness toward me. Dash was the best man I knew... Wow, a positive thought. Clearly, I'd let go of what had torn us apart. I couldn't tell where this current sweet smile landed. He either sensed my feelings or simply valued my generosity, but he lifted our joined hands and placed a kiss on my knuckles.

"I want to share with you that I'm not earning as much as I used to, and I've hired a paralegal to assist in the office, which impacts the profits. Amelia does her best, but she's more suited for answering phones and welcoming potential new clients. We'll need to rely on this income for some time, possibly even years, maybe longer," he said.

I nodded, maintaining my silence. How many different ways could I say that I wanted to live off the money I earned? Even now, with Scott taking so much money, I had way more than I wanted.

"Come home with me tonight," he murmured quietly. "Before you say no, I won't pressure you to stay. It's been too long since we've been together. I'm hard as hell, and you know only you can relieve me."

Since I felt the exact same way, my desire desperately nudged me to say yes. Yet, something held me back. Maybe it was the thought of Duke or Dixie, who only tolerated me being gone for the hours I had to work, or maybe I was the dumbest human being on the planet. The truth probably fell closer to the latter, but my mind insisted on upholding my boundaries and timeframes until we slowly began dating again.

"Not tonight." The words tasted like sawdust in my mouth.

"I'm disappointed," he replied, leaning in closer. "Have you eaten? Would you like to have dinner with me?"

No, I hadn't eaten and needed to get home to let the dogs out of their cramped quarters, but I found myself nodding. Neither of us moved to the other side of the booth. For the first time in years, I felt the connection we had once shared tugging me closer to him.

Dash

Two weeks later

I had a knack for being sneaky—or at least, I hoped I did. Hidden behind one of the highest sand dunes, I sat crisscross in wait. I had two treats already to be devoured. Initially, I aimed to win over Beau's dogs before moving back in with him. Now, I found I genuinely enjoyed Duke and Dixie. Many may say my actions bordered on stalkerish, and maybe they were right, but I chose to believe these were acceptable actions in my quest to win Beau back. Either way, this was my routine every Tuesday evening. To my knowledge, Beau didn't know I was here. The dogs, on the other hand, quickly sniffed me out, darting behind the dune with me to wolf down the treats and receive a full body rub.

Based on how well cared for and well trained they appeared, I deduced Beau fed them a nutritious diet, which led me to seek out homemade dog treats. I was spending quite a bit of money on organic fresh food treats.

This evening, when they darted around the dune to greet me, they came rushing toward me, taking the turn with skidding haste, tumbling into each other to get to me.

"Hi, you two," I whispered, extending my hands, no longer afraid that they'd gobble them up.

I offered another treat, petting each of their heads. "Make sure you keep taking care of our guy, until I can get there. Okay?"

We never had long. Beau kept an eye on his dogs. As if on cue, I heard his familiar whistle. They both eagerly grabbed the last treat and took off as they arrived, in a rush.

I sat there, digging my toes in the sand, dressed in shorts, a T-shirt, listening to the ocean churn. I was surprised that the seagulls hadn't spotted me yet. Eventually they would. Despite the tranquility of the moment, I rose to my feet but remained crouched to check if Beau had left. Sometimes, he lingered, playing with balls and frisbees, but not this evening.

I grabbed my sack and backpack and headed off in the opposite direction.

28: The Year
Beau

One year after separation

What I loved about this townhome was the ocean view from the front windows, and the small, gated backyard. One of my first purchases was a comfortable patio table and a Weber Jumbo Joe charcoal grill. Other than that, it was a dog haven. Toys and assorted dog agility equipment to keep them busy were scattered all over the place. Duke and Dixie spent a large part of their evenings here as long as I hung out here with them.

I currently sat at the table, researching the different climbing clubs in the area. It had been well over a year since I'd taken part in a climb. If I could drive to the mountain range, I think Duke and Dixie could take the trip with me. They were well trained. Since all my thoughts these days were centered on Dash, I planned to book a trip for the four of us after the dust wore off of our rusty start.

Dash.

My heart and my head finally aligned, seeking out my guy any time I could find him. I wasn't sure why I'd put such a long time restriction on us being apart. It seemed silly now. He'd actively shown me how much he'd changed back into the man he once was. Those changes had to be hard to make.

It had taken discipline and structure to keep Dash at a distance. I didn't have the strength to continue to hold him off. I'd met the goals I set for myself, I lived my life on my terms, paid my way, but it wasn't near as satisfying a place as I thought it might be.

I loved Dash, nothing had changed for me. An overwhelming love, an all in devotion to Dash, and yes I planned to make him work to be back in my life, but he'd be here with us in the near future, for sure.

My cell phone rang. Scott's name appeared on the screen. With the swipe of my thumb, I answered. The dogs took notice, standing at alert, which always made me smile. They never figured out where the ring came from. "Yo."

"What the fuck did you do?" Scott bellowed so loudly I jerked the phone from my ear.

"What?" I asked with the phone about six inches from my mouth.

"Is this some kind of joke?" I had two choices. I could pretend I didn't know or I could explain.

I decided on the latter, he seemed pretty freaked. "I came into some money, and I shared it with you and the girls."

"What the fuck," Scott said. My eyes closed and my chin hit my chest. He sounded frantic, which technically pleased me. The puffing of breath though might mean he was hyperventilating. "Brooks, I can't accept this. It's too much."

"Did you get the information on the girls?" I asked.

"What about the girls?"

I decided to let him figure that out on his own. "Lee, you're the best friend a guy could have. You make me feel like I'm family."

"That's the dumbest thing I've ever heard," Scott replied with anger, making me chuckle.

The doorbell rang, causing me to glance at the time. I'd scheduled a mobile dog grooming service to come by every Saturday around two in the afternoon. It was noon now, making them unusually early. Both dogs ears popped up again, and they came to my side of the small table. I pushed my laptop lid closed and rose.

"Then the only thing left to say is... *I win*." I couldn't contain my laughter. I was barely able to say, "Someone's at the door. I'll call you back." Duke and Dixie followed at my feet, ready to accompany me to the door to greet whoever was there. Generally the person on the other side of the door panicked when my good dogs tried to give their happy kisses to strangers.

"Place," I called, stopping them in their tracks. Based on the way they didn't immediately still, they weren't happy with my command. "Place..." I said again, firmer this time. They knew that meant they had to stay where they stood, no matter what happened from this point on, until I released them. The whining they were doing now meant they knew who was on the other side of the door and wanted to greet them.

That was a little weird. They weren't usually happy to see the groomer. They didn't like being separated to have their baths and de-shedding treatments. Without looking through the peephole, I pulled open the front door.

Dash stood there, a large suitcase at his feet and a garment bag hanging over his shoulder. He didn't wait to be invited in, rolling the suitcase over the threshold, while glancing around the townhome.

"It's pretty. I like the old meets the new. You decorated it nicely. Bohemian. I thought this would be how you made it."

The townhome wasn't that big. He kept going a few steps further, fully into the living room where the dogs were better able to see him. They whimpered in earnest as their bodies wiggled, tails wagging, but stayed where I'd left them. In the last year, I'd never seen them behave this way.

"What're you doing here?" I asked, once I found my voice.

Dash tossed the garment bag over the only chair in the living room as he started for the backyard. From inside his sporty windbreaker, he produced two large treats, taking them to the dogs. Prancing in place was the only way I could describe how they greeted Dash.

"Can you release their hold?" Dash asked, dropping to one knee in front of them to give each a treat.

"Release," I said, and they did instantly. Dixie leaped forward, knocking Dash to his butt. Duke was right there behind her, making sure Dash couldn't easily get up. Before I had time to give another command, Dash started laughing a joyful sound, taking Dixie in his arms. Duke had left the scene to grab my sandal by the door, carrying it in his mouth as he trailed back and forth between me and Dash. "They know you?"

"I saw y'all jogging one evening and set out to get to know them." Dash lifted a hand and arm to Duke, drawing him over for the same greeting he gave Dixie. "I only brought my necessities. Most of my clothes are at the office. I wasn't sure how much extra room you had," Dash explained, finally getting to his feet to face me.

"Are you saying you're moving in?" I asked, completely confused. We had only ever discussed dating once the year was up. I looked forward to the magic of being out with the one you loved, wooing them to your side of thinking.

"I waited a year," Dash said, coming closer to me. "This is the day you left me one year ago. The second worst day of my life."

"I meant we'd try to date again after a year," I said, still clutching the door. After watching him with my dogs, I wanted to shut the door, and lock him inside here with me.

"Oh, I misunderstood," he said, glancing all around the living room and into the kitchen. "You're letting the air conditioning out. Close the door."

Since the air conditioning wasn't on, I doubted we were losing any of the cool air inside the house but followed his instruction anyway. I wanted us to be a family. Dixie, Duke, Dash and me.

"So this is the living room and kitchen. I like the open concept." He turned to stare out into the backyard, both dogs at his feet as he rubbed their heads. "Is that fitness equipment for the dogs?" Dash gave me a cheeky grin. "Duke and Dixie. Great names by the way."

If I didn't love him so much, I'd question my safety with him here. Investigators had nothing on Dash's stalking ability.

I'd often envisioned him here with us. Mainly, I'd think of him talking about how small the townhome was. That he'd be able to walk the length of the living room in a few steps and complain, but that wasn't what I was seeing now.

"Where's the bedroom? Are there stairs I'm missing, or do we sleep on the fold-out couch?"

"The stairs are behind the kitchen. It's one room with a bathroom up there. Their beds take up a lot of room. And you can stay. Move in," I finally said, emotion clogging my words. I wasn't sure if the runaway feelings churning through me were detectable or not, but man, my insides were freaking the fuck out. I'd been a fool. Who cared about making it on my own if it meant Dash stayed on the outside. I was one hardheaded guy. Dash stared at me as I stared directly at him. Slowly, he came toward me, moving around the suitcase.

"Please put your ring back on. For the rest of our lives, I promise to put you first above all else. We'll make decisions together, live a more normal life that you're comfortable in."

I nodded my agreement as my world became complete once again.

Everything that I blocked for so long, all my love and devotion and desire to be with this man, broke free as Dash dug a hand in his pocket then produced the ring again. With an unsteady hand, I extended my fingers, spreading them wide. He slipped the ring back where it belonged. Once in place, Dash stepped into me.

I automatically circled his waist with one arm, bringing him flush against my chest. He tilted his chin up, and I tilted mine down to meet him. Inches from the kiss, his gaze connected with mine. "If you're unhappy, tell me. Don't just stay at the office all the time again."

Dash chuckled. The sound had a throaty quality that sent bubbles of energy coursing through me before it turned into more of a guttural groan. He tenderly cupped my jaw, his fingers tickling the shorter strands of my hair.

"After the severe loneliness I've faced and the insurmountable tears I've shed, I'll never be unhappy while you're with me. I love you. I want to change our commitment to marriage as soon as we can arrange a ceremony. Say yes."

"Of course, yes." I pressed my lips into his as fireworks exploded behind my closed eyes. All the emotion I hadn't let myself feel broke free as I dipped my tongue between his parted lips. *Home.* I was finally home again. I tightened my arms as if refusing to let him go again. It was him. Always him. Forever him. I'd tell him when we came up for a breath, if we ever did.

Dash suddenly pulled away, his gaze brimming with love as he pulled my arm from around him. I'd wondered how long it might take for him to notice my new tattoos. Something I'd done a couple of weeks ago on a whim. I turned my arm so he could see the stingray on my forearm and the palm tree on the inside of my upper arm. "Tell me about the tattoos, and I want children. I like your hair cut shorter too."

I tried to follow his mouth, urging him back to the kiss until his words made sense inside my head. "Children?"

The End.
Force, the final in the series, is coming April 21, 2025.

Note From The Author

Thank you for reading Fusion. For more information on future works visit kindlealexander.com and click the new release newsletter option, or friend me on all the major social networking sites.
Reviews and rankings help so much. Please consider doing so here.

Other Books by Kindle Alexander

If you enjoyed Fusion, then you won't want to miss Kindle
Alexander's bestselling novels:

Breakaway
Reservations
It's Complicated
Painted On My Heart
The Current Between Us (with Bonus Material)
Closet Confession
Secret
Texas Pride
Full Disclosure
Double Full
Full Domain
Always
Forever
Havoc
Order
Chaos
Justice
<u>A Wilder Inc. Story</u>
Secret
Breakaway

Level Up
<u>A Reservations Nightclub Story</u>
Reservations Book 1
It's Complicated Book 2
<u>Always & Forever Duet</u>
Always
Forever
<u>Nice Guys Novels</u>
Double Full
Full Disclosure
Full Domain
<u>Tattoos and Ties</u>
Havoc
Order
Chaos
Justice
Tattoos & Tinsel available 11/11/24
<u>Layne Family Duet</u>
The Current Between Us
Painted On My Heart
<u>Gravity</u>
Friction
Fusion
Force